NEST

ANYTA SUNDAY

First published as "Lenny for Your Thoughts" in 2013 by Anyta Sunday

Second Edition published as "nest" in 2016
Contact at Buerogemeinschaft ATP24, Am Treptower Park 24, 12435 Berlin, Germany

An Anyta Sunday publication
http://www.anytasunday.com

ISBN 978-3-947909-04-9

Cover Design 2016 Natasha Snow

For my lovely friend Lynda Lamb

It just happened.
I wasn't ready, but it didn't matter.
You smiled, and it knocked me from my nest, took my breath
away, and left me falling,
falling,
falling.

Part One

_____

Birds In Their Little Nests [Don't Always] Agree

(Then)

Carnival

(1995)

SIX YEARS OLD. I was a B-I-G B-O-Y, now. See? I could even spell it. I was going to school an' everything. But even though I was big, my hand was still small in Oma's as she put on the last black glove.

"Costume complete," she said, in a voice that sounded like a cough. Oma blinked a couple of times then kissed me with a whooping *smack* on the forehead.

"Ugh. Oma! Not the wet ones!" I wiped it off and grabbed the Zorro mask. My cape whipped in the wind as I darted to the rackety car that Oma drove. It was smaller than the other cars in Waldau and it smelled like dog fart. Not even Oma with her five squirts of perfume made it go away.

I quickly buckled into the front seat, poking my tongue out at my older sis Carolin, who was frowning at the rainbow colored dress Oma had made 'specially for her. I'd even helped put one of the buttons on! The button that Carolin was looking at right now—

"Hey!" I squealed and opened the door. "Why'd you rip that off? I did that one."

"'Xplains why it's crooked then." She flicked the button at my forehead and it hit my Zorro mask.

My lip wobbled. It often did around Carolin. Just because she was two years older, she thought she could be like Oma and do anything.

"Cry baby."

"Caro-*lin*," Oma said. Now her voice sounded like the scratches my teacher made on the blackboard when he was writing. "I've had quite enough of hearing you torment your brother. Apologize."

Oma had her hands on her hips. For the carnival she'd dressed up as superman—or I guess, super*woman*. Her red cape flagged in the wind and her curly grey hair bounced up and down like springs. The tight blue leggings and top sucked heaps of her wrinkles away.

"Carolin?" Oma inclined her head in warning.

My sister was silly. She stomped her foot and shook her head. "Why should I? My costume looks stupid now. He never should have helped! My friends will laugh at me."

Oma dropped her hands and her eyes got freaky. I even cowered in my seat. "Oh, your friends will laugh at you all right."

With that—and what *had* to be superhuman strength— Oma lifted my sis and set her on the roof of the car.

"What are you doing? Put me down!"

"Only once you apologize."

Carolin crossed her arms and narrowed her eyes at Oma and me. "No. I'll never say sorry. Never."

She did say sorry.

But only after Oma strapped her to the roof with old horse rope and drove us to school. It was a short trip—just five minutes down a gravelly road, but I reckon I held my breath the whole way.

I never wanted to be in Oma's bad books. *Ever.*

When she set Carolin down on the ground again, my sister hugged her tightly. "Please don't do that again."

Oma gently stroked her hair. She smiled that big soft smile that made me want to hug her too. "Be nice to your brother. Okay?"

"Yeah. I p...promise," Carolin said. "Anyway, it's not me you have to worry about. It's cousin Julian. He's a dick."

"Watch your mouth, girl," Oma said, sighing. She gave sis a kiss and looked at me over her shoulder. "Is Julian being mean to you?"

I hurriedly shook my head. *No. Nope.* If I told Oma that he chased after me at play, pinching me until he was bored, she'd march into school and...and...

Well, I wasn't really sure. But Oma did things differently from other parents and teachers. I didn't think she should do it here. "I'm B-I-G," I said. "I can handle Julian!"

My Zorro mask and cape made me feel stronger than normal. Like I could do anything; I could take on the world! Or, at the very least, my rat of a cousin.

Just then, I saw him on the playground at the top of the jungle bars wielding a silver cutlass. He scowled over at me, his face pinching together. He looked like a rat when he did that— a long, dark brown rat with a missing front tooth.

I really hoped that cutlass was made of cardboard and tinfoil. But I'd find out soon enough.

I kissed Oma goodbye and weaved through the crowd toward the main building. On my way I bumped into Ben splashing in a puddle.

"What are you doing?"

"Dog poo," he said with a groan. "The real stinky, mushy stuff."

I looked at the golden sludge on the edge of not one, but *both* shoes. It was the same color as Ben's short hair. I wondered if the poo also matched the dog's fur. Probably. "Must have been a Labrador."

Carolin, who'd followed behind me, started laughing at Ben, waving a hand in front of her nose. When I glared at her though, she stopped and darted past us, mumbling, "Later."

"Poo-poo to dog doo," I said. Oma had packed me extra shoes today since I was wearing black gumboots to fit my costume. "Want to wear my sport shoes?"

He stopped splashing and nodded miserably. "This day sucks. My costume didn't fit anymore."

I looked at the crooked cat—or mouse?—whiskers on his face. "You should have told Oma. She'd have made you something—and I could've put the buttons on it."

We sat on a wobbly bench outside the front of school. I could still see Julian, leaping onto the middle of the swing bridge. The yellow parrot stuck on his shoulder swung back and forth. I'd hate to be that bird. But if I was, I'd make sure I pecked Julian's shoulder until he cried.

Julian jerked his head toward me. I quickly looked away and pulled out my sport shoes from my bag. "Here Ben. Let's hurry inside."

The bell rang, and we skidded down the halls to class. Funny—even the teachers had dressed up! It was going to be a good day.

And it was. Until lunchtime…

Julian's cutlass wasn't cardboard.

It was plastic and the tip of it was sharp when Julian shoved under my armpit. I tried to roll away, but he stood on me, one of his muddy shoes pressing into my chest. "Get off!" I yelped at him *again*.

Ben lunged onto Julian's back, but Julian was strong. He made it look like he was giving Ben a piggyback ride at the same time as pinning me down. One smooth pirate was he!

"Mama said you crazies were at it again," Julian said. My

auntie wasn't very nice to our side of the family. "Is it true? Did your Oma make you have time-out on the roof?"

Ben lost his grip and slipped off Julian's shoulders. "Let him go!" He hit Julian's side until the cutlass arched in the air and pointed at his throat. Ben swallowed and stepped back.

I prayed for a teacher to come past, but this far back in the paddock, it wasn't likely. What would Zorro do right now?

I blinked up into Julian's eyes, the color of a haunted forest, like the one in our village. *I won't be afraid. I won't be afraid…*

I let out a warrior cry, latched both hands around his ankle and yanked. He stumbled off me but didn't fall. Still, I was quick enough to scramble to my feet. But just as Ben and I started running, a hand grabbed the back of my shirt and —*poboof*—the air was forced out of my lungs as Julian slammed me against him. He held the cutlass to my throat.

"Look at you. You *do* have a bit of gut-so."

"Let. Him. Go."

My eyes were squeezed shut, but at Carolin's voice, I opened them. She and a few of her girlfriends had fanned around us, holding jump ropes in their hands.

Ben was still running toward the school building, getting smaller and smaller by the second.

Carolin jerked the wooden handle of her jump rope toward Julian like an extra-long finger. She looked a little like Oma: not someone to mess with.

Julian laughed. But it was shaky. "What're you girls going to do about it? You're a joke."

Carolin gave a smile. "Oh, there'll be a joke all right."

Julian was made the punch line.

See, my cousin was big. But my sister? She was bigger. Her and her friends dragged Julian off me and led him down the grass plank, all the way to the playground. There they used their jump ropes and tied Julian to the side of the jungle bars.

I reckon Oma would have clapped.

"Say sorry to your cousin, Julian," Carolin said.

"I'm sorry you caught me," he spat.

"Your other cousin!"

Julian slowly turned his head to look at me. For the first time, he looked scared. His nose was even running a bit and his haunted-forest eyes had lightened to something much less frightening. I felt sorry for him.

I inched closer; it was my turn to wag my finger. "I don't like your games," I said, fumbling with the ropes until Julian was free.

He rubbed his wrists and wiped his nose on his sleeve. He didn't say sorry, but the way he looked at me, I knew he was feeling it.

Before he ran away, I said, "Don't you ever hurt me again, Julian."

Turned out he would, but not for another twelve years— and with a very different sort of weapon.

Unicorns Shitting Butterflies

(1996)

"My mama said your mama and papa didn't want you anymore."

I didn't like Nick. Neither did Carolin. *Nick the dick*, she'd mutter whenever the guy said something stupid. Or mean. Or like today: both.

I locked my legs around the jungle bars and lifted my hands toward the sky. Ben, next to me, nudged me in the ribs and whispered in that way everyone could hear: "What are you doing?"

A spooky breeze raced over me, like maybe it was a spirit or something. "I'm channeling me some Oma Niki." I giggled and said the new word I'd learned last weekend, again. "Channeling."

"Channeling," Ben repeated. "Don't you need a remote for that? Anyway, what's the point?"

"Well…" I thought about it. "See, Oma would know what to say, and I don't."

Nick threw bark up at us from the ground. At least, that's what I thought was hitting my shoulder and leg. Another of those cool breezes slid around me. It even smelled of our old car this time. Oma was getting closer.

"Hold my hand, Ben. Maybe that makes the channeling stronger!"

His sticky hand in mine made all the difference. This time the wind practically roared—

I opened my eyes and looked down, jumping a little as I saw that the roar was *real*. It was coming from Julian as he tackled Nick. Bark flew out of Nick's hand and he hit the ground.

"You pick on someone your own size!" I yelled at Nick.

Ben nudged me again. "I think he *is* your size."

Julian must have heard him, because he stopped pinning Nick down and looked over his shoulder at us. He was wearing bright red today, and he looked a lot like those men that waved flags in front of bulls—or, I guess not the man, but the actual flag. Huh.

With a small growl that was more like a cat's open-mouthed purr, he turned to the pale-faced Nick again. "Just leave Lenny alone."

And just like that, abracadabra, Julian the bully became *Julian Protector Extraordinaire*. A.K.A. the best cousin in the world.

One thing was for sure, Nick didn't throw any more bark at me that day.

At the end of school, me and Carolin were supposed to walk home, but she wanted to chat with her friends. Not with her "stupid little *boy*"—there was a lot of emphasis on that part —"brother". So I waited five minutes like she asked and started the cold trek home, kicking stones and trying to ping them against mailboxes.

A bike bell rang behind me and I jumped to the side as Julian screeched to a dusty halt. "Hi, Lenny."

"Um, are we friends now?" I liked to know these things.

Ben was my friend; I could play with him and joke about farting in plastic bags to try and save it. I wasn't sure about Julian though…

Julian shrugged and started to ride again, but slowly. "Nah."

"Okay."

I continued walking and kicking stones. Julian rode around me in wonky circles, chatting in a laughing voice that made the birds scatter from the trees.

"If you're not my friend," I asked, "why are you talking to me?"

Julian did another round. It was making me dizzy. "Dunno. Maybe we are friends."

I lifted a finger, pointing to him and the bike. He stopped like I wanted. Staring at him really hard, I crept closer. "Do you think farts are funny, Julian?"

He hooted and blew into the crease of his arm. A yes, then.

"Then I guess we can be friends."

We continued up the gravel road. At the bend before the river, Julian said, "What did Nick mean? About your parents not wanting you—?"

"Julian!" A female voice called. We both looked up to see my aunt—Julian's mama—waving at him from the bridge.

I got goose bumps seeing her, because she looked like a bigger version of my sister. They shared the same reddish hair and green eyes—just like our mama had. *Your mama and your auntie were sisters*, Oma had explained one time. *Carolin takes more after your mama. That's why they look similar.*

Julian swung off his bike and pushed it to meet her. I wasn't far behind him, and I hesitated at my aunt's sharp tone. "What did I tell you about talking to the Krause family?"

My cousin shrugged. "He's okay, Mama."

"Hello, Auntie Thomas," I said, glancing from Julian to my dusty shoes.

"Yes. Hello, Leonard." She stepped to the side so I could pass, and gestured for me to hurry along.

"Bye," I said, waving to Julian. He started to wave back but after a look from his mama, dropped his hands.

When I got home, I found Oma in the kitchen mashing potatoes, listening to the radio. She turned it down when she saw me. "How was school?"

"Dunno. Hey, Oma? Why doesn't Julian look very much like his mama?"

Oma pounded the masher against the pot and rested it on the bench. "Where'd that come from?"

I dropped my school bag at the leg of the table. "Auntie picked him up at the bridge."

Carolin yelled something from another room—some of her *girl*friends were here. Oma stood up and shut the door to the kitchen.

"Julian has some things that are the same—he has her green eyes, and chin, and definitely her mouth." She gave me a small smile. "You all have that mouth. Your sis, mama, auntie, cousin…"

I climbed onto a seat, grabbed at a piece of paper and a pen left there, and drew a pair of eyes. "Yeah, but those things look different on him."

Oma chuckled, came over and tousled my hair. Her minty breath bounced on the back of my head. "Of course they do. But like you take after my boy, Julian takes mostly after his papa. He's got Daniel's jaw and nose and hair color."

I colored in the irises, doing my best not to go out of the lines. "I didn't think Julian had a papa."

Oma let out a long breath that tunneled down the back of

my T-shirt, making me squirm. "He did have one. But not anymore."

"Like our mama and papa?" I asked.

"Yeah. Like that."

"I tried channeling you today, but you never came. I mean, I almost had you, but then you slipped away."

"Channeling me?" She moved toward the tin of cookies she kept on top of the fridge. "What for?"

"Nick said mama and papa didn't want us anymore. That's why they left."

"Leike!" Oma said, rolling her eyes. "That family is all the same."

Suddenly there was a big pile of chocolate chip cookies and milk in front of me. I grinned and picked up the cookie on top of the pile.

Oma looked at me with big, sad eyes, like the rabbit we kept in the back shed. It almost made me want to feed her carrots.

"Life sucks sometimes," she said. "It's not all unicorns shitting butterflies, you understand?" She dragged out a chair from the table and twisted it around. She liked sitting that way, resting her elbows on the metal back and two fists at her chin. Today she clasped her fingers together. Then shook them apart and sighed.

She explained everything. It went something like this: Once upon a time not very long ago, there was this giant wall that separated the land. My mama and papa wanted to get over the other side. They were planning for the whole family to get over. I was only a baby when they left me and my sis with Oma. They were meant to come back. Oma said they really, really wanted to. That we were all supposed to live happily ever after like in the fairytales. It was just that, well, they got a faulty unicorn.

It did not shit butterflies.

But it was all okay now, because they were up in the clouds watching. And we both had Oma there to look after us.

"You'll get your happily ever after, yet," Oma said, dabbing her eyes with the edge of the table cloth. "You'll see. I promised them that much."

Summer

(1997)

"Did your Oma really saddle up Herr Braun's horse and trot to the station for gas?" Ben asked.

"It was that or walking to the next village." I stared out of the tent flap toward the house where Oma was turning out the lights. When all but one was out, I looked up to the hundreds of stars winking above us.

"She's something else, your Oma."

"Yeah. I want to be as awesome as her one day."

Ben yawned, and I kicked my sleeping-bag-wrapped legs into his. We'd promised each other to stay up the whole night without falling asleep. "Don't close your eyes."

"I'm not," he said, but there was another yawn there, I could hear it.

"Tomorrow we should see if Herr Braun will let us ride his horses."

"Do we have to?"

"Are you scared?"

"No!" His "no" sounded pretty scared to me. Ben rolled over, facing the side of the tent, his back to me. "And please let's not spend more time with your sister. She's mean."

"Because she was strong enough to tackle you to the ground?"

"It knocked the wind out of me—and her carrot hair got stuck up my nose!"

"Don't call it carrot hair to her face," I said. "She'll hate you as much as her hair. Oma said it'll darken to a chestnut like mine when she's older, but I'm not sure I believe her. She keeps blinking when she says it."

"Your Oma kept blinking when she told me Mama would miss me this week. I think she just has something wrong with her eyes. She *is* old."

Oma was older than other parents, but she wasn't *that* old. Was she?

Ben stifled another yawn. "I just hope you don't have to move if, you know, her inner bird flies into the clouds."

"Inner bird?" I asked. "What do you mean?"

"Papa used to say everyone has a bird inside them, then, when they get really old, or unlucky, that bird leaves the person and goes to Heaven, where all these birds sit in beautiful nests in a really big tree and watch us from above." Ben let out a sigh that turned into *another* yawn. Sleepily, he added, "I hope Papa's nest has a good view."

I imagined all the birds tweeting their songs, my parents among them. A flutter rose inside me, and I patted by belly to calm my bird down. "I don't think I want Oma singing where I can't hear her."

Not for a long, long time, anyway.

"Are you asleep?" I asked, kicking Ben again. He grunted and mumbled something.

I explained the situation to him. How Oma had promised Carolin over and over that she wasn't going anywhere. That we were stuck with her for longer than we'd probably ever want. "So I think her bird is safe in its nest for now."

But Ben hadn't heard me. He was sleeping.

The traitor.

I sighed and my breath fogged in the air. The sound of a rustling came from the bushes to my left and I froze. Wild animal? In the backyard?

Or something else? A bird poacher?

"Psst!"

A panicked squeak slipped out of my mouth and I hurried to sit up. Before I could completely shove myself back into the tent and zip up, a bunch of shadows slithered over the lawn. Me and my inner bird quaked.

A slice of light from the house hit the shadows and they morphed into a single form. *Julian.* Just Julian.

I scrambled out of the tent, the sleeping bag coming off me. "What are you doing here? Thought your mama said you weren't allowed to come over!"

Julian handed me a heavy metal torch. "Battery went out; I hope you have one."

"I do, but—"

"What my mama don't know, don't hurt," Julian said. He sidled past me and rummaged in the tent.

He must have found my torch, because he came back out with a grin. He grabbed my hand and pulled me to the mini playground Oma had put in when I was five.

We sat on the swings and twisted the chains round and round. When they were taut, we lifted our feet and whirled. Night air rushed over my face and the stars blurred. I laughed and my inner bird fluttered so hard I thought it might escape.

Julian pulled my torch from his pocket and turned it on. Light hit under his chin, stretching his nose and darkening his eyes and mouth. His skin glowed like blood. "OoooOooh."

"Gah! Stop!" I said.

He laughed so loud it rumbled like our shuddering car—I

could *feel* it. I came off my swing and lunged at him. *My* turn with the torch.

I hit his chest and his *"ooof"* of air combed through my hair. We fell to the ground, Julian's feet still stuck on the swing, the rest of him on dry grass under me.

"Thanks for the soft landing," I said, earning a smack over the back of my head.

"It's puppy fat. Mama said it goes away."

I laughed again. Suddenly Julian was on top of me attacking with tickles, under my arms, my sides...I couldn't *breathe.* "Okay, I give up. I give up. Sorry, Julian! Anyway, the bigger you are the bigger your bird, right?"

Julian picked up the torch that had flown from his grip, and in the light I caught his grin. "You're speaking crazy like Oma." He shook his head. "Now, do you have a sleeping bag for me?"

I shook my head. "How was I supposed to know you were coming over?"

He clapped on hand on my shoulder. "From now on, always suppose I am." I followed him into the tent. He prodded Ben, but he was so out. "Doesn't matter," Julian said. "We'll share yours."

We only just fit in my small bag. Julian stole my pillow, so I rested my head on his arm. We were lying with our heads out of the tent, warm breezes swirling around us. The stars winked some more.

"Last year, I told my class that one day I wanted to go to the stars. Nick was a dick as usual, he laughed and said that I'd never get there."

Julian hummed. "I bet if you wanted to, if you *really* wanted to, you could get anywhere you want."

"Sweet."

"And..."

"Yeah?"

I felt him shrug. "And if you can't, maybe I can help you get there, little cuz."

"Oh yeah? How? Piggyback?"

Julian moved his arm from under me and shoved me half of the pillow. "If I have to."

We stayed like that, staring up at the night sky, our hair tangled together.

Ben stirred at my feet, and I told Julian about our inner birds.

"I think Ben is really brave," I said.

"Why's that?" Julian asked.

"Because even though his papa's bird flew to the sky, he doesn't cry. I know I'd cry if it happened to Oma. Maybe I'm just a real big wuss."

Julian seemed to be thinking about it. Then he said, "Yeah, Ben is brave. But you're not a wuss. I'd cry too if Mama was taken." He patted the back of my head, his finger catching in a knot. "And your Oma? Taken away? Not bloody likely. My mama said she thinks the old bag will outlive us all."

"Thanks," I said, hearing my own yawn as it mangled my words. "That's the best thing I've heard all night."

"Sure thing. Night, Lenny."

"Sweet dreams, Julian."

I DREAMED OF BIRDS that night—of my own singing to me from deep within. It said I had something good with my friends and to treasure them. And that whatever happened, I had to be careful with my heart.

"You know the inner bird is really your soul, don't you? But I'll play along. We'll have birds, Lenny. Birds that can sing to each other."

Something fluttered and twisted deep in my belly, and I

knew it was my bird, tweeting, *laughing*, promising to show me the magical heights of the sky called life.

"There's love to be seen, and sorrow, and forgiveness. We can navigate it together. It'll be just us against the world."

And it was.

Until it was taken from me.

Too Big to be an Elf

(1998)

Oma planted the six-foot Christmas tree in the middle of the basement, just off the kitchen. "Okay. Go for it, kids."

"Oma?" I said, checking out the roughly sawed trunk that had been stuffed in an old tri-pod stand. "Did you buy this from a Christmas tree market?"

"Where else would I get it?"

Carolin crouched by my side and stared at the base. She shook her head, and we both looked over at Ben standing behind the massive evergreen. Simultaneously, we rolled our eyes.

Carolin got up, dusting her faded purple jeans, then kissed Oma's cheek. "You're wicked."

Oma hooked one arm around my sister's neck, the other around mine, and then beckoned Ben to join in. We locked our heads together. "We're missing someone," Oma said.

"Julian," we all said.

"He said he'll come by as soon as he can sneak away from Aunty," I said.

"Bet I can help the process along," Oma said. "It's been a

23

while since I popped by for tea with your aunt. In the meantime, you get started on the tree. Ben?"

"Yes, Oma?"

"You're in charge while I'm gone."

"What?" Carolin tried to jerk out of the group hug, but Oma held her tight. "I'm older than he is!"

"Really? It's hard for me to remember. You don't often act like it."

Carolin growled. "I'm taller, too."

"Then *you* can get the decorations down from the attic," Oma said. "They're in boxes on top of the shelves."

"And watch out for the spiders," Ben chipped in, cheerily.

We broke the hug and, with scowls from Carolin and smirks from Ben, got started.

It was barely five minutes before Carolin came running down from the attic in hysterics, shaking her hair, shouting: "Get it off, get it off!"

Ben swaggered in behind her carrying two dusty boxes of decorations. I didn't miss his satisfied grin or the glance at the peacock feather resting on top of the boxes.

I plucked the feather up and snuck behind the still yelping Carolin. "Just hold still a sec," I said. "I think I see it."

Carolin whimpered, but froze. I touched the tip of the feather to her head and slowly brushed it down as I circled her.

She squealed, her eyes tightly shut.

"It's gone," I said.

She opened one eye, then the other. Then she saw me holding the peacock feather.

She snatched it off me and swiveled to Ben, who was putting the boxes on the table next to the tree.

"*You.*" It came out a low growl, and before Ben could dodge, Carolin had tackled him to the floor. Her hair flamed as bright as her rage.

"Truce!" Ben yelped as Carolin noogied his head.

Carolin finally climbed off him, and Ben sat up, brushing the dirt off his faded jeans. He fixed the button on his tartan flannel shirt, then glanced at me. "Thanks for all the help, *friend*. Next time Julian has you in a deathlock tickling your guts out, I'll just watch."

I smirked and helped him to his feet. "Let's get this tree jazzed up."

Carolin brought out a ladder and we decked each branch with our homemade decorations.

Ben rummaged in the box and pulled out the silvery-blue bird he'd made last year. He stared at it a long time, twisting and turning it, stroking the glued on feathers with his thumb. Carolin opened her hand palm up and waited for him to pass it over. When he did, she said softly, "This one is real nice."

She climbed the ladder, removed the glittery gold star we'd made earlier in the month, and placed the bird on top.

The gold star dropped onto my head. "Ours was wonky," she said.

It wasn't, but I nodded anyway and hung the star lower down. I finished with the fairy lights, but when I plugged them in, they didn't work.

"Broken," I said at the same time the door crashed open and Julian waltzed in wearing a large green-and-red-striped elf hat.

He looked ridiculous. He was far too big to be an elf—a good half-foot taller than Carolin, even.

But…at least in his green costume he wasn't sauntering about with his T-shirt in a knot halfway up his chest. The last few months, Julian had been building up his six-pack—or, he was *trying* to at least. Three times a week, I would sit on his feet, reading for school, while he did his hundred sit-ups, flicking me in the back of the head at every "up."

I only stuck with the stupid chore because Julian gave me

all of his homemade cookies for the week. "You didn't bring any cookies with you, did you?" I asked.

"No, hello?"

Ben laughed. "You know what they say: the way to a man's heart is through his stomach."

Julian and I looked at each other. I shrugged, and a little while after me, so did Julian.

I passed him the carton of wax figures we'd made last Christmas—fat candles carved into wizards and warriors, the wicks poking out the top. "Let's pin these to the tree and light them this year." That'd solve the broken fairy-light problem.

Julian picked up one of the warriors—my attempt at carving him. "It's like looking in the mirror."

It really wasn't. "That guy has a six-pack."

Julian hit his stomach. "Almost there."

"Sure you are."

He tugged the elf hat off his head and batted me with it.

Ben laughed. "This should be fun to *watch*."

I grabbed the elf hat and shoved it over Ben's head, laughing. "Good luck with that."

"Order!" Ben yelled, pulling it off. "I'm in charge here, remember? Let's get this tree done."

"Aye-aye, captain."

We marched around the tree putting up the last of the decorations. Only the Julian-warrior-wax-figure kept falling off and denting.

Julian picked it up. "Now it no longer looks like me."

"Pass it here," I said, gesturing for it. "I'll fix—"

The phone let out a shrieking ring.

Carolin held her finger up to Ben. "I'll take it," she said, and answered. "…Hello, Herr Leike, Carolin here…No, she's not home right now. Can I take a message? …Someone chopped down one of your trees? …No, I haven't seen anything suspicious. *No idea* who it could have been." She looked over at us, shaking her head, and all three of us did a synchronized grin. "…Merry Christmas to you and Nick."

"—the dick," we all finished after she hung up.

Oma picked that moment to enter the basement. "Language!" she said, then shook her head and honed in on the tree. She circled, once, twice, humming. Her gaze lingered on the bird at the top for the longest time. Then she nodded. "Excellent work. There are cookies in the kitchen. Follow me."

Carolin and Ben darted after her, and I was right at their heel.

Suddenly Julian grabbed a handful of my shirt and yanked me back. "You're staying here a sec."

"But—" *Cookies!*

I didn't finish. Julian was holding out a gift wrapped in elf-paper. "Okay," I said. "Presents trump cookies."

"I wanted to give it to you today. Mama is taking me to Berlin for Christmas and we leave tomorrow."

Hearing that made me a little less—actually, a lot less—hungry for cookies. It sucked. Julian had snuck over to Oma's every Christmas the last three years. This was breaking tradition. "Berlin, huh?"

"Yeah, it's going to be cool," he said, eyes lighting up. "The city is crammed with people and shops and buildings five times as big as our houses. There are heaps of stores that are filled with all the best, newest computer games and stuff! I'll bring you and Ben back something. Promise."

I pictured him sauntering the streets of Berlin having the time of his life, completely forgetting us.

"Stop looking like that abandoned pup under Black Bridge," he said. "When I can drive, we'll totally go for our own trip. Berlin. All three of us—and Carolin too, if she must."

"When you can drive? That's years away."

He nudged me in the ribs. "Maybe the present cheers you up?"

I studied the gift. I hoped it wasn't too nice. Carolin, Ben, and I had only made our gifts this year. Julian's was in my room —Ben and I had written and drawn a comic for him, starring the *Six-pack Savior* who fought against the evil *Rat-pack Rascals*.

We hoped he'd find it funny. That, or it'd stroke his ego.

"Go on, open it," Julian said, folding his arms and tapping his foot.

I ripped off the wrapping and jumped. "A wax carving kit!" I'd been going on and on about needing one to Oma, hoping she'd get one for me. I threw up my hand to high-five him. "Thanks, Cuz. You're the best."

"Okay," he said, sounding a little shy, his cheeks bright. "Cookie time. Oh wait…" He pulled the Julian-warrior figure from his pocket, handed it to me, and cocked his head slightly to one side. "Now you can really make it look like me."

And I tried too, but it didn't turn out so well.

Not that time at least.

But over the next years, I would keep trying…and one of them, the last of them, would be the reason things changed between us.

Movies

(1999)

"WHAT DO YOU think of Jen?" Ben asked. All three of us boys —Ben, Julian, and I—were crammed on the couch watching an episode of *Dawson's Creek*. My sister was a big fan and the three of us thought we'd check it out while she was at a sleepover. Then, once Oma hit the sack, we were going to watch the scary movie Julian had smuggled in. "Think she's kinda, you know, pretty? Maybe?"

Julian cocked his head and stared at the screen humming, a big frown cutting his brows.

I looked at her. She had boobs, which was what heaps of the boys chatted about at school. Nick and his friend Thomas were always stopping girls on their way into class and asking them to stand next to each other so they could compare.

I shrugged. "She has boobs."

"Yeah," Ben said with a long sigh.

I frowned and studied at the girl's chest until I was dizzy. I guess boobs were…interesting?

Julian shifted and hugged his legs. "That guy's voice is so gravelly and low." He deepened his voice, which had already dropped over the last year, and his words rumbled over my shoulder and into my ear. "I want to sound like that one day."

Ben and I laughed.

"Please tell me this isn't going to be a repeat of the Six Pack Phase?" I said. "I think we'd piss our pants laughing if you went around talking like that."

"Laugh all you like. I caught your pitiful attempt at sit-ups the other day, Lenny." He shoved his fist in my stomach and a whoop of air burst out of me. "Just as I thought. Nada. Not even close. You're all skin and bones."

He grabbed my hand and slapped it on his belly. "Feel that?" His stomach was hard-*ish*. "This is gonna be the year."

Ben and I looked at each other, rolling our eyes. "Sure."

We resumed watching, and I checked out the guy with the cool voice. He scrubbed his hands through his hair, then smiled up at the girl. A slow, lazy grin. For the second that smile lasted, I felt myself stir down low. It didn't happen often, rarely in fact, but sometimes it did.

I leaned forward just in case anything was visible; but it didn't last long.

For the next half an hour, we continued watching. The whole time, Ben squirmed like he wanted to say something, but kept changing his mind.

Then finally, as the credits rolled, he said in a small voice, "Guys?" He didn't take his gaze off the television.

"Yeah?"

"Ah, nothing. Never mind."

"What?"

He just shrugged. "Doesn't matter."

Julian and I looked at each other. His eyes held a mischievous sheen that I read all too well. In the small gap between us, Julian counted to three with his fingers. Each time one finger opened, it tickled over my hip. *One…Two…Three!*

We pounced and Ben was off the couch in seconds, yelling

and laughing and demanding we let him go. I stretched out his arms, and Julian, his legs.

Ben writhed. His eyes looked strange from this angle. Like a blue-eyed alien with a mouth on his pointy forehead. "You guys are going to pay for this. Pay, you hear me?"

"We'll let you go," I said.

"*After* you've spat it out," Julian said.

Ben strained against our hold. "Spat what out?"

"Whatever you were trying to say," I said.

"It really doesn't matter!"

Julian glanced at me and, at my nod, began the first round of tickle-torture.

"Fine! Fine!" Ben wheezed through his laughs. "Let me go. I'll talk."

We let him go. Ben's face was pink from laughing, and he took his time sitting up, straightening his T-shirt and flattening his hair with his palms. He stayed on the floor, wrapping his arms around his legs, and looked from Julian to me on the couch.

Ben opened his mouth again and a blush bloomed over his face, visible in the TV light. "You know Tina?" he blurted out. "I think she wants to go out with me."

"What makes you think that?" I asked.

"She wrote me a Valentine's note."

Julian coolly waggled his brows. "Sweet," he said. "You like her?"

"I dunno, I mean. She's nice. But...um..." He looked away, fidgeting with his fingers. "How do you ask a girl out?"

I shrugged. "Never done that before. Julian?"

Ben and I both turned to my cousin for advice. He was the oldest, the one who claimed to have all the answers to everything. It was him who set us both straight on the whole *Santa didn't exist* thing. And him who explained about sex and babies —which we'd all agreed sounded pretty gross.

The rose blush that'd crept over Ben's face was now creeping over Julian's. He shrugged. "Ask her and her friends to come to a movie with us. That's how other guys in my class do it. And make sure it's a scary one—that way you have an excuse to hold her."

I punched him in the arm. "Charming. You've done that before?"

"That's none of your business." He jumped off the couch and rummaged in his bag. "Is Oma in bed already?"

I went and checked, coming back with my thumbs up.

"Sweet. Now, let's watch *this* movie."

Two hours later, we climbed into my bed a bunch of shaking limbs. I tried to wedge myself in the middle, but Julian and Ben pushed me to the side next to the lamp. Ben lay in the center, and Julian on the far side, by the windows.

I switched off the lamp, drowning us in the night.

I tried to close my eyes, but they were riveted to the shadows in the room. Shadows that seemed to move. That seemed to whisper horrible, torturous things filled with blood and crawling body parts.

They promised me I wouldn't get a wink of sleep.

What the hell had possessed us to watch that movie? I growled out the answer as I tucked myself closer to Ben. "Julian."

"Yeah?" he whispered, lifting himself on one elbow to look over Ben at me.

"Nothing." *Stupid, stupid movie!*

We continued to stare at each other, only occasionally darting our gaze to those whispering shadows. At the very least, I was happy that Julian looked as freaked as I felt. After a long time—minutes? Hours?—Julian's eyelids fluttered shut. I yawned in agreement, praying for a dreamless sleep—

I yelped as something scuttled down the side of my cheek and shoved the blanket up over my face.

My yelping made the others jump, and suddenly all three of us were under the covers, our scared breaths keeping us warm.

It felt safer under here. The only thing…I needed to pee. But I *really* didn't want to walk downstairs on my own. "Shit!"

"Dammit," Julian said in that forced, low, husky voice.

"Fuck," Ben said, and laughed.

"Son of a bitch."

"Asshole."

"Fuck you, you fucking fuck."

"Moron."

"Dick-a-roo."

"Kiss my ass!"

I snorted at Julian's last one, and suddenly our swearing session switched to a crude one.

Ben took the lead. "Jerk off."

"Horny."

"Dirty whore."

"Balls."

"Vag."

"Cock."

And that reminded me of my pressing need. "Fuck, shit-a-brick, I need to pee."

Ben threw back the blankets. "So go."

I glanced at the dark outline of the door and the even darker hall behind it. A draft crawled over me and…was that the creaking of wood?

Maybe I could hold my pee in until morning?

Except all that laughing…

"One of you has to come with me," I said.

Julian laughed, and I threw my pillow at his head. "Ben. You come. Julian's so big and brave, he can stay here. *Alone.*"

He muttered into the blanket, "Ah, crap."

Ben and I shuffled off the bed and crept downstairs. Floorboards groaned under us and one of Oma's loud, engine-starting snores ripped through the air. Ben jumped, gripping my arm like there was no tomorrow.

"Next time pee out the window," he hissed. I dragged him into the bathroom with me.

"Press against the door so nothing comes in," I said, wishing we had a lock on the door.

I did my business in record time, washed my hands with a slap of soap and dash of water, and dried them on my shorts as Ben and I raced back up the stairs two at a time. With frightened, snorting giggles, we dove into the bed.

"I don't give a damn what you guys think," I said. "We're sleeping with the fucking nightlight tonight."

There were no complaints or laughs, just two audibly relieved sighs. I plugged one in by the desk and huddled back under the blankets.

Julian was the last to speak before we finally fell asleep. He punched his pillow, fluffing it up, and then rested his head, facing Ben and me. "Okay, I changed my mind," he said. "Don't invite the girl to a scary movie."

Birthdays and Fortunes

(2000)

I SCREWED UP a sketch I'd been doodling of Oma peering into her crystal ball at the kitchen table. It was all the scarves she wore that made it hard. I just couldn't seem to give them life. They looked too flat.

That was why I preferred making things three-dimensional, like with the clay, the moldings, and the wax.

I scrunched the paper into a tight ball and threw it at Carolin as she waltzed into the kitchen. It bounced off the curls she'd spent the last hour working on with a hot rolling iron.

"What the hell's with you?" she said, carefully pressing her hair to make sure her curls were in place.

I shrugged. "Nothing."

That was a lie.

Dammit, I just needed not to think about it. Who cared, anyway? It wasn't that much of a big deal...

Carolin bent to pick up the paper I'd chucked at her. She opened it on the table opposite Oma, who was still staring hard into the crystal, murmuring something. Carolin flattened the paper. "Where's the rest of you?" she asked.

"The rest of me?"

"You know, your two appendages, the ones usually stuck to your hip." She took the picture to the fridge and stuck it there with a banana magnet. "Ben? Julian?"

I scowled at her, then stood up from my chair and dragged it with a grating squeal back to the table. I didn't want to talk to Carolin about my "appendages."

Unfortunately, Oma did. She snagged my sleeve and pulled me close. "Ben's mama has taken him to see his father's side of the family. They have flown over here and are in Berlin for a week."

Carolin took an apple from the fruit bowl and polished it against her chest. "Right," she murmured, frowning, gaze cast down. She glanced at Oma, mouth opening as if she wanted to say something, but she shut it again, and shined the apple with more vigor. "And Julian?"

Oma let go of my sleeve to pat my arm.

"He's at a birthday party," I said, pulling away from her.

Oma shook her head, the setting sun stretching a warm glow over her, making her curls shine all creamy like moonlight. "Not just *any* party, either," she said gently. "It's Julian's. His thirteenth."

I caught Carolin's wince, and I couldn't bear to hear anything she had to say. So what Julian didn't invite me like he did the last years? I didn't care.

Not a bit.

"I've got homework," I said, and rushed up to my room, slamming my door behind me. I fell back onto my bed and stared at the ceiling, planning what I could do to make it less… grey. Less boring. Less lonely.

I rolled onto my side and fished under the bed for the soccer ball I had under there. I threw it against the lonely grey over and over, imagining the *thump-thump-thump* it made was music. When I got bored of that, I turned on the radio as loud as I could, then, back pressed once more to the mattress with my gangly legs in the air, I balanced the ball on the soles of my feet.

My bedroom door swung in, sending in a wicked gust of air. I started and the ball dropped on my face with a smack. A twang of pain had me blinking. "Shit." I sat up, lunged for the ball, and whirled it at Carolin—

Except it wasn't my sister.

Framed in my doorway, in the last of the evening light, was Julian in the T-shirt I'd had printed for him last Christmas.

The soccer ball smashed into his mid-section and I winced. Julian's face bloomed red as he swore and buckled over, dropping the plastic box he carried to the floor.

I leaped off the bed and moved over to him. "You okay?"

Julian went strangely quiet. Did it hurt so badly—?

Wham! His arms wrapped around my legs. He lifted me over his shoulder and tackled me onto the bed. The mattress met my back with a cushioned *thwump*, and a five-foot-ten Julian robbed the air from my lungs. "I'm sorry!" I wheezed.

He unwrapped his arms from my middle and rolled off me, laughing so hard his eyes squished together, crinkling slightly at the sides.

I punched him in the arm. "What the fuck? Did you fake the pain?"

He shook his head. "Balls...sting. But...your face... looked...startled...raccoon."

I hit him again, but this time not quite so hard, and my fist lingered on his chest and upper arm, slowly uncurling. "I hate you."

That cooled off Julian's laughter fast. "Yeah, about that..."

He pushed up on his elbows, and I drew my hand away, tucking it under my head. I couldn't hold Julian's focused gaze, so I looked up at my ceiling. My whole body was taut waiting for Julian to speak.

His mouth smacked a couple of times, then he sighed.

"What," I said, "cat got your tongue? Or maybe you're too exhausted after talking to your real friends all day."

I caught the blurry movement of Julian moving and felt the bed spring up as he got off it. I swallowed a sigh. Everything about this fucking day sucked major ass.

Something scraped on the floor and then came the distinct sound of a lid popping. Julian's footsteps slurped passed the side of the bed where my legs dangled and moved to the opposite side. Julian's side. Near the windows.

Closing my eyes, I felt the air stir behind me. It touched my skin in the lightest way, shifting one strand of my hair, and a shiver rippled over me.

The bed dipped and when I opened my eyes, Julian was staring down at me. "I hated that you and Ben weren't at my party. I like my other friends but it sucked without you two." He shrugged. "You know how Mama is."

I did. "We're not a bad influence."

"I know. But if she could, she'd keep me away for good. I whined for forever to get her to change her mind, but she said she thought I'd have grown out of inviting you. When I said *never*, she said she's looking out for my best interests. But," he said, shifting out of my sight for a second, "that didn't stop me from sneaking over here to give you some of this. Sit up."

I sat, twisting toward him. I spotted the cake and my tummy rumbled. Julian snorted and handed me a square piece of chocolate cake.

I snatched it from him and took a large, sticky, seriously chocolaty bite. "I *love* you."

"Knew you wouldn't hate me for long." The Julian smirk was back. He fished out another piece from his plastic box and ate too.

"Aren't you caked out by now?"

"I wanted to have my piece with you."

"Then do you have to get back to your party?" I said with a full mouth.

"Soonish, yeah. Uli has snuck over some peppermint schnapps, herby liquor, and some porn for later."

I was pretty sure I was going the color of peppermint myself. I hated missing out on all the fun. And, well, I'd never seen any porn before. I was curious.

I put down the rest of my cake on the plastic lid between us, then shuffled off the bed and gestured for Julian to follow. Downstairs, inside the hollow bench in the kitchen, I had his gift. It was nothing special, really. Just a CD I knew he wanted.

His hug made it seem like I'd given him the world. "You must have saved up ages for this," he said, glancing around our kitchen. Which I'd never really thought of as small until I he looked at it that way. Suddenly, I was huge, he was huger, and my kitchen was tiny: a doll's house, hosting giants.

And then the air grew warm. Really warm, and it felt like breathing through a straw. I suddenly couldn't stand Julian in our home anymore, cocking his head with those saddened forest eyes, looking at it—at *me*—like that.

"You're welcome," I said, pushing against his chest. I would have pushed him all the way down the hall and out the front door too, if Oma hadn't materialized.

Yes. Materialized. One second it was just Julian and I, alone in the shrinking kitchen, and the next, Oma was there, resting a firm hand on my shoulder, telling us both to sit our asses at the table. Now.

I did. Reluctantly. Refusing to look at my cousin.

I stared at the window. It was dark enough outside that the glass mirrored everything. I watched Oma's reflection as she reached out for the crystal ball in the center of the table and dragged it closer. Her bright green and pink scarf stood out, and for a moment the art of the scene was beautiful. Then I glanced at Julian's reflection. His head was twisted in my direction, shoulders hunching lightly as he sighed.

I blinked away and stared at my own reflection. Chestnut hair, tousled and unkempt; thin lips twitching in an ugly pout; and chin, jutting out—an exclamation of my pride.

"I can read into your futures," Oma said. "Would you like to know what I see?"

I folded my arms and shrugged, not wanting to appear as if I cared.

But I focused all my attention on Oma's reflection as she laid the tips of her fingers on the crystal ball and moved them in circles. Her eyes shut and her breathing deepened, turning into a hum. Then she snapped her eyes open and met my reflected gaze. I jerked in my chair, scraping it a few inches across the floor.

Julian leaned over, frowning. "You okay?"

I blinked back at Oma—her big eyes so much darker, so much bigger than usual. An eerie shiver rolled over me, and though I wanted to really badly, I couldn't look away. What did she know of my future?

"W...What do you see?" I asked, my voice barely more than a croak.

"I see both of your futures at once," she said.

Julian shifted on his seat.

"You do?" I asked.

"I do. Because they are intertwined."

"What does that mean?" I said, a nervous shiver sneaking through me.

"It means you'll be in each other's lives for a long time."

Julian shrugged. "That's nothing I didn't already know," he said. Then he leaned over the table toward Oma and whispered loudly:

"But I'm glad Lenny knows it now, too."

Kissy-kissy

(2001)

BEN was thirteen and a half before he plucked up the courage and asked Tina out. Properly, that was. They'd been holding hands and ringing each other in the evenings for months before that.

The scary movie idea that Julian had once had was moot, since none of us could have gotten in. So, on a cold and sunny winter's weekend, we went to a romantic comedy instead.

Oma dropped us off at the small theatre in the next village. The girls were waiting for us outside, huddled together in their pink coats and woolen hats. "Are those your dates?" Oma asked.

I pointed to Ben. "He has the date."

"And who's the lucky girl?"

"Tina," I said, pointing her out. "The tall one with the black hair."

Oma nodded and smacked her pink painted lips together. "Okay. Quick chat, boys."

I shrugged my shoulders at Ben and Julian's raised brows, and we turned our attention to Oma.

"I'll keep it simple. I don't want any girl getting pregnant, are we clear?"

We shook our heads vigorously. We'd learned enough at school (and from Julian) to know exactly what she was talking about, and *no way* were we ever going that far.

"Good," Oma said. "That's settled. Out you go then. Have fun. Ben, I hope you brushed your teeth."

Ben cupped a hand around his mouth and breathed into it, his expression paling. He rubbed his palms over his grey slacks. "Crap."

Oma chuckled, fished through her fake-alligator handbag and threw back a stick of gum.

Ben stuffed it in his mouth, and Julian clicked open both their belts. "You'll be fine," he said. Then he reached over and spiked Ben's hair. Ben tried to bat him away, but *good luck with that.* "Better."

"Great," I said, "now you're like a blond, slightly smaller version of Julian."

Julian gave a wicked smirk. "He should be so lucky."

"Right," Oma said. "Out. All of you. I'm looking forward to a few kid-less hours and that sale at Mystic Corner. I'll meet you here after your movie."

We squeezed out of the car and had barely hit the foot-path, when Oma hooted her freedom and screeched out from the curb.

"Seriously," Ben said. "Oma Niki is something else."

We met the girls at the corner, awkwardly danced our way to the ticket counter, bought tickets and popcorn, and filed into the darkened theatre.

Tina's friends sat at the side of the room, and Tina and Ben chose seats in the middle, near the back. Ben none-too-subtly motioned for Julian and I to sit behind him.

"Only if you don't mind jokes at your expense," Julian said

and sidled down the back row. I carefully picked my way after him, balancing a large coke and popcorn.

The lights dimmed as soon as I sat. I jammed the popcorn between my thighs, and Julian stole my coke. I nudged him in the ribs. "Get your own."

"You've got a whole liter," he said, straw poised at his mouth. "You're not going to drink it all."

His lips moved over the straw slowly, as if daring me to stop him. I swallowed, throat suddenly parched. I wanted—*needed*—to drink right away.

His cheeks hollowed as he sucked in, long and hard.

I snatched my coke back and pulled out the straw he'd molested. Julian chuckled and something in that soft sound made me hesitate. It was just a second—a buzzing second—but for a moment I wanted to stuff the straw back in and suck on it the way he had. The moment passed and I ripped off the lid and chugged the rest of the drink.

The fizz burned my throat and the back of my nose, and my eyes watered, but I powered through it. Julian watched me, his lips curling.

I finished and ripped out a burp that had Ben turning back to scowl at me.

Julian laughed, dug into his pocket and pulled out his wallet. Opening it, he pulled out a few coins. "You can buy us another one."

"Why should I buy it?" I said—*whispered*, since the movie had just begun.

Julian took the ice-filled remainder of my coke and placed it on his other side. Then he pressed the money into my hands. "Because after downing all that, you're going to need to piss real soon. Grab the drink on your way back."

Damn him, but Julian was right. Half the movie later, I was squirming in my seat, the popcorn jerking closer and closer to the edge. As if he knew exactly what was up, Julian snagged the popcorn box and placed it on his lap. He gestured me to go with a flick of his hand and a smooth smile.

When I got back, I handed him the coke and kept the change. He quickly summarized what I'd missed—not the movie, but Ben and Tina.

"They keep looking at each other when the other one isn't looking. Like this," he said and looked at the screen while I was left frowning at the side of his face. Then, when I glanced down to Ben, I caught Julian swiveling his head in my direction. As soon as I looked at him again, he jerked his gaze away.

I chuckled, then laughed louder when I caught Ben doing exactly that to Tina.

Julian continued lightly making fun of our friend, touching me the same way Ben did Tina (when he dared). I played along —even if Ben would give us shit later.

But, it was fun. I could...I don't know, somehow I could really see the thrill in all of it. The dark theater, the grazing touches that shot little sparks through the body and lingered in the gut...

Ben leaned over to Tina, cupped a hand to her ear and whispered something. When Julian did it, I just about leaped from the chair. He gripped my arm, keeping me from lurching upwards. His breath was warm and wet on my ear and it seemed to roll over my skin, down my neck. I raised my shoulder but it didn't stop the tickling, instead I knocked Julian's chin, bringing his lips crashing against my temple.

He chuckled and his breath somehow turned into a shiver that worked its way through my veins.

My dick stirred. Was this how Ben felt with Tina? Did he have all these prickly sparks randomly going off inside? Was this what it would feel like when I went out with my own...girl-friend, the first time?

When it was Tina's turn to whisper back to Ben, I did the same to Julian. I breathed heavily, hoping that weird feeling rolled over his skin too. He twitched and I stilled the popcorn between his legs before it knocked over Ben's head.

Then Ben and Tina inched closer, their heads closing in— Julian and I smirked, mimicking them until suddenly our breaths were mingling, and my heart was racing. His lips were right there, and I was staring at them. Really staring at them. A flash of Julian sucking on my straw almost made me lean in farther.

I hurriedly pulled away, then forced a casual snigger. Maybe we were taking this mocking thing a little too seriously.

A small frown cut between Julian's brows, and he rubbed it, looking away.

"Kissy-kissy," Julian said, sounding less enthusiastic than before. Or perhaps a little…parched?

Ben drew away from Tina and threw us both a look, effectively breaking the awkwardness that had suddenly wedged itself like a third seat between Julian and me.

We looked at each other out the corners of our eyes and laughed, smothering the sound in the crooks of our elbows. Then a kernel of popcorn hit the side of my face.

Julian smirked, and threw another one. Without taking my eyes off him, I reached over his lap and plucked some popcorn. I flicked a piece at him with a sly smile of my own. The first one hit his nose. The second, he caught in his mouth.

And that was that. For the rest of the movie, it was an all-out, popcorn flicking war.

Not That Drunk At All

(2002)

WE CRASHED NICK'S end-of-summer party. We didn't know it then, but it would become a yearly tradition.

Nickelback, strobe lights, and smuggled alcohol filled Nick's garage, but Ben, Julian and I didn't care to join the crowds in there. We hung out in the back garden. Close enough to see the chaos—and Nick making out with his girlfriend against the backside of the garage—but far enough away, behind a couple of apple trees, that he wouldn't catch us.

Julian leaned back in the garden chair and crossed his ankles. He looked at Ben and me toting a quarter bottle of hard liquor and his eyes gleamed with apprehension. His foot jiggled as much as my insides did.

I'd drank a couple of beers before, but this was a whole other level.

I poured some booze into a plastic cup, smelled the herby liquid, and raised my cup to Ben on the other end of the bench. I knocked mine back. It burned my throat and I spluttered, gasping for air.

A deep rumbling laugh escaped Julian.

Ben downed his shot with no more grace. His eyes bugged

and watered, and he was incapable of saying anything for a good five seconds. When he did, he shook his head, and the hair he'd been growing surfer-style came out of his hair tie.

"Gimme the bottle," he said, reaching over and picking it up. "I reckon I'd drink you and Julian both under the table."

Julian snatched it back. "Don't be so cocky. I've been drinking longer than both you guys." He took a long swig. A drop ran from the bottle and plopped onto his green T-shirt, darkening one small splotch by his collar. "Okay. Now you can go again."

Round and round the bottle went, our plastic cups quickly ditched for a straight-from-the-bottle experience. Each of us claimed we didn't feel any different. Maybe we had a high tolerance.

"I just feel good," Ben said. A new song came on in the distance and he stood up, jumped on the bench, and started rolling his body like all the girls would love a piece of his ass. He clapped his hands above his head and jerked his hips. His jeans were slung low on his hips, shiny boxers sticking out the top. I was afraid one hip-thrust too many and his jeans would slip off.

Actually, I wasn't that afraid. It was too funny a thought. Especially since his boxers were covered in puppies.

When Julian decided to join in, adding to the "let's bang the music" dance, I doubled over clutching my gut. Julian jumped on the middle of our bench, making it bend and wobble under me. I shifted onto the garden chair with the bottle and took another drag of liquor.

Ben started singing the lyrics, holding a pretend microphone to his mouth and squeezing his eyes shut. And Julian sent kisses to the invisible crowd they were dancing to.

I jumped to my feet and acted the crowd. I grabbed at the kisses, cupped them to my chest and cheek, and fluttered my eyelashes, trying not to snort.

We weren't drunk at all.

The chorus came, and Julian grabbed his T-shirt and pulled it off. Ben did the same and then, in a somewhat synchronized fashion, they whipped their T-shirts like lassos over their heads, bucking their hips.

Ben and Julian shared a look, then swung their T-shirts around their necks and ran their hands run down their chests.

Ben thrust out his chest showing off the *one* hair he had there.

"Oh Ben," I said mimicking a girl. "Can I have your autograph?" The snort I'd been holding erupted out of me. "Fuck guys, you look hilarious."

I took another long pull from the fast emptying bottle and glanced at Julian.

He was a touch broader than Ben and a half-foot taller. He'd still not managed the whole six-pack thing, but his shape tapered nicely to his waist and he had a flat stomach that sported a thin treasure trail.

I slowly lifted my gaze to find him watching me with that signature tilt of his head. My breath fled and I gripped the bottleneck tight. Hurriedly, I drained the rest of the liquor and focused on Ben and his crazy dancing, but Julian was still there in the corner of my eye. Watching.

"We need more alcohol!" I yelled.

"There's a half-bottle of whiskey under the chair," Ben said, pointing in time with his dance.

I grabbed it and unscrewed the top, then Julian and Ben whipped their shirts around their heads. "Let go in three," Julian counted down, "two…"

Then two things happened one after the other. Two things that would end up turning this night into a memory I'd never forget.

The first:

Ben let go of his shirt early. The blue material arched and

flew toward the nearest apple tree at the same moment two girls stepped out from behind it.

Whollop! His T-shirt hit the first girl and the plastic cup she held. The cup tipped, and red wine spilled down her white top.

Ben looked like he was torn between laughing and apologizing. He jumped off the bench and moved over to the girls, wearing his dimpled *forgive me* grin. Only, when he was two feet away, he stopped slurring *sorry* and froze.

From where I was, the girl's face had been partially hidden by a branch, but it soon became clear why Ben had stopped talking and moving and everything.

"Ben!" the girl shrieked, the voice very familiar and very mad.

Carolin.

The second:

Julian reined his shirt in just before it too hit someone. He jumped off the bench, gaze rooted toward our poor friend Ben.

But somehow his foot twisted funny and he lost his balance.

I saw it in slow motion; he was two feet away and falling toward me, and I knew we were both going down.

His head hit mine first, his *dammit* the only pocket of air to cushion us as we tumbled. My body thumped against his and the bottle of whiskey dropped.

Julian's arm wrapped around my waist, tightening me to him, his other arm outstretching to take the impact. Then he rolled us so he hit the dry, packed ground.

My face was glued to the side of his neck and part of his chest.

"Whoa." I peeled my head off him, hands pressed to his chest.

His eyes were closed, and he started shaking under my fingers. Shit. Had he really hurt himself? "You okay?"

I looked at his face and caught the twitch of his lips.

Laughing. He was laughing, eyes narrow slits as they watched me.

I scrambled off him, grabbing his T-shirt that had fallen next to us. I chucked it at his head. "Shirt on. We need to save Ben—Oh, no."

I'd looked over at Ben just in time to see him do the dumbest thing of his life. He reached out and started wiping Carolin's wine-stained chest with his hands. "It'll come out," he said. "I'm sure it will."

The slap she gave him resounded loudly around us. Julian and I both winced.

I hurried to Ben's side, throwing him a sympathetic smile and mouthing, "you good?" I folded my arms and stared at Carolin. "Hey sis. What's up?"

"You are so screwed," she said, and her friend sniggered. "Oma is going to—hell, I have no idea what she'll do to you. Sneaking out?" She leaned in and sniffed my mouth. "Drinking? It'll be at least two weeks of whatever she cooks up."

"You're not going to tell her," I hissed.

She narrowed her eyes in challenge, and then suddenly it morphed into a smile. "Sure. Okay," she said, "*if*…"

"If what?" Julian asked, rocking up next to me, his shirt on.

"*If* you invite me on your camping trip next weekend."

"You hate camping," I said, "Why—"

"I want the invite. In front of Oma. Then she'll think I'm out in the bushes with you lot—which, you will vouch for."

Still rubbing his cheek and casting Carolin dirty looks, Ben said, "Where will you actually be?"

"A concert with me and our boyfriends," the girl we'd all ignored said. I looked at the tall, leggy blonde wearing what looked like swim gear with a very short skirt over it.

"So, you going to invite me?" Carolin said, unbuttoning her top. She threw it at me. "Give me your T-shirt, Lenny."

"What? No way."

"To the shirt or the deal?"

Julian leaned an arm on my shoulder and said, "We'll invite you if you keep your mouth zipped about your brother drinking."

"Good. Now I can't go around with a stained camisole..." She gestured to the silky thing she was still wearing, which unfortunately was very thin and very see-through. I *really* didn't need to see my sister's lacy underthings.

"Here," Ben said, picking up his T-shirt at Carolin's feet. "You can wear mine. Seems only fair."

"Fine," she said to Ben. Then to me: "And because I love you, I'll give you a heads up." She pointed behind the apple tree. "Nick's seen you guys. He's coming over with some friends, and he looks pissed."

She did love me. I knew that. But the reason she gave us the heads up didn't have swat to do with love. It was because she needed that invite—an invite that could only happen if we weren't grounded. And for that, Nick couldn't catch us and tattle-tale...

We sprinted.

I dragged behind the other two so I could scoop up the whiskey bottle I'd dropped earlier. I didn't have time to find the lid, so I pressed the opening against my palm and ran. The alcohol splashed against my hand and, as I was vaulting over the low chicken wire fence, I wondered if the liquid seeping into my skin could get me drunk.

If, you know, we could get drunk *at all*. So far the alcohol hadn't done anything...dancing half-naked, and being chased off Leike's property...that was just another day.

Drunken hollering and the crashing sound of Nick and his friends hurtling over the long, grassy paddock followed us. Ben sped up, muttering between puffs about his pale skin making them a target in the moonlight. "Should never have given her my shirt!"

I snorted on a laugh, my legs aching from running so hard.

Julian, the fastest of us three and far ahead, doubled back for us. Seeing him trot toward Nick and his pitchfork-carrying sidekicks made me giggle. Hard.

"Shhh," Julian said, pulling me by the hand to the wire fence that led into the haunted woods. Ben and I stopped abruptly, giggles fast subsiding.

Everyone in Waldau knew the story of the kids that went in there and never came out. Some even said it was the true origins of Hansel and Gretel.

Needless to say, not one of us kids ever fucking went into the woods.

"Come this way."

"Are you kidding? Hell no."

Ben looked from the woods to Nick and company behind us. There was violence in the way their boots stamped on the grass, the way they seemed to lock eyes with us, the way they *charged*.

Ben shrugged and jumped the fence joining Julian.

I glanced at Julian's outstretched arm. Then I looked over his shoulder at the wood that seemed to grow darker and creep closer like it wanted to swallow us all whole.

"Rather the village riot," I said, taking a step back.

"Lenny," he warned, and when I didn't move, he swung a leg over the wire fence, grabbed me into a fireman's hold and, like I weighed nothing, hauled me over.

He didn't let me go until Nick and his friends' warrior cries had faded and we'd trekked a good ten minutes into the cavernous mouth of the forest.

Somehow, even with all the manhandling, I still managed to keep the whiskey bottle.

I finally slipped off Julian's shoulder, twigs snapping under my feet and making me jump. Ben sniggered and grabbed the whiskey from me. "There's no such thing as witches," he said, and guzzled from the bottle before pressing it into Julian's hand.

"Where are we going?" I said as I squeezed myself between them.

Ben wrapped an arm around my neck and started howling like a wolf or a ghost—it was hard to tell which. Either way, my answer was an elbow to his ribs.

He cracked up, spraying out of his mouth. Maybe *he* was drunk.

Julian veered to the left suddenly. "There...see?"

I peered through the gaps in the night-laced trees to the night-laced everything behind them. "This backs up onto my place," Julian said.

I made out the familiar roof in the distance. "Sweet. Let's get caught by auntie. That's so much better than Oma."

He clocked me over the back of the head. "Shut up." Then he grinned at us. "And we're not going inside the house."

"We're not?"

"Nope," he said, gesturing us to follow. "We're going to the shed out the back. There's a small bed, a couch, a television, and maybe even some leftover schnapps in there."

Yeah, there was all that, all right.

There was also porn.

But I wouldn't discover that until early the next year...

The Best and Worst and Longest Night Ever

(EARLY 2003)

I LITERALLY STUMBLED over Julian's porn collection.

At the bottom of a bottle of tequila, and halfway through a game of cards, Ben had conked out to the land of zzzzz's. When he started to tip towards the floor, Julian and I lifted and moved him to the bed. I draped the blanket over him, tucking it under his side. I didn't want him waking up to a cold.

As I stepped back from the bed, I bashed into a small shelf filled with computer games, videos and—

What would you know?

There was a video wedged between the back of the shelf and the wall, angled in such a way that I could make out part of the cover. A naked ass. "Huh." I bent over and picked it up. *A Hole Lot of Trouble to Cum.* I laughed, waving it at Julian. "What you *really* do out here, huh?"

Julian sank into the couch, crossing his ankle over his knee and resting his head back. He slowly faced me, a shit-eating grin on his face. Waggling his brows, he lifted his hand and curled a finger at me to come over. "Brilliant idea."

I hurtled the video at him and he caught it with a clap

between two hands. "Come on, Lenny. It's not like you've never watched porn before."

Actually, I hadn't.

I'd *tried* to check it out once last month but my sister had walked in. I'd only just changed the channel in time—and hadn't dared trying since.

Julian sat up straight, an alcohol induced twinkle in his eye. "You haven't?" There was something in the way he said it that sounded far too...excited. "Then this should be fun."

"Fun," I murmured. The same feeling I got when I was in a car and the road sloped suddenly and gravity started chasing me with its large tickly fingers—that exact feeling came over me. I swallowed as I stumbled toward the couch. "Fun. Yeah. Okay."

Things sloped even more when Julian stood, put the video in the player, and flicked the lights.

There was little light in the shed; enough to outline the both of us, but still dark enough to make it feel like we were curtained with privacy.

The film began, and not five minutes later, moans from the actors fucking filled the air, robbing me of breath and making my throat dry. I kept swallowing, equal parts embarrassed and fascinated as I watched the man's ass clench as he thrust into the woman he'd pinned on his desk.

A soft puff of air from Julian made me glance his way. He averted his gaze back to the screen.

As the male's thrusts picked up pace, Julian's expression darkened, lips edging toward a lust-filled place, and I felt myself stretching, wanting so badly to follow him there.

I couldn't help but press the heel of my palm over the sensitive swell in my jeans. Fuck. Watching this really made me want to jerk off. A quick peek at Julian made it clear he was just as hard. His hands were gripped on the arm of the couch and the remote.

"Maybe this isn't suck—*such*—a good idea," I mumbled.

Julian pressed pause and the screen stopped on a shot of the guy's cock mid-thrust. "What were you saying?" His voice carried laughter and a hint of nervousness. "Something about suck?"

I grabbed the small cushion that was between us and chucked it at him. "Laugh all you want, but Jesus, Julian, watching that is making me so fucking horny."

Julian's free hand moved to his crotch, where he openly rubbed himself. "Yeah. Me, too." He looked over at me, glancing down to where my hand was doing the same thing. He gulped, then shrugged it off. "It's not like we need to be shy about it or anything, right?"

He dropped the remote and arched himself off the couch, then he undid his jeans and shoved them to his knees. "I know you do it; you know I do it. Or do I have to remind you of the time you came running to me the first time you came, freaked out you had an infection?"

I wished there was another cushion to throw at him. But I was all out. Besides, at the rate my fingers were fumbling over my jeans to yank them off, I wouldn't have been able to. "Okay. Turn it back on! I'll imagine I'm with Jessica Kolb."

Julian frowned. "Jessica who?"

"Kolb," I said, and brought my cool hand to my shaft. "Girl that likes me."

Julian stilled the hand stroking himself. "First *I* heard of it. And?"

"And what?"

"Do you like her?"

I shrugged, and he resumed his stroking—the same slow-slow, ring-around-the-head pattern I worked on myself. I pulled my gaze from him and his slightly upward curving cock and rooted my sight back on the screen. "She's all right, I suppose."

"Huh." The movie started again. Positions were changed,

and I wasn't quite feeling it as I watched the woman bouncing up and down. Just as I was starting to go limp, the male flipped her over and started thrusting into her from behind. The way his hands gripped her hips...his ass flexing...the sweat rolling between his shoulder blades...

I moved my hand to the tip of my cock, teasing circles around the tip until I felt that buzz-thrill in my balls. I switched back to pumping, my hand sliding faster and faster.

I glanced at Julian, doing the same.

Faster, faster—

My legs tensed, and I choked on a moan as I came into my hand.

Julian worked up to his climax, head thrown back, his ragged breaths hitching. He jerked once more and then sagged, mouth hanging open. I couldn't be sure, but I thought he mouthed something; maybe the name of a crush? I tossed him the box of tissues I found instead.

He caught it, barely opening his eyes, and gave me a crooked smile. "Thanks."

"Can we turn it off?" The moans and cries of the actors were just awkward now.

Julian laughed. "Yeah. I think the remote fell on the floor."

I did up my pants and then fumbled in the dark for the remote, but I couldn't find it. Thinking it'd slipped under the couch, I got on all fours, head pressed to the carpet, my ass sticking up in the air.

This was the position Aunt Thomas caught me in when she burst through the shed door. An icy gust of wind tunneled into the room, and I jerked up, hitting the back of my head on the seat cushion, making it fly into Julian's horrified face.

I lunged to my feet, quickly taking in Julian's zipped-up state and allowing a semi-relieved breath, before I twisted toward my aunt.

She was blinking at the television screen. I didn't dare

follow her gaze. But the moans and "Oh, yeahs" and "Harders" were filling the suddenly very small shed very, very quickly.

I choked on the sounds as they came faster, threatening to drown me. Shit. Where was the remote?

I glanced at Julian again, hoping maybe he'd be able to make it stop. Or at least get his mama to look away. But, save for his Adam's apple jutting as swallowed, he had frozen. He clutched the cushion as he stared at his mama.

Aunt Thomas slowly turned toward us. "What's this?"

I had to break the spell. Had to get Julian back from wherever he was to the here-and-now. I moved to the television, feeling the resentment and dislike flickering over me as I passed Aunt Thomas and turned off the screen.

As soon as I did, darkness smothered us.

"Dammit," Julian whispered. Then Aunt Thomas found the light switch and we found ourselves in a bright, fluorescent reality.

A reality which was about to choke me so god-damned hard.

It came out in a whoosh of hurried breath: "It was Lenny's idea. He brought it over!"

I swung my head toward Julian at the same time Aunt Thomas swung her head to me. She said something, but I didn't hear her. My ears were ringing with the tinny sound of disbelief. This was my *friend*, the guy who'd stood up for me, the guy who made me laugh every day, the guy who snuck out of his house to spend time with me, the guy I *trusted* enough to jerk off with, the guy I…

"…your great aunt and cousins…wish you could choose family…not them…"

I balled my fists at my side, throat burning as I held back the angry words I wanted to spew at him just then.

I found my shoes and shoved them on, ignoring Aunt

Thomas as she told me to stay away and stop corrupting her son.

I reached for the door.

Julian dropped his cushion and lunged over the room to catch my arm. "Lenny!" he said, trying to pull me back in, his fingers digging into my bicep, his face close to mine.

"Let him leave, Julian," Aunt Thomas said. "You're better off without him. And we need to talk."

Julian's grip loosened on me, but just for a second, a very small second, then he was back to wrapping his arms around my chest so I wouldn't leave. "I'm sorry," he said, panicked, into my ear.

There was earnestness in his voice, and any other day, any other time, I would have shrugged this all off. Maybe even laughed. Who cared if Aunt Thomas thought it was my porn? She didn't like me anyway. It wouldn't have mattered.

And yet, tonight, it did.

Tonight it felt like something in me was crumpling inward and then trying to claw up my throat. Heat gathered at the back of my eyes making the half of my aunt I could see and the door blur. One second, I could feel every nuance of Julian's touch, the way his fingers skated up and down my arms, the nose that bumped on the back of my head, the prickles that came as he breathed in deeply. Then the next second everything was numb. I could have been asleep, dreaming this.

"You've got other friends," Aunt Thomas said softly.

And my throat was back to burning, jaw clenching. I elbowed Julian in the gut and tugged free. His surprised intake of breath hit the back of my neck, spurring me to get out of there faster, faster—before I threw up.

"Just shut up, Mama," he yelled as I raced into the frosty night. "Ground me for life, I don't fucking care, but don't tell me who my friends are!"

I was halfway down the grassy path, dew soaking into my shoes, when the shed door slammed.

"You get back here, Julian Jacob Thomas."

I quickened my pace, suddenly desperate to curl up in Oma's arms like I used to as a kid and let her rock away all the bad feelings.

"Lenny!"

I broke into a run.

"Lenny, *please!*"

I slammed through our gate, slipping on the gravel, and almost staked myself on the fence.

God dammit!

I pushed off the splintered wood and skidded toward the back door. I fumbled for my key and swore. I'd left it in Julian's shed.

I didn't dare bang on the door and wake Oma—she was finding it harder and harder to sleep and waking her would be cruel.

I doubled back into the yard. There was a spare key inside the fake rock by the cherry trees.

The crunching of steps came up behind me, along with Julian's panting breaths. "Lenny?" he said, reaching for me.

I lurched out of his reach.

"Stop!" He caught me under the frost-covered cherry trees, lifting the rock for the spare key. "This is stupid. Talk to me."

"Leave me alone."

"I'm sorry. I panicked back there."

A half-laugh, half-grunt popped out of my mouth. Maybe my throat was just too damn sore to hold it all in. "You don't say."

"Fuck you. You think you've never done anything stupid? What about when you told my class about the birthmark on my ass?"

"It's in the shape of Australia. We all thought it was cool."

"It was embarrassing. And private."

I pried at the crack in the rock, but my fingers were slick with dew and sweat and frustration. "So that makes it even?"

"Jesus, Lenny! That's not what I meant."

"Stupid rock!" I bashed it against the tree trunk and stubbed my fingers. I shut my eyes against the throb in my hand and the one deeper inside. When I opened them, I looked over at Julian looking at me, his wide eyes gleaming with regret. "What do you want?"

"You—"

Light suddenly streamed from the house, and Oma stormed out in her nightgown, rollers in her hair, and a—

Whatever Julian had been about to say morphed into: "Is Oma carrying a *knife*?"

She charged toward us, metal gleaming like in that cheesy horror film we'd watched when we were twelve.

We both jumped behind the thick cherry tree.

"Oma?" I called out, carefully peeking around the trunk. "What are you doing?"

At the edge of the light spilling on the grass, she stopped. A couple of seconds passed, and then she rubbed her head in the crook of her arm. When she noticed the knife she carried, she flinched.

"Sleepwalking again?" I called out. God, I hoped she'd only cut up tomatoes this time.

"Lenny? Is that you and Julian?"

We emerged from the tree. "You can go now," I hissed to Julian, but he kept right at my side.

Oma's eyes lost their fogginess awfully fast. She crossed her arms, knife gripped in her hand, pointing toward my feet. "What's going on here?"

"Nothing," I said.

Julian shifted from foot to foot, his gaze pleading with me. I looked away, toward our glowing house windows, wishing they could blind me of Julian's expression. No such luck.

"Right," Oma said, the sass back in her voice. She bent over and stabbed the knife into the dirt. "I don't know what's up with you two, but you're damn well going to sort it out."

She grabbed both of our ears and pulled us inside the house. Julian and I went in, yipping with pain. Then she let our ears go and ushered us up the stairs, past my room.

"Oma? What are you doing?"

Oma pulled down the hidden stairs that led to the attic. "Up you go."

"Into the attic?"

She smacked Julian's backside until he started creaking his way up the stairs. Then she pinned me with a look, and I ducked my head to my chest and slumped up after him.

"When can we come out?" I said, staring down at Oma.

"That's up to you two."

Then she shut us in the attic.

"I don't want to be up here in this spider-infested hole," Julian said softly, "but I think Oma's right. We need to sort this out."

I opened my mouth to argue, and Julian pressed his warm palm over my lips. His thumb grazed over my chin sending a flood of goosebumps down my neck.

"I don't want to wake up tomorrow to this crap between us," he said. "So let it out."

He dropped his hand, and I shoved his chest. Let it out? He said it like it were so easy, but the feelings were a mess inside. I couldn't make heads or tails of it. I couldn't just *let it out*.

I shoved him again and he folded back toward a bookshelf full of dusty, teetering boxes. I did it a third time. His back hit the shelves, and still I tried shoving him farther. He caught my hands, looking me right in the eyes, something quivering there. My rapid breathing slowed and I swallowed. His favorite gladiator T-shirt was balled in my hands, and our come-crusted jeans were rubbing at the zip.

Hurriedly, I leaped back, ripping my gaze downward, to his bare feet, red and white from the cold.

I kept backing away until I hit the slanted windows on the opposite wall. Julian tried to follow and a box fell from the shelf. Christmas decorations spilled over the floor, a barricade between Julian and me.

Julian hesitated, picked something up, and shoved it into his pocket. Then he looked up at me and sighed. "Lenny," he said softly.

I shook my head. The air was clammy and suffocating. I couldn't—I just couldn't stay in here. I yanked open the window and a cold breeze gusted into the attic.

Moonlight bounced off the glass onto Julian, who was moving toward me. I ducked through the window frame and onto the roof. Crouching carefully, I sat on the nobbled, ice-covered tiles. Cold seeped through my jeans and I embraced the numbness.

"Lenny, please." Julian clambered out the window.

I picked at a wedge of ice and threw it into the garden below. It tinkered over the corrugated iron scraps of our old rabbit cages.

Julian's feet inched into view, raw, and naked, and walking over the ice. *To get to me.*

And just like that my anger melted.

"You'll get frostbite," I said. When he didn't move, I hooked my thumbs in my shoes and slipped them off. "Put these on."

"You'll freeze."

"I'm wearing socks."

Julian dipped a foot into one of the shoes—

Then his foot slipped on the ice.

He toppled sideways, slamming against the roof, tiles snapping under him as he skidded off the side.

"Julian!" I cried, frantically crawling to the edge.

Somehow, my cousin had found purchase on the gutter, and dangled precariously over the tetanus bomb that were bunny cages waiting below him.

I grabbed Julian's wrists and held on as tightly as I could. "Say something." I grunted, as I pulled. "Anything." *As long as you're okay.*

"Fucking damn."

"Yeah, that'll do."

I heaved, pushing my feet on the gutter for leverage, praying it wouldn't snap.

Julian wedged a knee onto the roof and squirmed to safety. He collapsed next to me, hugging the roof tiles.

"I'm sorry," I said, smoothing my fingers over his cheek below a nasty scratch. "It was dumb to come out here. Does it hurt? God, I'm sorry."

He rumbled with a small laugh and sat up. "It takes nearly falling off a roof for you to talk to me? I have to remember that."

I hit his shoulder, playfully. Whatever I'd felt before didn't matter anymore. Julian hadn't plummeted off the roof to his death. He was okay.

We were going to be okay.

I helped him inside the attic.

Julian touched his cheek with the back of his hand, wincing. Then he patted down the rest of his body, lingering on his pocket.

"All still there?" I asked.

He nodded and sat on the floor under the windowsill. He patted the space next to him, and I sat, tucking my knees under my chin.

"You *have* to forgive me," he said and the arrogance in his tone brought back my anger.

"Because I almost killed you? Because I'm your cousin?"

"Because you're my best friend."

His words robbed me of any fight I had left. I rested my forehead on my knees and leaned against him.

Julian's arm swung around my shoulders and stayed there. After a couple of minutes, he shifted. "I think I want to collapse into bed now. Shall we call Oma?"

Five minutes later, we were in bed, me on my side, Julian on his. "You think we have to worry about Oma coming in here with a knife?" he asked with a yawn.

"Will that movie haunt us forever?"

"Snuggle closer if you're scared."

I wasn't scared, but I snuggled closer anyway.

THE NEXT MORNING, we woke to Ben standing at the side of the bed, hands on hips, scowling down at us. "What the fuck was that last night?"

Oh shit. Ben!

Julian and I shared the same horrified expression and sat up.

I went to apologize, but Ben wasn't finished. "You watched porn without me? Cold, guys. Cold."

I raised my hand for permission to speak. Ben narrowed his eyes. "Go ahead. Give me your excuses."

"At least you were saved from having your aunt or mama walk in on you."

Ben ran a hand through his long hair. "Yeah, I caught all that. Pretended I was asleep the whole time." He found my sketchbook on the bedside table and chucked it at Julian. "Dude, your mama was crying for ages."

Julian grew quiet. I fished for his hand under the covers and bumped it in sympathy. He cleared his throat. "Sorry you were stuck with that, man."

Ben shrugged it off. "I'm used to it." He shook his head. "But no more porn with friends without me, okay?"

Julian and I nodded.

"Good. Is your sister still asleep you think?"

I shrugged. "She does love to sleep in."

Ben clapped his hands together. "Payback time," he said, and hightailed out the room.

A minute later we heard screaming and laughing and some more screaming. Sounded like Ben got his revenge.

Julian shifted and swung his legs out of the bed, and then he looked at me over his shoulder, eyes still sleepy, hair tousled, his scratch painfully red. "Are we still good?"

"Yeah."

"Lenny…" Julian swiveled toward me, mouth parting. Then he licked his bottom lip and bit down on it.

"Yeah?"

He shrugged. "I'm glad."

I caught his hand before he stood. "About the birthmark thing," I said as Julian briefly knotted his fingers with mine before letting go again. "You have to forgive me for that."

"I have."

"You have?"

"You still don't get it. I forgave you the moment you did it."

I leaned back against my shallow headboard and watched him as he rose from the bed and stretched. "Because we're best friends?" I asked.

He dropped his arms with a grunt and swung them back and forth. "Because you make me mad but I can never stay mad at you long, Lenny."

Lenny For Your Thoughts

"I TOLD YOU I'd take you here one day," Julian said, tucking his linked fingers under his head. He peeked at me out the corner of his eye and then we both stared up at the trees and afternoon summer sky. River water lapped next to us, its calm disturbed as Ben dunked his feet in.

Somewhere around us my sister was on the phone, trying to convince her boyfriend to get his hungover ass out of bed and meet us at the island in Treptower Park.

In Berlin.

I was finally here.

I ripped out a handful of grass at my side and threw it up, letting the slight breeze scatter it over Julian's face. He spluttered as a strand caught in his mouth, and I sniggered, earning me a nice swat to my side.

"I like it here," I said, trying to breathe in the whole vibe of the place. "Maybe one day I'll live here."

The leaves rustled and shifted, letting through more light. I didn't turn my head, but I could feel Julian's gaze on me. He was always quiet whenever I asked him what he was going to do once he'd finished school, whether he wanted to travel, what he wanted to be, where he wanted to live…he rarely answered, and when he did, it was short and gruff.

Mostly his answer was he didn't know, and he didn't want to think about it.

So I wasn't surprised when he didn't respond.

Carolin stormed out from behind the trees, her feet close to stomping all over us. I flinched and pushed back onto my elbows. "You all right?"

She paced at the edge of the water, from Ben to a little grey paddleboat someone had ditched. "Is this what you're all like?" she said, glaring at each of us guys in turn.

"Well that depends," Ben said, braving up. "Like what?"

Carolin looked like she wanted to hit something and I was afraid Ben might be it. He didn't have his surfer's hair to protect him from the sting anymore either. He'd chopped it off real short on the longest day of summer.

"Like one moment you're all 'Ohhh Carolin, you're so amazing, I think I love you. You're smart, you're beautiful—and that body! Wow.'"

Ben choked on his tongue and started coughing, his cheeks blooming red.

Carolin thumped his back and then continued pacing. "Then you finally—cover your ears, Lenny."

"Shove off. I'm almost sixteen, you don't have to protect me anymore."

She threw her hands above her head. "Fine. Whatever. Then I let him *fuck me six ways to Sunday*"—she glared at me. And I really wished I'd listened to her. Ugh. Too late to cover my ears now—"And he sounded like he was having a great time. But then he suddenly went all cold. He never says nice things about me anymore, and last night I swear he was checking out that Italian girl with the feather necklace."

"The one who smokes in rings?" Ben asked, waggling his brows at me. "Because she was hot—"

Wholptz. Julian and I rolled our eyes. We'd seen that slap coming a mile away.

But either she didn't hit him very hard, or Ben sucked in his usual annoyed cry, because he reached out and tugged her until she crumpled next to him.

Then—a first—she leaned on him, letting him take her weight, burrowing her face into his sleeve, maybe to wipe away her tears.

Bunched up in his arms, my sister didn't look two years older than Ben. In fact, for a refreshing second, she looked like she could have been the younger one.

I stared, the scene burning into my mind: Ben, jeans rolled up, feet bathing in the Spree River. Carolin, with her red hair that flowed down her back, glowing more and more with every stroke Ben gave it.

I blinked to Julian watching them through a looped piece of grass. He moved the grass as if magnifying the scene, and then faced me. "They're sweet," Julian said. "Never thought I'd see the day."

I chuckled. That was for sure. The two of them were always teasing and winding each other up—it was their thing. But it was nice to see they could put that aside as well.

Of course, it didn't last long.

My sister sighed. There came a muffled, "It's just...*I* want to be the hot one."

Ben twirled a lock of her hair around his finger and let it go. "Well, we can't *all* be the hot one."

Carolin reared back, shoving him in the chest. "Seriously? You guys *suck*."

Julian cracked up, spurring me to laughs. "Ben, you stupid fuck," he wheezed, throwing his grass away and rolling over to push himself up.

He strode over to Carolin, took her hand and twisted her into a dance. "Since you don't look anything like his mother, this would be better coming from Ben, but seeing as we've established he doesn't have any sense when it comes to these things, I'll take over."

He spun her again and she let him lead her around the grass. "No, not all guys are like your boyfriend. We don't all suck—though we'll agree Ben might be an exception to that. You are beautiful, tall, graceful, and you sing like a charm. You're also funny and you know what I love most about you?"

Carolin looked like she was struggling to hold her smile, her eyes tearing. She shook her head.

"You care about your brother. Don't think I'll ever forget the time you and your friends tied me to the playground for being mean to him. If it weren't for your ass-kicking, I'd never have found the bestest friends ever."

"Yeah, but you'd have come around eventually. We're cousins," Carolin sniffed. "You sort of have to like us by default."

Julian decided it was his turn to do a spin and rolled himself into her arm and quickly out again. "No. Not true. If it were, my mama would also like your family."

She looked to the river and then back to Julian, his shadow falling over her face. "You really love me?"

He stopped dancing. Behind him, Ben slumped his shoulders and skimmed a stone on the river.

"Of course. All three of us do."

Carolin folded her arms. "Well, two of you maybe." She glared at Ben's back. "But then we can't *all* be loved, either, right?"

My cell phone buzzed, vibrating in my pocket. I took it out and read the text.

"Jessica?" Carolin asked.

Julian stared at me over her shoulder, then whisked away to sit next to Ben.

"Yeah," I said. "She wants to know if we're having fun."

I stuffed the phone back in my pocket.

"Aren't you going to answer?"

I shrugged. "Later."

"Are you two serious?" she asked, sitting at my feet.

Serious? Hardly. Sure, we spent a bit of time together, but not that much. Just the occasional Friday night. "I like her."

"Yeah, you do," Ben threw over his shoulder, "because with her, you're getting heaps of action." If he could have jerked his hips, he would have. But as it was, two things stopped him. One, how he was sitting. And two, Julian shoving him into the water.

"Bleck, gross," Ben said, spluttering. "What was that for?"

"You need to grow up," Julian said tightly.

"And you're setting a fantastic example," Ben said.

I laughed, jumped up to join the fray, and bowled into Julian's side, hurtling into the slimy, weedy river. Ben splashed our faces as soon as we popped through the surface.

Julian hauled in a deep breath and dove under the water. His arms slid around my waist and I was yanked under. As soon as he let me go, I grabbed him, locked my legs around his, and drew him close. Bubbles burst out of our mouths, bumping together on their rise upwards.

Another pair of legs wandered close, and almost like we could read minds, Julian and I both grabbed Ben and pulled him under.

"All right boys," my sister said, when we came up for air. "You let Ben go. Right now."

Ben sent us a cocky grin once he was back on land, then turned the same dimpled smile on my sister. She returned the smile, coming really close to him. Kiss-close. And then she pressed both palms to his chest and shoved him backwards.

Julian and I parted as Ben's arms windmilled and he fell back into the water with a loud slap. Carolin dusted her hands. "*Now* I feel better."

It took us a good couple of hours to get dry again. Thankfully, we could hang our clothes from the trees.

A paddleboat caught my attention as we redressed; it floated there, tied to the base of a chestnut. It would easily fit the four of us, two up front and two behind…

Ben read my mind, and suddenly we were all piling into the boat, Ben and Carolin singing loudly.

"So," Julian said to me as we settled in the front and he handed me a paddle, "you want to live in Berlin?"

"Yeah. Someday."

Ben's singing screeched to a tone that was better left untouched, and Julian's lips quirked into a smile that pulled at something deep inside. It was simple, sincere, and comfortable —like wearing a hug. I wanted more of it.

A blush creeped up my neck and I glanced toward the water reflecting a group of soaring birds against a pink sky.

Julian gently nudged his leg against mine. "Do you think about the future a lot?"

"Sometimes."

"Can I ask you something?"

I nodded, not taking my gaze off the water, white-knuckling the paddle as if it might stop the tingles racing up my leg.

Julian spoke softly, "In your future…where am I in it?"

It was something I'd never questioned before. Not really. I'd imagined all the places I wanted to go, the things I wanted to see and do, but I never wondered who I'd be doing them with or without. In my mind Julian and Ben were always with me.

I shifted, breaking our contact, and felt the cool bite of the next breeze. "This is why you don't like talking about it."

The answer stared back at me in his wet, dull eyes, and the trembling of his chin that he tried and failed to shrug off. "Let's get back," he said. "I don't think my clothes are as dry as I thought they were."

We paddled back. Ben, Julian, and Carolin hopped out of

the boat and headed toward the bridge on the other side of the island. I stayed rooted to the seat of the paddleboat and watched as the three of them shrank into the distance.

When Julian turned and realized I wasn't with them, he came back for me. Like I knew he would.

Like I wanted him to.

Like I didn't want him to.

I stared at the water, where a drop of rain rippled the surface. Looking up, a few drops landed on my nose and mouth.

The sky rapidly darkened, and the tree branches cried overhead, casting darker, longer shadows.

Julian leaned back against the tree he'd slung the boat rope around. He stood there for a long time watching me, raindrops pattering onto his hair and rolling off onto his shoulders.

He crossed his arms and dropped them again. Held my gaze, then dropped that too.

What was he thinking? How did he know just to be here and not say anything?

My voice cracked. "Penny for your thoughts?"

He blinked at me, and his lips wobbled into a smile. "Lenny for my thoughts?"

"I didn't say—"

"I like that," he said and stretched out an arm for me.

I stared at him, the branches above showering him with large dollops of spring rain. One dollop splashed on his nose and ran down his cheek. I took his offered hand and pulled myself out of the boat, coming nose to nose with him.

"So?" I asked. "Your thoughts?"

He hesitated and pulled back a half step. "I'm glad we came up here. Berlin suits you. Maybe you will live here one day. Maybe I will, too."

I hiccupped on a breath. God, I was glad for the rain. Glad it would cover the tear slipping out the corner of my eye.

"Now," Julian said, "do I get my Lenny?"

"Yeah," I said, and let him lead me back to the bridge where Carolin and Ben waited in the middle, Ben holding his jacket over both their heads.

At the base of the bridge, I snagged Julian's sleeve, drawing him around. "What Ben said before," I said. "…it isn't true. I don't get heaps of action."

"None of my business," Julian said, and then gave a rough, cracked laugh. "Though I do recall a certain pink T-shirt incident…"

"It's just, the thing is…" I fumbled for words to describe this thing that was on the tip of my tongue, on the very outskirts of my consciousness. I took in a breath—

Then it whistled out of me, no words the wiser. "Never mind," I said, and stepped onto the bridge. "It doesn't matter."

But it did.

And it would.

Same Blood, Same Lips, Same Chin

CHRISTMAS 2005

"STRIP GUYS," I said peeking over my sketch block. "I want this kinky."

Julian peeled off his top.

"What the hell are you doing?" I threw my pencil at him, laughing. "I was having you all on." I waved a hand toward Carolin, hunched over her cultural studies books at the corner table of my newly converted art-shed. "You think I want to see my sis naked?"

"Oh, but it's okay to see the rest of us naked?" Ben quipped, grinning. He nudged Julian in the side. "Dude, none of us need to see what you're packing. Put your T-shirt back on."

My sister snorted, dropping her booklet, and came over to us at the bigger, paint-and-plaster-splattered table. "Having us all naked and sprawled over each other might be a little incestuous too," she said, laughing, "don't you think?"

Julian suddenly looked down at his T-shirt balled loosely in his hand. "Yeah. I guess."

"I get it, man," Ben said, thumping him on the back. "You hear kinky and it's impossible to think straight."

"Seriously," Carolin drawled, pinching the back of Ben's neck. "How *did* I live half a year without this?"

Ben pecked a kiss to her cheek and lifted her into a tight hug that made her squeal. "You couldn't, that's why you're back from uni."

"Put me down, Benjamin!" Somewhere in the last couple of years Ben and I had both sprung up and broadened, and my sister, once so proud of being bigger than us, had to lift her chin to look us in the eye.

Ben held the backs of her thighs against his stomach, and Carolin braced her hands against his shoulders, her hair curtaining parts of his face where it fell. He blew the strands away, looking up at her. I grabbed a piece of charcoal and began sketching; their forms were perfect in the soft light I'd set up.

"Seriously," she said, but more gently this time. "Put me down."

"Not before you tell us the truth. Admit it, you were homesick. You missed us. You can't live without us."

I hoped I captured the moment fast enough, before Ben finally let her go. My hand moved swiftly over the paper, the charcoal making a rough scratchy sound. Julian shifted to my side, smoothing his T-shirt over his stomach. What did he think of my work? It was rough, I knew, but did he like it?

As if he could read my thoughts, he nodded. "Like it, Lenny."

"Put me down," Carolin said, "and I'll admit the truth."

Slowly Ben loosened his grip, letting her slide down his front. He only let go when he was sure both her feet were firmly on the floor.

Carolin gave a funny little smile and blinked rapidly. Then she shrugged and her smile turned mischievous. "The truth is, I'm back for *Christmas*. That's all."

"Sure-sure," Julian said, resting an arm on my shoulder.

His hand disturbed my line of sight—and concentration—and I shrugged him off, but his touch lingered, warm and shivery.

"Just for the record," Ben said, snagging Carolin's hand as she backed away from him. "I didn't miss you, either."

And there they went again, just like old times...

It took me an hour to get the sketches for the portraits done. "Good," I said, chucking the pencil on the table. "This year's part is practically done."

For my art class, I had to provide a portfolio of work, show-casing my abilities. From photography, to pencil, and brush-work. The next-and-last school year, we could work with any medium we wanted. I'd discussed my year project idea with the teacher, and she agreed that if I wanted, I could begin imme-diately.

I fidgeted as Julian, Ben and Carolin stretched and shook their stiff limbs. One of them was going to have to help me with it. "I need a volunteer for my masterpiece," I said.

"Oh, I bet it *is* kinky this time," Ben said. "Look at the way our Lenny is blushing."

"Fuck off," I said, stowing my sketch block away. "This is about art, nothing else. I'd get Oma to do it, but she's got a cold and I don't want it getting worse."

"If you can do it with Oma, it can't be anything too scan-dalous," Carolin said.

"Have you met your Oma?" Ben said, and Carolin conceded him that point with a grin.

"What's the project?" Carolin asked.

I bit my lip, skipping my gaze over her shoulder to Julian and quickly back again. "I want to sculpt a replica of an ancient statue."

"An ancient statue?" Carolin said, perching herself on the table.

Ben shoved her over and sat too.

Only Julian continued standing in the middle of the room,

arms crossed, watching me carefully. I shivered under his gaze, because I didn't know what he was thinking, and I wanted to. Because I wanted him to want to know what my statue was about, and I really, really didn't want him to offer to be my model.

I focused on my sister as she tied her hair back into a knot. "I want to replicate one of the classics in wax."

"That's a big project, isn't it?"

"Yeah, and I have a year-and-a-half to do it."

Ben whistled. "Dude, I got a cramp after just an hour."

"The model part won't take that long. A few hours at the most, with a couple of people assisting me—once I've got a plaster cast ready, I can do it on my own from there. It's like the molds of your face I've done in the past. But bigger."

"Which classic are you doing?" Julian asked, tilting his head.

"That depends on the model. Male or female."

"And if it's male?"

I swallowed.

Ben grinned, cheering with a fist to the air. "I *knew* it'd get kinky."

I scowled at him. "Is that you volunteering?"

Ben dropped his arm.

"Look, it's fine." I shrugged. "I'll hire a professional, someone who won't read into it as anything but art."

"With what money?" my sister said, laughing.

I glanced at Julian and he held my gaze, refusing to let it go. "Guys," he said, "can I speak to Lenny privately for a bit?"

If they were curious, they didn't say anything. They slipped off the table and shuffled away, Carolin saying to Ben, "Hey, I need to drive to the Christmas Market for a tree before Oma takes an axe to the Leike's again. Want to tag along?"

"I'm there for the heavy lifting, aren't I?"

"You bet."

Once the door shut behind them, Julian picked his way over to me, standing on the opposite side of my easel. Along the wooden board at the top, he laid his arms and rested his chin.

"Lenny," he said. "You know you don't have to get a professional." His gaze lingered on my face, sending a flutter through my chest that swooped suddenly deeper inside. "I'll be your David."

"How'd you—?"

"Because," he said, raising one brow, "as someone once told me, Michelangelo was an Italian artist and his David was inspired by the Greek style."

"So you do listen when I ramble about art."

"About art and a whole lot more." He straightened and stepped back, the glow of the lamp haloing his dark hair. "It would be the perfect fit for your theme, so, yeah, I'll do it."

"I...I've already got your head in a mold, so I'll only need..." I swallowed.

Julian looked down at himself. "The rest of me?"

That bird soared and dove again. "Yeah."

He curled his finger, beckoning me to move over to him. I went, the floor suddenly uneven under my feet and I tripped into him. I quickly pulled back, and tried to raise one eyebrow at him like Oma, my sister, or Ben would have done, but the traitorous second brow rose with it.

Julian gave a small laugh that whispered over my nose. "You've been blushing all afternoon."

And before I could answer, before that next inevitable wave of heat washed over me, Julian stilled my fidgeting hands and kissed me.

I was looking down when he did it, startled by the firm way he gripped my hands. Then his lips were on one half of my mouth, warm and hard.

And then soft, hesitant, pulling away—

It was like with that one touch, my bird twisted out of control. The air seemed to thicken around me, gluing me to the floor, and though the bird inside screamed for me to move, for me to follow, I couldn't get unstuck.

And then his lips left, the pressure on my hands disappeared, and cool outside air sailed in as Julian slinked away.

And I stood there. Staring. Only when Oma called me in for coffee did I move.

On automatic, I went inside, and sat, and drank. I didn't feel any of it. Taste any of it. Hear any of it.

Until…

"What are you smiling about?" Oma said, buttering a piece of walnut bread.

Smiling. I was, wasn't I? How could I not be?

Oma pulled off the one eyebrow thing.

I lowered my grainy, sweet coffee. "Actually…" I laughed, and my bird fluttered. "I'm in a really good mood."

"Certainly seems so," she said, and then coughed into the crook of her arm. "What were you up to out there?"

I picked at a small hole in the table cloth. I was sitting in the seat Julian usually sat at when he came around and fiddling with the same hole he'd run his thumbs over in circles that morning. "Uh, just figuring out the details of my next art project."

Among other things.

The barest touch of his lips on mine…

I stared into my cup as I recalled Julian's hands pressed into mine. If I thought about it now, the kiss had been in that firm, needing touch too.

"Well I'll let you bathe in it while I'm off for a drive," Oma said, patting my shoulder as she got up. She left the kitchen and came back. "You haven't seen my axe, have you?"

~

THINGS SEEMED TO happen around me.

I wasn't there.

I mean, I *was*, but only in body. The rest of me was rolling around in thoughts, memories, and that moment with Julian…

All the moments with Julian.

Ben and Carolin got back with the tree and half decorated it with me staring into space next to them, twiddling my thumbs, pacing.

All I wanted was to see Julian again. To kiss him back.

I wanted to slide my hand around the back of his head and taste his lips. More than that, I wanted to feel his tongue too and see what it felt like to slide my body against his.

But at the same time, I wanted to hide under my bed, and sink into the cold wooden floor, never to come out again. What would I say? What was supposed to happen next?

And when Ben asked, "Where'd your cousin go?" All I heard was the "cousin", and I wanted to choke up the bird Julian had sang to and make it go away. Because it wasn't just that he was a boy.

He was family too. We shared the same blood, same lips, same chin.

"Next one!" Carolin called, opening her hand, palm up under Ben's nose.

"Stop putting your hands in my face," he grumbled, passing her one of my old wax warriors.

"Next one!"

This time Ben didn't complain about the hand that almost banged his nose. No. Instead, he opened his mouth and captured her thumb in his mouth.

My sister jumped so violently, she knocked over the tree, which I caught with my shoulder and steadied.

With widened eyes, she looked at Ben and her thumb. Ben slowly pulled his lips off her, teeth scraping over her skin. The shiver Carolin gave would have been noticeable the next village over.

Ben smacked his lips together. "Now will you stop shoving your hands in my face?"

I picked up two of my old wax figures that'd fallen with the tree. I'd already managed to lose a couple of them over the years, and I didn't want to lose any more.

When I looked up, Ben had his head bowed. He smiled at his old bird decoration and gave a small laugh mixed with a sigh before handing it to Carolin. Just like all the years before, she placed it on top.

"Thank you," Ben murmured.

We finished the tree, and I ran up to my room, desperate to get rid of the energy building inside. I paced and gritted my teeth, one moment heading for the door, the next retreating to the window, where I looked out, wishing I could see around the bend in the road to his house.

"Fuck it." I stormed back downstairs, out the house, and didn't stop until I was at Julian's, knocking.

I jerked back in surprise when Aunt Thomas answered. I'd had it in my head that no one else but Julian could answer.

"Leonard," she said, planting herself firmly in the middle of the doorway. "What are you doing here?"

I stumbled at the ice in her tone. "I…I need to see Julian."

"Julian isn't feeling very well right now. He needs to be alone."

I peered over her shoulder, wishing I could see all the way to Julian's room. He was sick?

Shit. I should have come quicker. Should have followed him right away!

"Can I just have five minutes? I won't be long. But I really need to speak to him."

"Have a nice evening, Leonard," she said, closing the door. "Tell your Oma I send my regards."

The lock snipped into place.

"Julian!" I shouted, banging my palms on the brown painted door.

Like hell I was going to let Aunt Thomas stand in the way. I had something to say.

I'd say it.

"Julian!" I tried again.

I ran to the side of his house and skulked in the shadow of the large hedge separating his place from the cemetery.

I pulled out my phone and dialed his.

Julian didn't pick up. I tried three times. Nothing.

But he was up there in his room. Every now and then, I saw him through the window, pacing, much like I had been all afternoon.

I found stones and threw them up until finally, *finally*, he looked out. Even from here, I saw his pain. Rarely had I seen Julian swollen with tears, and the sight tugged at my heart, made me want to cry too. He was meant to be *smiling*, dammit. The both of us.

Holding his gaze, I rang him again. He pulled the phone from his person and brought it to his ear. His breath tunneled down the line, and he kept his focus on me.

"Julian," I said—pleaded. "Come down here."

He shook his head.

"But I need you to."

He shut his eyes, and after a moment, shook his head again.

"Are you sick?"

His voice croaked. "I'll be fine."

"So you *are* sick?"

"I spoke with my mama, Lenny," he said it so quietly, it was hard to hear. "She told me something."

"About our kiss—?"

"No. Not really. Not about you."

The tension in my shoulders dropped.

"She got upset," he continued. "So angry, and then so sad. And then she told me about my papa. Told me why she hates your family."

The tension rolled back, thick, hard, and fast.

"He followed your parents. He was meant to turn them in, but he didn't, for my mama. He tried to stop them instead. The grenade, it killed him too. Mama had told your mama and papa they were selfish to try leaving. Told them nothing good would come of it. But she loved her sister, and when they really were going through with it, she sent my papa after them." Julian sniffed. "Mama said whenever she sees you, she sees your father taking away her sister. Her husband—my papa."

I didn't know what to say—or whether I could around the lump in my throat.

"Come down, *please*."

"There's something else you should know." Julian broke our connection by glancing to the side. "I never should have kissed you."

"But—"

"I didn't mean it. I was just curious. I love you as a cousin, as a friend, but that's it. Nothing else."

Now it was my turn to turn away. I couldn't bear if he saw the tears in my eyes—if he knew it had meant something to me. That for a single second, everything had been right—like I'd been clicked into place.

"Are things going to be weird between us now?" I managed through a tight throat.

I didn't dare look at him.

In the stretched silence, I tried to pick out all the details in the hedge—where the leaves were bent and battered, where birds had nested, how many gravestones I could count through the branches.

"I don't want it to be," Julian finally said. "Can we pretend it didn't happen?"

I closed my eyes and tears trickled down my cheeks, curving under my chin and dribbling down my neck like they didn't want to let go. "Is that what you really want?"

"…yes."

BUT DESPITE THOSE WORDS, things were awkward after that. Julian always had things to do, other friends to meet, mysterious highly contagious illnesses…

For those months I missed him, dreamed of him, hated him, loved him, and loathed him.

I did everything to rid him from my mind. And by the following summer, I had managed.

And then Ben left to spend the summer with his papa's family.

The Moment Nick the Dick became Nick the Okay Kind of Guy

EVERY SUMMER, without fail, we went camping.

We packed our tent and supplies in backpacks, rode our bikes to the *Thüringer Wald*, then walked to our spot—a clearing where two hillsides met, with a small stream of water ribboning the base.

Last year, Nick-the-dick and his friends had stumbled on our spot too, deliberately pitching their tents on the flat hilltop opposite us. We'd spent the rest of the weekend trying to get rid of each other.

This year, I accidentally invited them to come. Which was why there were three tents pitched—the third, mine, a good hundred yards into the wood, where the ground was flat and not too soggy.

"Hey," a husky male voice said behind me, and I leaped up from zipping my tent.

"Oh, Theo, you gave me a fright."

Theo and I had met at the beginning of summer; he was some distant cousin of Nick's and was living with him for three months. He'd winked at me at the village beer rally and I'd winked back.

I liked him because his eyes were blue and his hair was sandy, and he didn't look like he could get stubble if he tried, and his hands were soft like he bathed them in moisturizer, and he wore just a hint of musk that hid the smell of his sweat.

I liked him because when I was with him, there was nothing to remind me of Julian.

Theo slipped his arms around my waist and pressed me against his front. His lips found my neck and he sucked on my skin. I tried to sink into his hold, but we were still new at this and I felt stiff and awkward. I hid a wince at the hickey he was giving me and murmured into it instead.

It'd get better. These things took time, after all.

"We're going to have so much fun this weekend," he said, his tone oozing lust that both excited and repelled me. "I'm so glad you invited us up here."

Actually, I'd only sort-of invited him. With Ben gone for the summer, and Julian acting cold toward me, I didn't want to go alone—and breaking tradition was out of the question.

I'd mentioned this to Theo, and a week later he, Nick, and a buddy had followed me into the woods.

A deer snapped over foliage in the distance—a sound that had once freaked Ben and I out, but one we had long gotten used to. This was no haunted wood.

God, I missed Ben.

He had always been there with his charm and cheeky wit. Without him, I was a compass with a broken arrow.

"What are you thinking, Len?" Theo asked, turning me to face him.

I'd told him to call me Len, but each time he did, it made me blink. His heated gaze dropped to my mouth, and I knew he wasn't looking for an actual answer to his question. Or he was, only he'd supposed he knew the answer.

He stilled my head in both hands and attacked my mouth in a rough, wet kiss. His tongue probed as if to feel every inch inside, and my tongue tackled his to get him out of there—*a losing battle.*

I pushed against his chest to draw him away so I could breathe. He withdrew, lightly bumping our heads together, and smiled.

Another sound came from the not-too-far distance.

I knew before seeing him. Knew from the strangled gasp that cut through the warm air. From the way the hairs at the back of my neck prickled. And from the urgent need to rip myself out of Theo's arms.

Julian stood in a gap in the trees on the muddy path leading to the hilltops, his pack piled high, pots hanging at the sides, his boots and legs caked with splashes of dirt, and T-shirt plastered to his chest with sweat. His eyes darkened to a haunted shade of green.

For the first time in over six months, he really looked at me. A hundred different things passed over his face at once, and none of them settled. "Lenny," he mouthed, the sound not coming out.

Theo shifted at my side. "I thought you said he wasn't coming."

"I didn't think he'd want to camp this year," I said, voice uneven.

Julian eyed Theo in a way that made me shiver, then strode toward us. "It's tradition," he said. "And maybe it's the last time I can do it before I leave for military service."

Julian still hadn't ceased his glare at Theo, and I moved a step between them.

"This is Theo," I said. "We're…" *Boyfriends? No. Dating? Not really. Kissers? What the fuck?* "We're close. But keep it quiet, Nick and Thomas don't know, okay?"

"Nick-the-dick's here too? What's going on Lenny? Are these your new friends now?"

"Fuck you," I said, and turned my back on him. Theo held Julian off when he tried to come closer.

"Maybe you'd better find another place to camp," Theo said.

Julian's wounded voice hit my back. "Do you want me to leave?"

Yes. No. Absolutely. I opened my mouth and shut it again, then shrugged.

"Fine," he said. "But I'm not packing in and going home."

Theo wrapped his arms around me and kissed me hard. I kissed him back harder, wanting, needing Julian to see.

I glimpsed over Theo's shoulder, snagging Julian's gaze. He watched us for a moment before bowing his head and retreating. I'd wanted to hurt him; wanted him to be reminded of our last real moment together.

But with each of his steps into the wood, the bird I'd thought I'd stitched back together began to break apart.

ONCE WE'D FINISHED a noodle dinner, Nick, Thomas and Theo brought out the booze and started drinking. Nick and Theo were sharing a tent, so I knew if I left now, I'd have at least a few hours to myself before Nick was asleep and Theo snuck off to find me. I yawned and, after a "later" mouthed by Theo, treaded into the forest, alone and relieved.

I bypassed my tent and in the dim late-evening light, wandered down the muddy path until I reached the tree Ben, Julian, and I had tagged with our initials. From there I went off the beaten path to where I knew Julian would be: down a slippery slope to the one-tent cove at the bottom. I used the trees as crutches until there were none anymore and I was sliding down the hill.

"Damn—"

Just when I thought I'd crash face-first to the ground next to the tent, Julian was there, pulling me into open arms, steadying me.

He didn't say anything, just planted me upright, firm fingers slowly lessening their grip, then skating off my arm and waist.

"It's not what I want," I said. "I didn't want you to leave. I hate it when you do that."

He looked at me and then moved to a line of old stumps close to the entrance to his tent. He sat on one and scrubbed his hair.

In the fifteen minutes since leaving the others, the sky had greyed. Wood shadows lay thick around us, cloaking us— making me stronger.

"How long have you been with him?" Julian asked.

"Why does that matter?"

He inhaled sharply, and I waited for him to argue that *yes, it did matter*, but he breathed out slowly, closing his eyes.

I sat on a damp stump across from him, the coolness quickly leaking through my shorts and numbing my thighs.

"So you really are..." he didn't finish, but I knew what he was asking.

"Yes. I think I've known a long time, but it was only when..."—*You kissed me*—"that I admitted it to myself."

Julian muttered a curse, picked up an old twig from the ground and chucked it hard up the bank behind us.

"Is it so bad that I like guys?"

Julian moved off his stump and unzipped his tent. He went in and came back with a flask. He guzzled its contents and wiped his mouth, missing a drop of alcohol that rolled down his chin.

"No," he said. And then he threw the flask back into the opened tent. "Yes."

"No? Yes? Which is it?"

"Have you slept with him? Do you love him?"

I leaped off my stump, getting right into his face. "What the fuck does that matter?"

"It doesn't." He said it hurriedly, then broke away from my gaze and stared at the stump. His Adam's apple jutted out as he swallowed. "Why did you come find me?"

His answer throbbed painfully in my gut. What *had* I been hoping for? Why had I come to find Julian? "I just don't know anymore," I said, backing away from him. "I...I wish I hadn't."

I LEFT JULIAN AND SCRAMBLED BACK TO MY TENT. In the middle of the night, Theo snuck in. His body landed heavy and insistent on mine. "I'm sleeping," I moaned.

"It's finally just the two of us," he said. "We have the whole night." His hand reached into my sleeping bag and cupped my crotch. "I've brought condoms and stuff."

His breath was sour with whiskey and his hand was cold as he fished under my boxers. I didn't want my first time to be with someone who was drunk. Someone who was diving right to the prize. Someone who was...who...

Who wasn't Julian.

Fuck it!

"What's up, Len?" He peeled back my sleeping bag and drew down my boxers, kissing a path down my chest toward—

"Theo, no. I don't want this."

"It's about to get really good, I promise."

"No!"

Theo stopped and was shifting off me when suddenly something lunged into the opened tent flap, grabbed him and hauled him outside.

I yanked up my boxers as I followed, coming out in time

to see a fist crunch against Theo's cheek. His head swung with the force and a splattering of blood flew from his mouth.

My gaze took in Julian's pumping fist, and the murderous look on his face as he shook Theo, about to hit him again. "Don't you fucking touch him. Ever. Again. Are we clear?"

Theo touched his face, wincing, then roiling with anger he pushed Julian back and threw his own punch. "Fuck off. That's Len's choice."

"Well you don't seem to fucking listen to his choice. No, means no, you fuck."

"Hey-hey," I said, finally unfrozen enough to push myself between them. "Break it up. Nobody was hurt, Julian."

"But he was *about* to hurt you." Julian lunged again. Two guys intent on hitting each other was more than I could deal with. I grabbed Julian, wrapping my arms around his chest, and tugged him back.

"Why do you even care?" Theo hissed.

"He's my cousin! I fucking care. I have to."

Cousin. I squeezed back the burning behind my eyes. Then I crushed Julian harder against me as I pulled him away.

Theo punched Julian again. Theo's fist met Julian's arm and I felt the force of it as it knocked us both back a step.

Suddenly a beam of light appeared, and Nick was there. "What the fuck?" Nick said, shoving himself between the two of them. He grabbed Theo when he tackled again. "Cool it, T."

"Who is this shit, anyway?" Theo spat to his side, then looked up at Julian. "What were you doing lurking in the fucking woods outside Lenny's tent?"

What *had* he been doing so close to my tent?

"I could ask the same about you, T." And the way he glanced over at me, I just knew he *knew*. And that was the moment Nick-the-dick became Nick-the-okay-kind-of-guy.

Nick shrugged his shoulders. "But I *won't* ask." He looked back to Theo and spoke in a low voice. "You done now?"

"He started it."

"I don't give a shit who started it. Are you done?"

Theo shrugged out of his grip. "Yeah."

Nick turned to us. "You done, Julian?"

Julian's hair whispered over my forehead as he nodded, and I gripped him a little tighter. "Yeah, we're done."

Theo's gaze burned into me, firing me with questions that I couldn't answer. He grunted and turned on his heel. The last I saw of him was his profile in Nick's flashlight as they slunk back to their tent.

Julian pried gently at my hands, freeing himself. Without a word, he went into my tent, found my flashlight, and rummaged around. The box of condoms and lube came hurtling out the opening and into the brush. Then he threw me a shirt, some pants, and my shoes.

My voice had difficulty making it past the knot in my throat. "What are you doing?"

He came out, drawing the strings on my backpack. He rolled it to my feet. "I lied. It matters."

My breath caught.

He thrust the flashlight in my hand, and began yanking up tent pegs. "I came camping because it matters. You matter." He stopped and looked over at me, voice softening. "I miss you, Lenny. You're my best friend."

Finally, my limbs had unfrozen enough to help him with my tent. I yanked up a tent peg. "I was always right here. You didn't have to miss me."

He hesitated, then resumed packing the tent. In under ten minutes, it was in its bag and Julian was attaching it to my pack. He swung it over his shoulder and looked at me. A hundred things flickered in his expression. I felt his regret, pain, hope. He opened his mouth to speak, but his voice was lost.

I moved toward him and nodded. Some things were too hard to say. "I missed you too, Julian."

We spent the rest of the night in his tent, talking. It started off timid, a few small stories of things we'd both been up to, but as the night deepened and tiredness dulled our inhibitions, we reminisced. He told me about a morning a few months back when he'd gone to a party and woken up without pants on and one shoe missing in the middle of the woods. And another time, when he'd come to see me, to finally talk, but I'd been out with 'other friends', and when I came back laughing and roughhousing . . . he'd grown bitter, sad; he convinced himself I didn't need him anymore.

In turn, I told him about the time I tackled Oma into a hug when I spotted her outside the school. She never normally picked me up, so when I saw her talking to my art teacher, I just had to squeeze her. Turned out it wasn't Oma and I'd just given some other granny the fright of her life.

I told him that sometimes I went to the attic and climbed onto the roof hoping that I might turn around and find him coming out after me.

Julian draped an arm over his face then and sighed. "Sorry, Lenny," he said, the apology warming my chest. "I'm so goddamned sorry."

Soon after, we drifted off and in the morning, I woke to Julian mumbling deep in his sleep. Sometime in the night we'd curled up against each other, me cocooned in his embrace, his breath combing my hair.

I twisted slowly and he shifted onto his back, mouth parting. His chest rose and fell in a slow rhythm, and I wished I could see what he was dreaming.

Lifting myself onto my elbow, I watched him.

Julian. He was back in my life.

Finally.

Then I did something I never told him about. Something that I thought about every day we spent together after that as we revived our old friendship, before he left for the army. Something I thought about every time I worked on new wax pieces. Something that I closed my eyes to every night for the next year. Something I thought about every time I brought myself to release.

I carefully lifted myself until I hovered over him. We were so close I could feel his stubble gently scratch my chin. Then with the softest press of my lips to his, I kissed one half of his mouth. Just like he'd done to me at Christmas.

Two halves now.

That had to make a whole.

Goodbye. Again

"I HATE THAT you're in the Army," I said, easing my foot off the gas and rolling the car into the train station parking lot.

"It's not so bad," Julian said, rubbing his palms over his camouflage pants. He clicked open his belt and pulled up his shirt, reveling a six pack. "Finally got these babies."

Ben thumped him on the shoulder from the back seat, while I struggled to look away; willing my cock not to stir.

"Damn," Ben said, "maybe I should reconsider doing civil service."

"Besides," Julian said, covering his smooth skin and dark treasure trail, "it's only another couple of months—then I can move on with my life, what I *really* want to study."

I rubbed my thumbs over the grainy steering wheel. I hated that he only came back every few weekends. Hated it for this moment, where I had to say goodbye. Again. "When are you back?"

"I'll make sure I'm back for your last day of school. I'm sure Nick will be celebrating; we'll make like every other year."

"Only if we can find an escape route that doesn't involve dashing through the haunted woods."

Ben snorted. "Still scared of that place? We've got to get that out of you, Lenny boy."

"Ah, shit," Julian said, glancing out at the tracks, "that's my train."

We opened doors and stumbled out, moving toward the platform. I trailed behind, a part of me hoping maybe Julian would slow down too. Maybe he'd miss his train. Maybe he wouldn't have to go.

But we made it to the platform on time, the large clock ticking slowly above our heads. Ben swung an arm around Julian and hugged him. "See you in a month, man. Don't shoot your major off."

Julian snorted, and patted the back of Ben's semi-long hair —looked like he was trying to go surfer style again.

Ben stepped back and it was my turn.

Julian cocked his head to the side, the way he always did, beckoning me closer. Like all the visits before, our hugs were stiff, awkward. I moved in the same direction as he did and ended up bumping foreheads.

I let out a soft curse and he grinned, cupped the back of my head and steered me into the hug. My legs were angled wrong and I couldn't support my weight, and Julian's chuckle in my ear robbed me of breath.

"It'll get easier," he said, and I wondered if he meant *it'll get easier saying goodbye* or *it'll get easier because soon I'm coming home*.

I wished it was the latter, but after the army he was off to Mannheim to study. The next couple of years were only going to be a series of goodbyes for us.

I pulled away before I breathed in his scent and my throat clogged up. "Bring us back graduation presents."

Ben looped an arm around my neck, and that's the way we stood, waving to Julian as he and the train left.

"Actually, I'm glad we're doing social work," Ben said once we were in the car, driving back down the pothole-covered streets to Oma's. "I want to be able to help you out with Oma if you need it. With her eyesight getting so bad and all… In fact, I've been thinking…"

I glanced at him running a hand through his hair as he stared hard out of the window. "I want to move in with you. Just for the year and a bit. I'll pay rent and everything."

I screeched the car to a halt at the side of the road, pulled up the brake, and turned to Ben. "Don't you dare pay any fucking rent."

His eyes sheened with emotion, then he nodded and looked out of the car at the village.

Houses lined up, the old with the new that tried to look like the old. Pastor Dieter walked his pet dog past the small bakery toward our old weather-beaten, window-smashed elementary school, overgrown with weeds and tagged to death. The grass fields in the distance rolled with the wind and the small river sparkled in the light. The haunted wood that we all ran into every year didn't look quite so scary from here.

Herr Leike glared at us as he passed in his new Audi; my sister's old high school friend rolled a stroller up a windy path; and somewhere, Oma was making some kind of trouble or other.

It wasn't all pretty, it wasn't all horrible. It was the place that'd once seemed larger than it was. The place Ben had broken his arm climbing an old Linden in the graveyard. The place where every village festival, we'd dress up and eat and drink beer. The place where Ben discovered that the top of the pastor's flat roof was the perfect spot to spy on everyone in the village square. The place we could both walk around blind-folded and not get lost.

His official address might have been one village over, but his home was here.

"You belong here, man."

Ben took in all the details of our home, sighing, a smile slowly warming his face.

I banged my head back against the headrest. Ben was the only other person in the world that could make me look forward to a day when Julian wasn't in it.

"I hope you don't mind my sister's old room," I said. "Though you won't be able to change much."

"Sweet," Ben said, and his cheeky tone was back. "I can go through all her shit."

"Do and you die."

"Maybe finding out her secrets will be worth it."

Secrets. The word felt a weight around my bird's leg. And suddenly, urgently, I needed to release it. I stared at Ben's dimpled smile and hauled in a breath.

"Ben?"

"Yeah?"

"I've got a secret." He waited for me to continue. My bird fluttered, and then the words gushed out. "I'm not interested in women."

His smile stayed mostly intact as he processed that. Only a small frown cut into his brow. "Oh," he breathed, and a blush crept up his neck. "Ohh. I get it. You're interested in *me*."

He said it so seriously and gently, like he was preparing the best way to let me down. It didn't cross his mind that I wouldn't be interested in him, because Ben had this wonderful ego, where every girl loved him. Now I swung that way? The same rules had to apply.

I laughed so hard my body shook in the seat and the old car rumbled. I wiped away a tear welling out the corner of my eye. Ben waited patiently for me to finish, but it took a while— because I wasn't just laughing at my dear Ben, I was laughing off all my nervousness and anticipation. Laughing off a life-time of hiding this truth.

I lifted the brake and rolled the car back onto the street. "Ben, you made my fucking year."

"Is that a yes?"

"No, Ben. No. Trust me, I'm not interested."

"Just in other guys?"

I almost shook my head, but refrained. *No, not* others. *Just one.*

But that secret wasn't ready to come out.

Lenny

S UMMER. *SUPPOSEDLY.* Hard to tell when the rain pelted down, soaking through my thin T-shirt and shorts. I scrambled down the hill, slipped on a patch of mud and landed on my ass, my breath punched out of me.

I sat, wiped at the water collecting at my brow, and shook my dripping hair. To think it'd been sunny when I'd started this hike.

Ah, there was no use. I let the rain do its thing; at least the water was warm-ish. I looked down on Waldau, towards my house. Had Ben already left for our shift at the old folk's home? And Julian? Had he watched me run off up here sucking in my sob?

I rubbed furiously at the crease between my brows, as if I could make the feeling go away. But it bubbled inside. It was too much having Julian back in Waldau for the summer. He kept talking about the friends he'd made over the course of his first year at Uni. He kept bloody smiling, his stupid, beautiful green gaze drifting off into the distance. What was he thinking? Had he finally met someone?

But of course he had. *Look at him!*

He fit his skin now, he was tall and broad, his eyes looked like they'd seen and knew so much more, and he was *confident*— the boy in him I knew so well was fading, and who did that leave behind? Someone I didn't know. Someone who'd grown up a few years without me.

He'd gone off and seen the world, and I was here doing the same thing as everyday: my civil service, my wax hobby, and taking turns with Ben to help Oma get used to her hip replacement. And it looked like it was going to stay that way for a while.

I shut my eyes and, with the rain drowning out the sound, I let the yell out. I should be happy; I should be cheering. This made me the crappiest friend in the world.

Ben had gotten his acceptance into the Free University of Berlin, and would be leaving at the end of the summer. When he'd told us, he'd rung up Carolin on speed dial and put her on speakerphone so we'd all hear the good news at the same time.

"I'm coming to Berlin, Caro." His eyes shone with pride and relief that he was finally taking that next step. "I told you you'd never be rid of me."

Oma snatched him into a hug. "But I'll be finally rid of you," she said, blinking hard, "Can't stand you always asking how I am. It's meant to be my job, you know."

Ben squeezed her back, kissing her soft bouncy curls, just behind her ear.

Then it was Julian's turn. He gave Ben a high-five and they banged their shoulders together.

Ben looked at me over his shoulder and then dropped his gaze. The air snapped with Carolin's breath tunneling down the line, and time stretched, waiting for me to break it. For me to jump up and noogie the crap out of his golden bangs while I told him how proud I was.

I forced a smile, hoping the heat behind my eyes wouldn't give me away. We were so used to touching, Ben and I, it was another part of our daily conversation, but now I'd forgotten how to do it. I looked around the room like it might offer me a reprieve. That's when I focused on the wooden clock chiming in the corner of the room.

"We're going to be late for our shift," I said.

Ben's shoulders fell, and Oma frowned at me. "Lenny," Carolin reprimanded softly. Julian looked at me with his all-knowing, experienced eyes, and cocked his head. Just so.

I strained the smile some more, and backed out of the room, through the kitchen, and then raced out the back door…

Now I ripped out handfuls of wet grass, the smell fresh and strong in my hands. I threw them, and a breeze blew them back over my neck, my chest, my lap.

"Lenny!"

His deep voice sliced its way through the rain and, like it always did, my blood pounded in my veins. I slowly raised my head. At first I only saw his feet and Oma's red umbrella as he came up the steep incline. It leveled out on the stretch where I sat, and soon I saw all of him, water rolling off the umbrella with every step.

"Lenny," he said again a few yards away.

"I don't want to talk about it," I said. "Not yet."

He nodded and when he reached my side, he knelt down, sitting back on his haunches in the muddy grass, and covered both our heads with the umbrella.

The rain pitter-pattered on the material in a rhythm that almost drowned out my thoughts. Almost. But…I stared up at my Julian, who'd become a man, who was staring at me as if I might be someone different too.

But I hadn't changed. "It's just me. I'm the same."

He shook his head and, with his free hand, reached out and plucked a long piece of grass off my neck. A tickle raced after the grass where it had rested against my skin.

"I bet Aunt Thomas is amazed at how you turned out," I said to him, forcing myself not to touch my neck.

Julian stilled, something unreadable crossing his face, then he flicked the grass away. "She says I remind her of Papa."

He stared at my soaked T-shirt as he said it, and then he pulled off another two straws of grass. Instead of flicking them away, he placed them on his thigh, making an L.

His fingers skated over my stomach as he plucked more of the grass, making an E and then an N. The rain made a hollow in my T-shirt where my bellybutton was, and Julian dug his pinkie in there like we used to do in our tickle fights as kids. Except this time, I didn't laugh. This time my skin simmered at his touch and my cock hardened.

Julian withdrew his fingers and tortured me further by pinching the remaining grass from my thighs. My skin under the thin material prickled with the touch. N and /—the last strand he needed lay on my inner thigh.

I watched him eye it, watched him as he hesitated to take it, watched as his fingers twitched, inching closer—

I snagged his hand and brought it gently to the last piece, his thumb grazing over my bulge. His gaze flew to mine, and I didn't let him speak, didn't let him swallow. I was tired of dreaming, tired of hoping, tired of waiting for him to *see*.

I leaned forward and kissed him.

My wet lips met his soft mouth and I trembled as I pulled myself closer, hands firm on his upper arm and the back of his head. I opened to taste him, capturing his bottom lip and sucking gently.

He dropped the umbrella to the side and let the rain wash over us.

A warm sigh left him and his lips parted some more.

Crushing myself closer, I shifted onto my knees, one hand slipping off his shoulder to his LENNY covered thigh. I clutched him and the grass. Us. A moan slipped out of me, needy and passionate. I couldn't rein it in, and Julian wasn't stopping me.

But he wasn't giving it back either, he was just taking it, accepting what he knew I needed.

I kissed him harder, searching for the zeal he was supposed to have, but he didn't offer it.

My eyes welled with tears, mingling and falling with the rain. I ran my mouth along his jaw, down his neck, down the arm that just hung at his side. Hooking two thumbs under his T-shirt, I dragged it up and over his head. Rain matted the hair on his chest and glistened over his skin. I pressed my fingers to every inch of him, squelching my doubts with my lips to his nipple. Julian's breath hitched, and his head rolled back.

"Lenny—"

I lifted my lips to his to stop whatever he was going to say. I didn't want this conversation with words but with the grass between his skin and mine, the wet summer air sticking to us, and the smell of his body with the lightest traces of sweat and soap.

I wanted to touch him everywhere, until he was turned inside out and all his thoughts would be there for me to *feel*.

I twisted and carefully pushed him to the ground. He looked up at me with green eyes that watered from…from the *rain*?

My T-shirt had half-ridden up my stomach, and I pulled it off and laid it under his head. Then I kissed him again, and for a second I felt him tilt his groin against me. I lengthened myself over him, pressing our hard crotches together. I smiled —he wanted this too.

Then my smile faded. So why did he refuse to hold me? To kiss me back? To feel every inch of me as I did to him?

I kicked away my sandals and pried his off with my bare feet. I rested my feet on his. Grass grated between our thighs as

I gently thrust against him. Our chests rolled slickly together, and my heart was beating so damn fast, Julian had to feel it.

I kissed him again. I wanted this to keep going, wanted it to go farther, wanted to reach down, fish into his shorts and grasp Julian's cock—no, I wanted both our pants to our knees as our cocks slid together and we came over each other's stomachs.

I let out a sob and pinched his nipple hard for not being with me in this moment. For not giving it back. He sucked in a breath that whistled through his teeth.

Then I pushed off him, rolling onto the mud. But suddenly Julian locked his arms around me and we rolled together. With him on top of me, he whispered into my ear. "Finish it."

Then he rolled us back the way we'd been.

With angry, needy thrusts, I finished, and he did too. Come leaked through our shorts, warming us as we lay there, neither moving, neither talking.

My ragged breath bounced unevenly off the crook of his neck. "Why'd you let me—?"

"Because you were sad about Ben leaving. Because you needed to."

"And you didn't?"

His answer hit the hairs at the nape of my neck. "I can't."

"Why—"

"Because we're fucking *first cousins*, okay!" He pushed me off him and grabbed his T-shirt. "And I'm not that way!" I lay back in the mud where I'd fallen and watched him shove into his shirt. He reached down, lifted me up, thrust my T-shirt and the umbrella into my hands. "I have to get back home, take mama out like I promised."

And all the passion he'd held back with me came back to him as he hurtled down the hill and around the bend.

The last I'd hear from him for months was his *fuck!* bellowing in the wind.

Reality. It sucks

HE CAME BACK for New Year's.

He was across the village square, dancing with his mama as firecrackers exploded over them. I watched with Carolin and Ben from the pastor's rooftop.

The night sky illuminated with color and then clouded with smoke, and the entire time, I watched *him*.

He kissed his mama's cheek, bought her a drink, and spun her into a dance, laughing when she did. Then he moved over to Oma having a shot of liquor with Pastor Dieter on the bench outside the church and kissed her cheek. He held out a hand, offering her a dance, and she picked up her cane and smacked it at his ass.

He laughed, waved to them both, then went back to his mama for another twirl. His mama said something to him that made him cross his arms and frown at her. It was just after that he glanced up to us on the roof.

Of course he knew we'd be there.

Even as far as across the square I caught the subtle tilt of his head to the side. Even from here, I felt his gaze whispering across my skin.

I left before midnight, went to bed and stared into the dark. When the firecrackers boomed collectively, I knew it was 00:00, 2009.

At 00:01, my floorboards creaked and a shadow fell heavy into my room. I knew by his darkened shape in the doorway who it was. I shut my eyes and feigned sleep.

Julian's feet padded lightly over to me.

Something brushed the back of my hand that rested on the covers by my side. Julian's fingertips? It tickled, but I kept still, breathing slowly in and out.

He sighed lightly, then the bed dipped as he sat down. I heard the scuffle as his shoes came off and my heart raced like crazy. Still I pretended to sleep. Then Julian was quiet, unmoving, as if trying to decide whether to shake me awake or lie down and sleep.

I swallowed, and hoped he didn't hear it.

Maybe he did, maybe he didn't, but he shifted, and suddenly his warm weight was on me, pressing firmly, his legs between mine through the sheets.

Still, I didn't move, didn't dare open my eyes in case I broke this connection. But I wanted him to know I didn't mind, that he was welcome there, that he should stay. So I shifted my hand, nudging his. *Continue. Finish it.*

That's when he let out a little whimper and rolled off me. "No," he whispered, then he got up and left.

And that was the last I saw of him for a year and a half. Six months into it, after not returning my e-mails or any of my calls, I finally understood. It was the end.

No, not the end—there'd have to be a beginning for that.

It just never was.

Everything I thought…well, they were just that. *Thoughts.* In the mind. Not based in reality.

I *wanted* reality.

BERLIN GAVE IT to me.

I danced in a crowd, in a beautiful neo-gothic church-turned-club. *Die Kathedrale.* Light glittered through the stained glass windows around the arched frame of the church doors.

It was beautiful and it was so Berlin, and I wanted that to be enough. But something inside of me wouldn't let go. I lived in a nostalgic blur—Julian always on my mind, no matter how hard I tried to push him out.

The guy I was dancing with trod on my foot and a sharp pain snapped something real into me. Suddenly, the blur was gone and I *felt* the way our bodies bumped together. Tasted the sweat and beer in the air around us. Heard his breath as it whooshed down my neck. Smelled his shampoo as he kissed and sucked my neck.

I saw the want in his eyes, the way he eye-fucked my body, and I wanted it too.

I pressed into him, willing him to step on my foot again. To keep me in the right-here-and-now.

The stained glass light shimmered in the air, wrapping itself around us.

"Leonard," he said the name I'd given him back at the bar. "God, yes, Leonard."

The name sounded harsh and real and that was what I needed. "I want you," he said in my ear. "I want to take you back to my place and fuck you."

He kissed me again, and I let him lead me off the dance floor and out into the night...

It was a taste of reality, that night.

It sucked.

Not Jealous, You Moron

A FTER A SHIFT at the old folk's residence, I came home and collapsed at the table across from Oma and her crystal ball.

She'd tied a scarf around her head and wore cherry earrings—wait a sec—"Are those actual cherries?"

She looked up at me, her eyes rimmed thick with brown eyeliner. "There are too many of them to know what to do with."

"How'd you—you know what, I don't want to know."

She smiled but it fell when the front door opened, bashing against the wall.

I hurried to the entrance. What the—

Blotchy-eyed Carolin stood there, hunched over crying, and Ben stood next to her, rubbing her back, visibly shaking.

"What happened?" I asked.

"I don't...I don't know. She just rolled up at my place, bawling and telling me to drive her home right away."

I helped him guide her into the kitchen and sat her down.

Oma was already up, boiling water for some tea.

Ben and I knelt either side of her. "What happened?" he

asked, brushing back her cropped hair with a tenderness that made me miss him more.

Her bottom lip wobbled and she looked at me, and then focused on Ben. "Dave was supposed to love me."

Ben's grip on her calf whitened. "Did that fucker hurt you?"

"Don't call him that. I love him." She hit his shoulder, but he didn't budge. Instead, he rubbed her shoulder and neck, and then brushed away one of her tears.

"No dice, Caro. If he makes you hurt like this, I'll call him whatever I want."

That made my sister cry harder.

I rubbed her knee. "Hey, it'll be all right."

But even as I said it, I heard the lie. You could wish it to be all right. You could pretend. But it would always lurk somewhere inside, ready to rear its head when you least needed it to.

Oma brought over Carolin's cup of tea, rested it on the table in front of her, then bent and kissed the top of her head. "Ah, dear, I wish I could take the pain away."

"I just want...I just need..." She sniffed, and wiped her nose on her sleeve. Then she pushed back her chair to the middle of the room with a deafening screech, and lifted her arms out for a hug. For a team hug. Like old times.

We huddled together, all our breaths mingling until Carolin's shaking sobs stopped.

After that, we cozied around the table, drinking tea. Carolin pointed to Oma's crystal ball. "Please," she said, "read my future love life?"

Oma looked at each of us in turn, then at the ball. Drawing circles over it, Oma hummed, and Carolin and Ben both shivered at the same time. Oma concentrated hard on something. "Ah, it's very special, Carolin. It's not just romance you'll have. No, you'll have a love *story*."

It was just what Carolin needed to hear. I saw it in the way her eyes lit up, heard it in the relieved breath that tunneled out of her as she bowed her head toward her tea.

"Now mine," Ben said. It was the first time he'd ever asked for a reading. All three of us looked up at him.

"Really?" I asked.

"I want to know."

"To know what?" I jibbed. "How many girls will confess their love to you? How many hearts you'll break?"

Ben's jaw clenched and it was his turn to stare into his teacup.

Oma hummed, fingers tracing a pattern on the crystal ball. "I see family, Ben," she said. "And I see you the happiest you've ever been because of it."

Ben stared harder at his tea, then choked on a soft thank you.

I sank back in my chair feeling like a dick. Ben might have jumped from girlfriend to girlfriend but he always treated them well and never promised them the world. But...he wanted more, didn't he? He wanted what had been so broken in his life —a family.

Warmth seeped through my work uniform as I hugged my tea to my chest and caught his gaze. *Don't you know you already have us as a family?*

Ben swallowed and took a long drink.

The crystal ball glittered in the kitchen light as Oma moved it to the side of the table. And the farther it moved from me, the more I needed it nearer. Needed it to tell me my future. Would I ever move on from Julian? Would I ever find a man who *I* could call family?

"Wait," I said, and Ben, Carolin, and Oma looked up at me. "What can you read about my love life?"

Oma dragged the crystal ball back to her. After a long moment, she looked at me over the top of it. *Are you sure?* her gaze seemed to ask. I inclined my head. "The ball says you'll tell us about your love life when you're ready."

"But does it…can you see…the guy I'll be with?"

My sister was the only one to give an audible gasp, but she quickly swallowed it. "Lenny?" she said. "You're gay?"

I didn't need to say anything; I just looked at her, and she nodded. "Wow. I never…okay."

She swung her head toward Ben. There was a moment where they spoke without speaking, their eyes reading each other the way good friends and family could, and then she said, slowly, "You knew."

"Does that matter?"

She nodded. "Yeah, it does."

"Why?" He frowned and his gaze grew dark. "This isn't something to be competitive about, Carolin." Then he stood up suddenly. "Not everything has to be a competition."

Carolin was quick on her feet, shoving his chest. "I'm not jealous, you moron."

Ben captured her hands and held her there. "Then why does it matter?"

"Because you *knew*," she said, and her tears were back, "and you've been there for him, and you didn't run off, and even though you're straight you still touch him fondly and let him jump all over you just the way you always have. And you kept his secrets…you love him."

Ben hooked a finger under her chin and urged her to look at him. Then he glanced at me before continuing, "Lenny's Lenny and always will be. Why is this a problem?"

She shook her head, locks of hair coming out of her knot. "It isn't." And then she lifted herself on the tips of her toes and kissed him on the cheek. "It just makes me see how much I love you."

"You love me?" he said, and his voice cracked.

Carolin hesitated and then playfully punched him in the

arm and laughed. "Not like *that*. You really *do* want all the girls to love you."

I couldn't be sure, because it was only fleeting, but I thought I caught Ben wince.

My sister didn't notice as she spun out of his grasp and came over to kiss my cheek, in just the same way she'd done with Ben. "I know a bunch of gay guys in Berlin," she whispered. "When you come up again, I'll introduce you to some of them."

Then she hugged Oma and slunk off to her room. Ben excused himself, car keys jangling in his hands, ready to go.

Oma shook her head and looked at the crystal again, and I held my breath, waiting for her response. Maybe she'd pluck one of her earrings out, eat the fruit, and while the stone was still in her mouth, ask me if I'd had my cherry plucked already.

Or maybe, when she thought I wasn't looking, she'd shudder, hiding her disgust from me because she loved me, but didn't understand.

She did neither. Instead she smiled. "My brother preferred men too," she said. "Of course, his love story was tragic. Yours won't be."

"Why? What happened?"

"The war. He and his lover died side by side."

"I'm sorry, Oma. You've seen too much death."

"But I've seen and will continue to see so much love."

I paused, and leaned in. "How do you know that? Have you seen the guy I'll end up with?"

She sighed. "The crystal ball only tells me that you'll tell us when you've found him."

The Feel Of A Bird Losing Its Wings

I WAS PAST PAIN.

After years of wanting and waiting and *hoping*, seeing him again—seeing him with *her*…life had finally done it. It'd torn the wings off my bird for good.

And it didn't hurt like I feared it would.

There was just…nothing anymore. No clarity; I couldn't see right, taste right, hear right, smell right, feel right. Every sense had been numbed.

So when Julian stood on a pew and announced it at the end of mass, in the bustling church, to all of us at once like we were just *the rest of village that they'd better tell*, I became one of the hundred that pushed forward to congratulate him.

I simply followed the others, copying them.

I kissed her soft delicate cheek. Murmured, *"You're a lucky woman."* She smiled at me, and the numbness threatened to swallow me when I saw just how beautiful, and petite, and graceful, and so unlike me she was.

My aunt stood next to her, and for the first time, she reached out and shook my offered hand, her smile triumphant, broad, splitting her face, and I hoped I'd never see such a thing on my sister, ever.

"You must be proud," I mumbled.

"And happy," she said.

"And happy."

"For so many reasons."

A shudder rolled through me and I jerked my hand away. She laughed softly and moved on to accept Herr Leike's congratulations behind me.

Julian swallowed when he lifted his gaze from Frau Rohr and met mine. His Adam's apple jutted out, and he blinked. Somewhere inside, there was a stir of anger, but the numbness quickly drowned it out.

I held out my hand and stared at his chest. "Congratulations."

His hand bypassed mine and he grasped me into a hug, his hands warmly sliding over my numb skin to make it prickle. He whispered in my ear. "I didn't think you were here. I...wanted to tell you myself. I—" He squeezed me, fingers pressing tightly and not tightly enough. "*Sorry*. Thank you...for understanding."

I didn't understand his apology, and nor did I care to.

Haunted Woods

Fog stretched and curled out of the haunted woods. Trees reared up into the sky, darker than the night, and high-pitched screams carried on an icy breeze.

I shivered, even with Ben's arm around my neck and his warm body next to mine. One of his metal gladiator bracelets scratched the lobe of my ear. He leaned in to whisper and his helmet knocked my head. Pulling it out of the way, he said, "Dude, are you actually going to do it alone? Or do you need me to go with you?"

My answer was to shrug his arm off, snap my Zorro mask over my eyes, and whip my fleece-lined cape. The cold air tunneled around my thin black shirt and pants, and the effect I was going for was lost in a shiver.

"Do you need *me* to go with *you?*" I said shifting my foot over a small piece of grit that had found its way into my boot.

Ahead of us, Thomas (from Nick and Thomas—Twin Vikings) doubled over and laughed as his poor eleven-year-old sister came out of the woods with snot hanging out her nose and tears in her eyes.

Nick's fiancée scowled at Nick until he whacked Thomas over the back of the head.

"Told you you wouldn't be able to handle it," Thomas said, and scooped her up to his side. "I'll take you home."

Ben leaned back against the wire fence separating the quaint village and paddocks from the cave of this hungry wood. I wasn't entirely convinced a witch didn't live in there. I mean, one part of me knew it was just folklore…

But didn't folklore originate from an actual event?

"Where are your gloves?" Ben suddenly asked as I rubbed my hands together.

"Sis told me I had to be the gentleman; she needed them for her costume."

Ben straightened and the wire fence buckled back into its original shape. He searched the small village crowd gathered at the fringe of the woods. "Where is Caro?"

I scanned the colorfully costumed crowd. "Don't know, she said we'd know when she arrived."

Ben's cuffs clanged against his armor as he twisted toward the paddocks behind us. "Do you know what her costume is? —Holy. Shit."

I heard a braying, and followed Ben's gaze.

I stumbled back, choking out a cry of surprise that was mixed with a laugh. My sister had commandeered one of Herr Braun's horses and was cantering across the grassy paddock. Her leather boots glistened in the moonlight, along with her red hair whipping behind her, and the jockey helmet she wore.

She reached us and stopped, patting the sleek brown of the horse's neck. "Nice one, Kasper."

Looking down at us, she smiled. "Told you you'd find me."

Ben slid his helmet back as he looked up at her. His breath clouded between them. "Caro," he said, gracefully sliding over the fence and offering her a hand down. "Trust me. I'd always find you."

She swung off the horse and batted away his offered hand. Her cheeks were flushed from riding and the wind must have been strong, because she kept blinking. She drew the reins over Kasper's head and handed them to Ben. "Let's find a quieter spot to tie him up."

At the same time she said that, a hand clasped down on my shoulder and Nick's voice was in my ear. "Your turn, Krause."

I gulped. "In a sec, Leike." To Ben and Carolin, I said, "You guys going to be all right? Or do you want to go together?"

Carolin tucked her jockey whip into her boot and shook her head. She looked at me with a knowing smirk. "Have fun in there. If we're not here to see you come out, we'll meet back at the Leike's after-party."

"Don't piss your pants," Ben added with a wink.

"I'm twenty-three, I think I can handle it." Hopefully. I'd bailed last year. The only reason I'd made it out this year was because Ben had promised it would be harmless fun.

But looking at the fog coming out of the deep woods, I wasn't feeling it.

"Ready?" Nick asked. "Or are you going to chicken out again?"

"I promise not to scream like you did when Oma had a night terror."

"She wielded a knife! It was aimed at my manhood!"

Nick grumbled as he led me into the trees. Fog shifted around my feet and I forced myself not to gulp as Nick took out a long silky scarf and beckoned me to take off the Zorro mask. "How'd you do the fog?" I asked.

"Dry ice lining the path. Heaps of it."

The scarf came up around my face and then tightened over my eyes. As Nick did up the knot, he gave me a quick run-down of what would happen.

"I'll spin you ten times so you don't know what direction

you'll be heading in. Then Tina will lead you five minutes into the wood. There will be no speaking. There you'll have to count to thirty before taking off your scarf. When you have, you'll be alone. Just you and the Gruffalo in the deep dark woods, got it?"

The scarf pinched at the skin between my brows and nervous sweat beaded at the back of my neck. Nevertheless, I nodded.

"There are florescent tags on the trees that will lead you back," Nick said, "as well as a heap of delightful things to creep the shit out of you along the way." He thumped me hard on the back and my cape jerked to my throat. "Looking forward to seeing you on the other side," he said, far too cheerily.

Bastard.

Nick spun me more than ten times. By the end of it, I almost lost my footing trying to stay upright. I couldn't see him, but I could picture his cheeky grin.

"Okay," came Tina's delicate voice as she picked up my hand.

"We're going in?" I asked, but she didn't answer, just tugged me a step forward. Something snapped, shadows raced across the lids over my eyes and I cowered in my step and flailed my free hand out to push away from the tree—but there was no tree there.

I shuffled next to Tina, not lifting my feet off the ground. I thought my other senses would heighten to make up for the lack of sight, but all I could concentrate on was the ringing in my ears. And the pounding of my heart. And—

Tina suddenly let go of my hand. Surely we couldn't be there already, could we? I could count the seconds to every double pound of my heart, and we hadn't been out here longer than a minute.

"Tina?" I asked. There was no response.

I tried to peel off the blindfold when a hand touched mine, gently tugging it down again. "Between you and me," I said to Tina, "I don't think Nick's walk of terrors can beat this little walk to get to it."

She changed her grip on my hand and I wondered at how quickly her hands had warmed, and then...her skin felt rougher and her palm must've been my size, or bigger even—

"Oh," I said, "is this one of Nick's tricks? To swap the lead? I get it, when I take off my blindfold, you'll be some freaky figure in the fog that shouldn't be there. And I'll scream, and Nick who undoubtedly has this all recorded will hold it against me for many years to come."

The only answer was the subtlest squeeze of fingers as he —I was sure it was a guy now—tightened his grip. The way he did it, with the tips of his fingernails biting into my skin, was like a scale of piano keys being played up my arm.

The ringing in my ears disappeared, replaced by the small puffs that came out of our mouths.

I wanted to say his name. There was only one person that could make me *see* him just by the pattern of his breaths. But it couldn't be him. Julian wasn't in Waldau. This touch on my hand...it was the blindfold and the icy air and the mushy uneven ground teasing me, *haunting* me by bringing back his ghost.

"Tina," I said, because my body so badly wanted to believe the lie it was creating. "Just one word. Please?"

But she said nothing, and it remained Julian's hand in mine.

Tears filled my eyes and soon the blindfold rubbed wetly over the top of my nose. How much I wanted it to be his hand! How much I wanted to tell him everything that had happened since he'd left.

I'd tell him about Oma having correctly foretold three deaths of the village elderly. How her sight had worsened and she couldn't live completely on her own anymore. How she asked after him nearly every week, even when it was obvious he wasn't coming back.

I'd tell him how Ben was halfway through his studies and had just moved out of his student flat into his own apartment, and managed to visit us every other month. How he'd offered to postpone his studies to give me more help at home.

I'd tell him how Carolin had offered the same, and how I couldn't let them do it. They were so close to finishing. It didn't make sense.

And I'd tell him how I had just started to make a side business of my wax creations, selling them online.

I clutched his hand, mine clammy and nervous, and thought of the things I wouldn't tell him. Like going to bed every night unable to sleep, imagining him with his fiancée. Like waking in the morning hoping somehow I'd dreamed it all, and he'd be there, one arm slung over my waist and his snores in my hair. Like touching myself, picturing he was there, kissing and stroking me, and loving me back.

We stopped, and I knew we'd made it to the beginning of Nick's path. I twisted, reaching out to touch him, to feel his profile, but his other hand caught mine. There was one final squeeze and breath whispering over my cheek, then he let go.

Footsteps crunched away from me. I could have yanked the blindfold off right away, but my fingers fumbled on the material. I couldn't do it. Didn't want to know. Because for the first time since that moment in the church, the thick layer of numbness that'd cloaked me had faded.

I touched my hand where Julian's ghost had held it. It still tingled.

Something I thought I'd never feel again.

Part Two

FLYING THE NEST

(NOW)

Moving On

THE TOUCH LINGERED ON MY HAND. No matter how hard I washed it over the months, I couldn't get it to stop tingling with the memory of how his ghost had held it.

And the farther I tried to run away from it, the more it chased me. Like now, where I was checking out a house for rent in Berlin.

"Why here?"

The owner sounded curt, disbelieving, but there was curiosity in there too. I sighed and took in the old German house, with its red tiled roof and dark brown supporting beams making squares and crosses on the white façade.

Rubbing my palm over my jeans, I turned to the owner, Herr Koch, who lived next door. He was an older man—in his late sixties, perhaps—sporting a cap that did nothing to recapture his youth. His eyes narrowed on me as he waited for my answer.

"Why Berlin?" I said. "Because I love the city. It's creative, and I like how people take the old and make it new."

Melancholia was overrated here. You took the past and made it your future.

You moved on.

Which was exactly what I needed to do. Maybe when I managed, I'd be rid of the tingle for good.

I moved up the path, my satchel bouncing against my thigh, and made my way inside the house again. I couldn't believe how similar to home this place was.

It would do fine. Just fine.

"No," Herr Koch said, the floor creaking under him as he followed me into the kitchen, which overlooked the front yard. "Not Berlin, why do you want to rent out here and not live in the center like other kids your age?"

"I'd be moving in with my Oma, so the quiet out here is better. And it's only a half-hour train ride to town."

"Oma, huh," he murmured, the curtness disappearing.

I nodded and breathed in the freshly painted scent of the white walls. If I closed my eyes, I could imagine the room a light green, with a round table near the windows and a large East German cabinet against the wall at the back, my Oma sitting in her favorite velvet-cushioned chair, crystal ball before her.

The place was practically perfect; the living room wasn't quite right, a little too small. But if the wall to the small study came down, it would work.

Herr Koch readjusted his cap. "I don't want this place to be used for parties, and the garden must be tended to."

"Does that mean I'm getting it?"

"Just a second, Herr Krause," he said to me. "I need proof you can afford this place."

I opened my satchel and pulled out the paperwork. He scanned over it, but his growing frown made me nervous.

"I know I work freelance, but that income, coupled with what I'll get renting out our place in the village, I think it can work. I mean, I *know* I'll make it work. Six hundred euros a month. Doable."

Herr Koch tipped the front of his cap down, layering his eyes in shadow and studied the papers again. He cleared his throat. "I was looking for six hundred in cold rent. What I see here, you could only just manage that warm."

"Heating wasn't included?" I choked on the question and Herr Koch winced.

"No, it wasn't."

"But maybe——" I started. "I mean, could we meet in the middle somehow? If you give me a couple of days, I'm sure I can figure out a way to make it work."

"There are other places around here," he said, handing me my papers. "You could try the house around the corner."

I shook my head. I'd already seen that house. It was nothing like my place in Waldau. "It's not right. This one is. Well, if I removed the wall between the living room and study, it will be."

The curiosity in the man's voice was back. "You'd be ripping out walls?"

"Yeah. Just the one."

"Why?"

"I want to move my Oma to Berlin. I need a place that looks the same. You know…so it feels familiar. *Homely*."

"You're blinking," Herr Koch murmured suspiciously. Did he know there might be more to the story? "Homely, eh?"

"Yeah."

"And this is the place is it?"

I looked around once more, picturing family photos on the wall and Oma's crystal ball catching and reflecting light around the room. "Yep. Has homely written all over it."

"I'll tell you what, Herr Krause," he said, his lips twitching at the edges. "I'll rent you the place——"

"You will?" I said, ripping into a grin that made the man's lips twitch.

"With a *three month* contract. For now."

"Three months? But that's—"

"That's my offer. Take it or leave it."

LATER THAT NIGHT, I sat in *Die Kathedrale* with a cool bottle of beer in my hand, waiting for my best friend. Ben had called me an hour ago while I was writing to-do lists and had begged me to meet him for a quick drink. Thirty minutes from my new house—or it would be when I signed the contract tomorrow—I was here.

The barman raised a brow at me, probably to ask if there was something wrong with my Pilsner. I shook my head, finally took a sip, and glanced again at the arched doors. Streetlight filtered through the stained-glass windows surrounding the frame, and fractioned light fell onto the mass of dancing, drinking Berliners.

I could see myself a few years ago, dancing on the same floor, lips rubbing against lips, sweaty skin sliding against sweaty skin, hips grinding against hips...*Leonard. God, yes, Leonard.*

I shivered.

The way the light from those stained-glass windows had touched me then had given me the feeling something was going to happen that night. Nothing good, just inevitable.

I'd ended up losing my virginity.

Tonight the windows had the same ethereal glow that seemed to be whispering for me to come closer, so it could tell me secrets about what it could foresee... Well, I had my Oma and her crystal ball for finding that out. And I didn't want to be reminded of my supposed future.

Ah, there you are!

Ben squeezed his way through the crowd. He found me at the bar and gave a nod. His step was slow and heavy looking.

Another shiver rolled over me as the stained light hit his blond hair, coloring it red and green and the same blue as his eyes.

I took a longer drink of beer. I should have suggested to Ben that we meet somewhere else. Should have known I couldn't handle this place again. I thought I was ready to let go of the past and embrace a new beginning. Thought just by coming here, I'd be able to find peace with that part of my past.

I thought wrong. The tingle on my hand had intensified along with a jaw-clenching anger. It wasn't his decision, but I blamed Julian for that night. Blamed him for the almost lifeless bird that huddled deep inside and didn't dare to leave the safety of the nest.

"Hey, Ben," I said, then caught the barman's attention, motioning for a second beer. I didn't know what was up, but my friend looked like he could use a drink. Pronto.

Ben collapsed onto the stool I'd saved for him. He didn't look or sound his usual vibrant self. "Know it's late, Lenny. Thanks for meeting me here."

"What happened?"

I slid some money over to the barman when the second beer came. Ben took the bottle, murmured a "thanks," and sighed.

"Is it something to do with that girl you're seeing?" I asked. What was her name? Olivia?

There was a moment of quiet, and then he spoke. Yep, all the party had left his words, all right. "Yeah, she—I'm pretty sure she's going to dump me. But…she's *the one*, dammit."

I resisted a sharp desire to snap at him; she was never going to be "the one" because if she were, wouldn't Ben have introduced her to me by now? No, this had to be just another of his girls…

I rested my arms on the sticky bar and looked at him. "I'm sorry, man. Someone will come along who's perfect for you."

"But they *have* and I've just fucked it up."

"If it's meant to be, it'll be. You can't miss rightness like that, and when it comes, you'll just know, yeah?" But I didn't believe it. I'd lost faith in those words.

"How come you're suddenly such a know-it-all?"

"Oma's the know-it-all."

Of course, when telling me the same thing, she'd said: *love will bite you in the ass like a fucking mosquito, and once it's tasted you, dear, it just won't want to stop.* She'd snapped her cane against my ass to emphasis the point.

Ben grunted. "How is Oma doing, anyway?"

Other than her eyesight and the knife wielding night-terrors, she was just the same as always. "Good. I'm heading back to Waldau tomorrow after I—" I shut my mouth.

Ben thought I was in Berlin to pick up some supplies for my wax artwork. I'd yet to tell him I was looking for places to rent.

"After what?" Ben asked.

I shook my head. I couldn't tell him until after I'd signed the contract. After I knew for sure the plan was really happening and he couldn't stop me. "Nothing. Hey, let's get back to you. You look like a wreck."

Ben gave a short laugh and ran his hand through his hair, managing to spike it up in the middle. "I don't know. I just needed to get out for a drink, I think." He sighed, picked up his bottle and chugged half its contents.

"If you need a break," I said. "There's the village festival this Saturday. We can check it out. Hey, maybe Caro will come down too. I'm already leaving tomorrow, but you can give her a lift."

Ben lowered his bottle to the bar, frowning at it. "Um…"

I swiveled on my stool, facing him better. "Don't tell me you're having one of your spats. You don't really hate her, you know."

He gave a strained chuckle. "No. I don't. But—"

"Then it's settled, you'll drive the both of you down there. We'll go to the festival and...and...and then"—all going well —"there's something I want your help with."

"Planting more wax mushrooms in the backyard?"

"Nope. Something much bigger."

"Fine. But..."

I raised my brows at him. "Fine butt? Why thank you."

"Stupid fuck." He grinned and nudged me in the side. "Look, thing is, you might not like it, but if I come down there, I'm going to have to see Julian."

The name, though it played on repeat in my head, hearing it aloud was a punch to my gut. "He's...home?"

Why hadn't I known? Wait, that was clear. The only reason I wouldn't know was if he was purposefully avoiding me.

"You didn't know?" Ben said, frowning.

"No," I said bluntly, pressing my beer bottle against the ache in my chest. "Since when?"

"This is awkward. He's been home for a couple of weeks at least." Colored light brushed over the side of Ben's face, and the beat of the music pushed its way through my skin. I wasn't sure I wanted to hear what else he was about to say. I looked away as he continued, "I don't know why you hate him so much, Lenny, he's your cousin. Whatever you fought about... it's been years. He's finished his degree. We've all changed."

"What are you saying, Ben?"

"I'm saying: give him a second chance. We were all best friends once."

What he was telling me was true, but as I looked toward the dance floor, I couldn't help but shake my head. Maybe it was being in this club, remembering what had led me to *that* night, but I could only think of the shitty memories between us. The *not* friend moments.

"Even if we were once, it'll never be like that again."

Waldau

I was back in Waldau. Back to work.

Sort of.

My plaster molding of an antique birdcage stared back at me, waiting for the wax-swirling stage to begin. The sooner I got it done, the sooner I got paid.

I thought I'd be more productive after signing the three-month contract with Herr Koch. Thought I'd be more motivated to get work done and scrape a few hundred euros together.

I sighed and slumped forward in my chair, resting my elbows on the work table. If I was going to get this cage done and move on to the next project, I really needed to get layering.

Right then.

Time to start already.

First though, I really had to sweep the workshop...clean up a little...and then—yes, maybe I'd go for a walk before I confined myself to the small space for the next eight hours.

I trudged over the backyard toward the house. A cold,

misty rain sprayed over my face; a reminder fall was almost upon us.

"Oma?" I called, ducking into the basement, which I'd made into a living area after a slip on the spiraling stairs had sent Oma to the hospital. I moved into the kitchen. "Oma?"

The clip-clop of her cane on the tiled floor told me she was close. Then—*wham*—the door flew in, slamming into the wall and bouncing off again.

Oma held her cane up to still it. "I want this door gone," she said. "We need beads. Lots of colorful beads."

She moved to the table, her flowing floral skirt dusting the floor and her bangles jingling. Stray grey curls peeked out from under the scarf she'd tied around her head. Today's colors were blues, purples and oranges, and she'd decided on an off-shoulder shirt, which had to be making her cold.

Yesterday's scarf lay abandoned on the bench at the window. I skirted behind the dining table and picked it up. My fingers stilled on the silky material when Oma spoke.

"I have a bone to pick with you, Leonard Krause. When were you going to tell me Julian was back in Waldau?"

I turned slowly, forcing a smile. "You're the fortune teller. Weren't you supposed to be warning me?"

Oma shoved her thick glasses up her nose, raising one brow. Her lenses magnified the smudgy, liberally applied eyeliner. Even with her glasses, she was practically blind. But she knew the basement and garden like the back of her hand —and since she *rarely* left the house, that was all she needed to know.

"I had to find out from Nick when he came around with the bread this morning," she said.

I slipped the scarf around her shoulders and tied a clumsy knot in the front. "I didn't know until last night, either."

She huffed. "Well, when you see him—"

"*If* I see him."

She cackled as if I'd told a joke. "When you see him, you tell him to get his ass over here and have lunch with us. His fiancée, too."

I blinked hard several times. "I doubt he'll be coming over any time soon."

"We'll see. Are you working?"

"Thought I'd take a walk first."

"Put on some music before you go. I'm going to sit in my chair and meditate."

I did what she asked. Oma really had a thing about needing time alone. I switched on some music and it tinkered about the kitchen. "Call if you need anything."

I grabbed my blue umbrella, but the catch had broken and it failed to open. Reluctantly, I took the only other option: a rust-red one that'd been hanging by the front door, unused since the day...

I shook off the memory and opened it as I stepped out into the garden. That was all in the past now, and I was moving on, remember?

I stalked my way up to the top of the hill bordering the village. Soon this sight would be gone. Soon I'd be surrounded by apartments, bars, cafes, graffiti art...soon, I'd be living in Berlin. With Oma.

Grass and shrubs thickened the higher I climbed, almost covering the path. Not too many people walked up this way, which was good, because it made it mine. The place where I'd go to just...think.

The rain hardened, its sound over my head suddenly bringing back the image of Julian plucking grass off me, spelling my name on his thigh, then that frustrating, wonderful, sad, beautiful moment as I rocked against him to release.

I slowed and focused on the view: my home, the neighbors', and the church with its defunct clock tower; the main road winding through the village past the bakery and pub; and beyond, the stream that snaked close to my old—now abandoned—elementary school.

All the roofs in Waldau were red or grey, the facades mostly traditional white with the supporting beams in dark brown.

From here it looked quaint.

From here, I liked it.

My gaze fell to the house around the corner from ours, trimmed with a thick hedge on three sides. I stared at it until the white and brown of the house blurred muddy and ugly, and so unlike the memories made there.

I sighed.

How was it Julian was back and I still hadn't bumped into him? Sure I'd been gone two days, but that left twelve others. Waldau was a small village—everyone saw everyone nearly every day.

Could it be he was avoiding me? And if he was, shouldn't I be glad? I didn't *want* to see him, after all.

I gripped the umbrella, bowed my head away from the view and trudged uphill. I'd only gone a few steps when a voice cut cleanly through a light, grassy breeze.

"It's not raining."

I snapped my head up and my step faltered.

And there he was.

The tall, dark nightmare of my dreams. With a dark, frayed T-shirt that clung to his chest and long pants that were half stuffed into heavy boots.

I swallowed hard, my hiking boots sinking into the muddy ground, gluing me to the spot. Wearily, I watched him move toward me, his forest-green eyes crinkling with a smile.

Julian.

Closer now, he slowed to a stop. His gaze quickly raked over me—like he was taking stock of any changes since we'd last met. There were plenty of changes too, only most he couldn't see and I would *never* reveal to him.

He refocused on my umbrella, staring at it a few beats too long, and then his smile wavered and he cocked his head slightly to one side—a detail I used to think everyone noticed. "It's not raining anymore."

I opened my mouth and shut it again, then shook my head as a damned blush warmed my neck. I rubbed my thumb over the umbrella's plastic handle to stop my hand from shaking.

Julian carefully stepped forward, arms lifting as if to sweep me into a hug. "It's been a while."

My breathing hitched and I yanked down the umbrella between us. Julian halted as I pushed the dewy umbrella against his chest. "Nine months," I said. "Fasching carnival."

He glanced at his muddy boots and then to the clearing sky. A welcoming blue split the grey sky ahead, and for a second I knew—just *knew* what he was thinking: *if somehow we could catch up to it, maybe things would be all blue skies again.* The way it used to be.

I knew he was thinking that because I'd spent a good part of the last few years wishing the same thing. I felt it strongly: that wish for Oma to stay healthy, that wish to move out of Waldau to Berlin, that wish not to be quite so alone any more.

I felt it so strongly that I knew what the feeling *looked* like. And it was right there, quivering between Julian's brows and escaping in his quiet sigh.

He flitted his gaze to mine. "Fasching carnival. You—you knew it was me, then?"

I briefly shut my eyes and remembered the darkness, the touch of a hand in mine, the whisper of breath. I hadn't known for certain it was him until later that night. But really, *honestly*, deep down, I'd known the whole time. "What are you doing back here, Julian?"

His name on my tongue came out an accusation, and I heard it. So did he, because he finally stepped back from the umbrella. "Just here for a bit. Until I sort out my next move."

"Is your…" I could barely finish the thought, let alone the actual sentence. I cleared my suddenly burning throat. "Is your fiancée here too?"

Julian did his head-cocking thing again, and I squirmed under his study. "Would it be a problem if she was?"

I hesitated too long to say it. It came out wavering and pathetic. "No."

"Lenny," he said softly.

I pried my feet from the sucking mud, batting my opened umbrella in his direction as he stepped forward once more.

"Don't. I've got to get back. Oma will worry."

I swept past him before he could respond and beelined down the narrow path, cutting across the hill that joined with the neighbor's paddocks and fringed the haunted woods.

I didn't dare look back, because I was *sort of* afraid he'd be watching me.

And *wholly* afraid that he wasn't.

Village Festival

THE SMALL MERRY-GO-ROUND Pastor Dieter had organized for the village kids chimed its last round behind us. The square was still packed with people—mostly locals, but the daytime part of the festival was winding down. Mamas were already taking their little ones to bed. The rest of us would continue drinking until the wee hours of the night.

Sitting on a picnic bench with the pastor opposite us, Ben snuck one arm around my neck and his other around my sister and hooted toward the summer evening sky. "You're kidding, right?"

His head knocked against mine and he looked up at me, waiting for me to take it all back. But I wasn't. This was the plan.

My sister Carolin plucked Ben's arm from her neck and dropped it unceremoniously on the tagged table top, causing his beer to splash.

Ben winced, but then ignored it, running his beer-stained hand through his short golden hair. "Pastor? You're going through with this?"

He rubbed his thumb and index finger over his white

moustache that reached down the side of his mouth. "I leave the week after Nick Leike's wedding. If you know the name of this pastor that will be taking over the house calls, I'll do my part and tell Frau Krause who her replacement will be."

"I couldn't do this without you," I said, reaching over and shaking his hand. He clasped mine between both of his.

"The most of us love Frau Krause, she'll be missed in Waldau. But while I think you've done wonderfully looking after her, I think it's good that you're taking care of yourself and your needs too."

"Thanks, Pastor Dieter."

Before he let go of my hand and stood, he gave an encouraging smile. "Good luck in Berlin. And if you use my roof tonight, please don't leave muddy prints. It was only painted at the beginning of summer."

With that—the first ever admission he knew we snuck up onto his roof—he wished us a good evening and vacated to talk to Frau Rohr on the other side of the square.

"He's like Oma," Ben said. "He knows everything."

I laughed and raised my beer to that. Just as the cool liquid touched my tongue, I saw him. He tapped his beer bottle with Aunt Thomas's under a string of red and orange lights hanging from the local bar to the top of the church gates.

There was something about the way his gaze roamed over the square that had my skin prickling. Who was he looking for? His fiancée, no doubt. His gaze was closer to us now…

Please don't see us. Please don't—

"Guys," I said, "how about we head to the pastor's roof? Now."

Ben drained his beer and was the first to leap up from the bench. "Let's."

Carolin stood with ten times the amount of grace. I blinked from her to Aunt Thomas across the square. They stood at the same angle and with the distance it was hard to tell the difference between them. The same red hair rolled off their shoulders and their pointed noses were held up the same way. As if they weren't particularly pleased.

My sister shook her head. "I think I'm going home to bed."

"No." Ben snatched her hand. "It's *tradition*."

That was the moment Julian's searching gaze found me. I hurriedly looked to the left, hoping I'd been quick enough he hadn't caught me watching him.

I sidled around the bench and, in three large strides, ducked behind a tree outlined in fairy lights next to the merry-go-round.

Through a gap in the trunk and under a white horse's neck, I spotted them both again. His mama jerked the bottleneck of her beer toward Julian as if telling him off for something. Julian looked to his side. Then my aunt shook her head and reached out, running a hand down his coat sleeve.

Julian took another sip of his beer, trashed the bottle in the metal bin behind him, and kissed his mama's cheek.

His mama watched him walk away, and moved out of sight.

"Come on, guys," I hissed, waving Carolin and Ben over.

Carolin hesitated, and Ben growled. "Fine. If that's the way you want it." Then he proceeded to pick her up and sling her over his shoulder.

Way to draw attention to us, Ben!

Carolin hit the back of his legs, demanding to be let go, but he sucked it all in and smirked at me.

Those two were worse than siblings.

I led us around a corner, glancing behind me to make sure Julian hadn't followed. Clear. For now.

"This isn't the quickest way," Ben said, puffing as we trudged up a steep incline.

I pretended I hadn't heard him and ushered him down the narrow alleyway that cut behind the bakery to the street across from the pastor's place.

Ben dumped Carolin down at the side of the house and immediately stretched his back.

"Your own fault," my sister said, and climbed up the metal railing to the roof.

"But I got her here," Ben said, clapping a hand to my shoulder. Then he spoke loud enough that it carried to the roof. "So it was worth it."

He raced up after her, the rails protesting under him, mud flinging from his shoe onto my cheek. I wiped the sludge off and used the hem of my T-shirt to get rid of the smear.

The slapping sound of lonely footsteps came from the street, and then a shadow extended on the footpath under the streetlight.

Julian? Shit. I wouldn't have time to climb up without being spotted. I scurried down the side of the house to the nook with the garbage cans.

The footsteps followed. I measured the distance from the top of a garbage can to the roof. Could I make it?

"*There* you are."

"Gah!" My whole body jerked like I'd been pronged with something electric. I twisted, heart erratically punching my chest. "W…Where'd you come from?"

Julian shoved his hands into his shorts pockets as he studied me. Boy his eyes were green, even in the shadows that layered us it was easy to make out the color.

He frowned, and I jerked my gaze to the dingy corner behind the pastor's home.

"Were you…hiding from me, Lenny?"

I shook my head. *Yes, yes I was.*

He stepped toward me. "Why?"

Why? *Why?* I looked at him sharply.

He held my stare, though, as if demanding me to get it all out.

And I wanted to. Wanted to shove him away and out of

Waldau. Wanted to scream at him until I had nothing left inside. Wanted to pull out my bird and make him see just how badly he'd hurt it. "I really wasn't hiding."

"So what exactly are you doing in this dark corner with these overflowing garbage cans?"

"I was…I was…" I focused my gaze behind Julian on the pastor's ginger cat taking a leak in the shrubs. "I was just, you know, taking a piss."

"Behind the *pastor*'s house?"

"I was really, really bursting."

Julian gave me a funny look where his brow twitched, and then he stepped toward me. Without my umbrella this time, I had nothing to keep him at a distance. I slunk a step backwards, feeling the coolness of stone as I hit the wall.

Cocking his head, Julian studied me. "Do you remember the time when you had Jessica Kolb over? You were approaching third base when I strolled in. Your Oma was seconds behind me. You rolled Jessica off your bed and shoved her under it. Do you remember what happened next?"

"It's vaguely familiar." I knew every excruciating detail. Well, everything but Jessica's full name, that was.

Julian's voice grew softer, fringed with a little sadness too. Though I couldn't be sure. "You had no shirt on, so you grabbed the first thing you saw. *Jessica*'s T-shirt. Only your Oma walked in before you could squeeze into it—which, by the way, I still wish to this day I'd seen—do you remember what your Oma said?"

I shrugged. "Not sure."

Julian folded his arms. Like my Oma, he did the one eyebrow thing really well. "Your Oma said, 'What on earth are you doing without a shirt?' Do you know what you said then, Lenny?"

Heat rose to my cheeks. Even after all this time, I could still feel the embarrassment. "No idea."

"You told your Oma it was *mine*. That was the reason I'd come around. To get back my T-shirt. Then—and this was the cherry on top of that moment—you handed it to me and said 'thanks for the loaner'."

"What's your point?" I pushed off the wall and moved, but then my legs betrayed me by freezing right in front of him.

Julian's breath hitched.

We stared at one another and time seemed to be dissolving between us, trying to take us back to *then*.

He reached out and tentatively slid his finger under my chin and made me look at him. I wished I could bat him away, could jerk back from his touch, but the tip of his finger touching me was like the tickle of dry grass poking inside my ear, the part of the rollercoaster ride that dipped down suddenly...

I dug my hands deep in my pockets to hide my shiver and rub off the tingle on my palm.

Julian's voice dropped, on the threshold of a whisper. "The T-shirt was about four sizes too small for me." He hesitated, then added, "It was also pink."

He dropped his finger, but he was so close I felt the heat of him, like standing at the far edges of a bonfire; the warmth licked my skin in a way that made me want to get closer.

Which was exactly the reaction I didn't want. Julian was dangerous.

"The *point* is," he said, "you've always been a bad liar."

Bad liar.

Did that mean he knew how much I couldn't stand to be around him? That every minute—every bleeding *second*—I was stabbed with the good, the beautiful, and the best memories of my life? That just looking at him reminded me of a place we once were and could never be again?

"Lenny." He sighed. "We *need* to talk. I can't stand it like this between us."

Then why so long without contact? Why could you stand it then?

I shook my head; it'd taken too long to build up my walls, I couldn't let him crash into them again. I wouldn't be the crumbling mess I was when I realized Julian would never...

"Julian!"

That was the moment my friends decided to make an appearance.

Ben popped his head over the gutter above our heads. "There you are. Hey Julian, you guys coming up here, or what?"

"No," I said, staring steadily at Julian as I brushed past him to the path. "Sorry, but we're done here."

That Would Be Continuing

SUNDAY MORNING, sometime after nine, I ducked out of the village bakery with a bag of rolls under my arm and my phone jammed between my ear and shoulder. I awkwardly stuffed change into my wallet and into my jean's pocket.

"Yes, that's right. I want the wall between the study and the living room to come down."

I was thankful the contractor had gotten back to me so quickly—and on a Sunday, no less.

"I need to check it out to make sure it's nothing structural, but considering how big you say the wall is, I think you'll be looking at around 400 euros."

I headed up the hill, wishing the morning sun warming my back would keep me calm as I swallowed that figure. "Um, 400?"

"That's only an estimate."

He must have heard my hesitation, because he was quick to add, "But we can get it done early next week for you."

Well that was something. "All right. I'll talk to my landlord about getting a key to you when you go around."

"How's Tuesday work for you?"

"That'll be fine," I said, and ended the call.

"Lenny." I heard my name being spoken, but it was muffled as if the sun had soaked through and softened its edges.

I turned, the light blinding on my face as a figure emerged in front of it, reaching out his hand.

Julian's dark hair was tipped golden in the morning light and he smiled hesitantly as he closed the last few steps between us.

"How many times do I have to tell you to go away?"

"Yeah…only, you dropped some change," he said, opening his palm for me to take it.

I stared at it. He opened his hand more, fingers spreading slightly, pennies sliding down his palm.

There may have been no ulterior motives behind it, and I might have only been imagining he wanted to snap his hand around mine and demand we talk, but I couldn't risk reaching out and taking the money. Touching him was too tempting.

"Keep it," I said.

"It's not a trap," he said softly, leaning over, taking the hand hanging by my side and dropping the change in the center of my palm. He closed my fingers around it, and a second later his tingling touch disappeared.

When I didn't offer any more conversation, he gave one last smile, nodded his head, and crossed the street.

We were both heading in the same direction, both a good five minutes from our homes.

I shifted the rolls under my other arm and followed Julian into the shade. I could at least be civil.

"Thank you," I said as I approached his side.

He must have seen me coming, because he didn't jump. Just slowed his gait. "I'm sorry about last night."

We took a right, toward the village square and into the sun. I strolled next to him, something in the air and the warmth of the morning reminding me of the years we did this walking back from elementary school.

We'd held less back then. Had been so carefree with what was on our minds—how we felt. It was simpler then. I blinked down at my worn brown sandals. Suddenly, I needed that childhood honesty back.

"Julian," I said. "I can't stand it like this between us either. But neither of us can turn back time."

The church bells rang: a reminder of Sunday service.

"No," he said, stopping and facing me. A warm breeze ruffled his hair and lightly billowed his T-shirt. "We can't turn back time. I can't change what happened or how badly I acted. But we could—if there's a chance—we could decide how we want to continue."

And my six-year-old self was back, all earnestness and bluntness. "I don't want to continue."

His face fell. I expected him to nod and slowly walk away from me, but he didn't. Something desperate clung to him and he shook his head. "I've got something for you. Let me give that to you first, before…" …*you make any decisions.*

"Ben, Carolin and Oma are waiting," I said, squeezing the bag of rolls under my arm.

"Please," he said.

And because he was *him*, and I was me, I couldn't hold back.

I wished I could have. Wished at the very least I might have hesitated. But I didn't. What was left of my bird pulled me toward him, and I followed him to his place.

"You remembered that Jessica's name," I said as we walked down the side of his house. This had been on my mind all night. How did he remember that day with such clarity?

He lifted a hand and ran them over the hedge. "So did you."

"No, you remembered her *full* name. I didn't."

He dropped his arm. "Yeah, well, some things get stuck in your head."

"She wasn't even in your year."

He moved out to the backyard and pointed toward his old shed. And I wondered if he was pointing to give me an answer, but then he said, "My house truck is behind that."

"House truck?" Now that he said it, I could see the wooden structure jutting out from behind his shed.

With a quick glance back at me, he explained, "After Uni, I needed to hit the road for a while. Clear my head and just... well, this was the cheapest way."

The truck came properly into view. It looked like someone had stuck a cabin on a trailer. And was that a... "You have a chimney?"

Julian moved up a set of collapsible steps and opened the door. "Do you want to take a look?"

Yes. I did.

But I didn't want to see how he and his fiancée lived. Inside that truck was the bed they shared, the life they lived. Maybe the woman herself, sprawled half-naked in their sheets.

I shook my head and moved into the shadow of the shed, and leaned on its side. He gestured toward the truck, asking me if I was sure. When I didn't move, he ducked inside and came back clutching a dark square case in his hand.

"How come?" I called over to him as he shut the door.

His hand stilled on the handle, his back tensing visibly. "How come, what?"

"Don't play stupid," I said. "How come you remembered her name?"

He faced me, coming down the steps and over the grass. "How about you let everything out, and I'll answer you."

"Good bye then, Julian."

A female voice sliced over my back from behind, startling me. I pushed off the shed and turned to face Aunt Thomas.

"Leonard. What are you doing here?"

"Nice to see you too, Aunt Thomas."

Her smile stiffened. "Julian, love, I was just off to Sunday service. Did you want to join me?"

"No," he said, coolly. "I'd rather not."

She pressed her dress, as if to rid it of creases that weren't there. "Well. Maybe next week." With a stiff nod, she turned, only to pause and say to me, "I'll pray for you."

When she left, Julian raised a brow. "What was that about?"

I moved the rolls to my other arm, the bag crackling. "Most of the villagers know about me. Not all are as accepting as others."

He winced and looked at the case in his hand. In what looked a practiced move, he rubbed the corner with his thumb. Round and round. "Has being…has it been difficult?"

I waited a long breeze and two church bells until his eyes met mine. "That wasn't what was difficult."

He swallowed. "Can we talk about it?"

I cast my gaze to the drying grass, poking between the slits in my sandals, brushing against my toes. "That would be continuing."

Julian stepped into the shade with me and handed me a leather case, slightly worn around the edges. "Take it. Think about it."

I took it.

By the time I got home, the case was sweaty in my hand. I dropped the bag of rolls into the basket that Carolin had set up for breakfast, amongst the cheeses, and salamis, and fruit.

Ben seemed in a chipper mood. He bumped hips with mine, whistling. Carolin brought a jug of coffee to the table, scowling.

"How is it you stepped with the right foot out of bed this morning?" she asked Ben, grabbing a mug and filling it with the steamy black liquid. She added a splash of cream and passed it to him, then poured another for herself.

Ben smiled at me, and then winked at Carolin. "Had this wonderful dream. Oma was even in it. She was telling our fortunes. She said one day I'd be the happiest I've ever been because I'm part of a family."

"That wasn't a dream," I said, almost barging into Oma as I retreated toward the hall with my case. "She actually said that."

"What did I say?" she said, tying a scarf into a knot under her chin. "And what do I smell? It's delicious."

Carolin answered her at the same time Ben threw a dish-cloth in my face. Under his breath he said, "It can be both— memory and dream—you know?"

He picked up the cloth from my feet and slung it around my neck. That's when he caught sight of my case.

"What's this?" he said, bumping it out of my grip. With anything else, I would have laughed, would have joked along with him, but Julian had given it to me. And whatever it was, it was a part of our story.

"No. Don't."

Ben hesitated at my tone and eyed up the case. "Now I'm even more curious." I saw his reluctance as he handed it back to me, and it took him a moment to let go. "Maybe you'll show me later?"

Maybe one day.

But right now, it was just for me. I jerked my thumb toward the bathroom. "Gotta whizz. Back for breakfast in a sec."

Instead of the bathroom, I snuck into the backyard, moving toward the cherry trees. I leaned against the trunk of the first tree, in a slice of the same sunlight that had haloed Julian not even an hour earlier.

Would whatever was inside change my mind? Did I even want my mind to change?

By the way my heart raced, the way my breathing quick-ened and bird dove out my feet, the answer to that last question definitely wasn't a no.

With clammy fingers I opened the case. My breath shud-dered out of me, and I was torn between a sob and a smile.

Staring back at me, cushioned in silk, was the Julian-wax-warrior figure I thought I'd lost years ago.

Closer to Saying Yes

DOWN THE LINE, Herr Koch sounded more amused than anything. But it wasn't amusement in my favor.

"I gave you two sets of keys. You'll have to find your own way of getting them to the builders."

With the phone jammed between my ear and shoulder, I gripped the opened box of beads that'd arrived yesterday for Oma's new kitchen door and shoved it next to the wax bird-cage I'd been wrapping. "Yes, but, if you'd just help me out here—"

"No-no, that's not my job. Good luck. I look forward to seeing you around, Herr Krause."

He hung up.

Shit.

I hurriedly tried to think of a way... Yes, maybe that'd work. I'd give Ben a set of keys and beg him to drive back to Berlin and oversee things. Surely he'd do it, he was going back up in two days anyway, what was one day earlier?

I called Ben.

"Yeah?"

"Hey, I have a favor to ask..."

Within an hour, Ben came by for the keys. "Caro said she's coming up to help," he said, slipping the keys and a list of to-dos in his pocket.

"You have no idea how much this is helping me," I said, wrapping the finished birdcage.

Ben folded his arms. "No, I think *you* have no idea how much *we want to be helping*."

I looked at him running a hand through his hair. He seemed a mixture of happy and tired. I could see the happy in the way the skin at his eyes pulled together and his lip twitched, but the tired was in his heavy voice and the way his shoulders slumped. "Lenny," he said, holding my gaze, "there's something I want to talk to you about—"

"*Back in here*," came Oma's voice, and we heard the clack of her cane against the stone path I'd laid in the ground a couple of years ago to help her navigate her way. "Always working, he is."

"Never mind," Ben said. He slapped his hand over the pocket with the keys. "I'm going to get to it. We'll be back down at the end of the week."

"Thanks."

But he was already out the door. I heard a murmur of voices just outside my shed, as I quickly slid the packed birdcage out of the way and placed the box of beads under the table.

A rap came at the door.

My wounded bird stirred slightly—it'd been a little more active since meeting Julian on the hill—and I lurched to my feet. Without hearing his voice, his step, or anything *him*, I knew Oma was leading Julian to my shed.

"Yeah," I called out, the daylight coming in as Oma and Julian stepped over the threshold.

Oma planted her cane on the floor and leaned on it as she

waved an arm around the shed. "This is where the magic happens."

I gave a short laugh, glancing at Julian over Oma's shoulder. His face shone, and he bit his lip, worrying it as he looked around the room—everywhere but at me. Was he nervous to meet my eye? Or was he searching for the wax warrior he'd given me?

"I wouldn't go as far as that, Oma."

Finally, his gaze settled on mine and a slither of optimism wavered in the twitch under his eye.

"I'll leave you boys to it," she said. "Pastor Dieter is waiting for me in the kitchen. He likes me, he does. I suspect no one else spikes his coffee just the way I do."

Julian shifted from foot to foot, and then snagged Oma into a hug as she turned to leave. "Sorry it's been so long," he said, words muffled in her hair.

"Better late than never, dear." She whacked her cane on his ass with a hearty *snap*. "Be good."

The door had almost closed behind her when she threw over her shoulder, "And lunch tomorrow. Show up."

We waited for the sound of her cane to disappear, Julian brushing a hand over his butt and wincing.

I shoved my hands in my pockets and moved to the table. I wasn't sure how things were supposed to go between us. A part of me still wanted to shove him away and run for the hills. Another part of me wearily eyed him; it liked what it saw, but wasn't sure it could be trusted. And yet another part—the smallest—didn't give a damn if I got hurt again, it wanted me to jump on him and demand he never, ever leave again. "So…you're visiting."

"Ben asked if I'd come around and give you a hand with your move."

He shuffled farther into the room, and I freed my hands and crouched to the box I'd shoved under the table. I slid it out. Colorful beads and long strips of cord looked up at me. I'd only threaded five cords of Oma's door so far. "Ben told you?"

"Just a bit...

Julian hesitated and I looked up at him. "What else did he say?"

He crouched beside me and I quickly stood. "He's playing mediator," Julian said as he pushed himself upright again. "He wants us back the way we used to be."

I moved across the room and opened the long, brown painted cabinet where I kept all my molds. The opened door was supposed to keep him at a distance. Was supposed to buffer him from me.

But instead, I caught sight of the wax warrior I'd stowed on the middle shelf, next to the mold of his face. Wherever I turned he was there.

I reached out to touch it, but pulled back; I couldn't do that with Julian moving next to me. It was too personal, somehow. Like I'd be showing him the pain he'd inflicted on me, and I didn't want him to see that. Didn't want him to see I still cared.

I let out a slow breath and turned to him watching me.

Resting against the cabinet door, he fidgeted, then straightened, searching the shed again. "You've so many more molds now," he said. "We never talked about it, but I always wanted to know...did you ever finish, you know, that big project for art?"

"No," I said.

A quiet moment followed, and then: "Sorry."

I stared at him, exasperated; on the brink of telling him to leave; on the brink of melting into an embrace. "How would you see us continuing, Julian?"

His fingers picked at the flaking paint on the door. He looked from me to it and back again. His eyes met mine filled with assurance—a green that reminded me of leaves in spring. "I...I miss us. I want us to be friends again."

And it was beautiful, and not enough, and more than I was sure I could give him.

"I have this checklist," I said, slinking back to the table and thrusting it at him. "On it are all the things I need to do to move Oma and me to Berlin."

"That's a long list."

"Yeah. And I don't have much time or money to do it all." I jerked a thumb in the direction of our house. "I still haven't found a close enough replica of the wallpaper used in our entrance way, I have somehow got to move all the furniture from here to there…and I have to finish…"

I stopped, laughing, and hauled the box of beads to the tabletop. "There's so much to do, and before I can do more of it, I have to do this."

He peered into the box. "What is it?"

"She wants beads instead of a kitchen door."

"Why not buy something pre-made?"

I drew out the stool I'd been sitting on earlier and perched on it. "Penance," I said, taking out one of the cords, half lined with glass beads.

He sat on a matching stool to my side. I took a handful of beads and, one by one, slipped them on the cord.

"Penance, eh?" Julian said, then he took a fresh cord from the box and copied me, tying a knot at one end first. For a few minutes we worked together like that, each feigning intense concentration on the beads and cord.

When our breath had fogged the air enough that I couldn't think straight anymore, I spoke. "So, where does your fiancée think you are?"

Julian rested his cord on the table. "Lenny, I know I'm the villain in all this, but stop it. That's unfair."

"Stop what?"

He rubbed his nose. "Is this the price I have to pay? Will

you only be my friend again if I broke things off with my fiancée?"

He pushed himself up from his stool, and I dropped my cord to catch his arm. The beads I'd threaded *pinged* to the floor.

"Yes," I choked out. "I...I just don't know how to have what we had with anyone else around." I tightened my grip, his skin cool under my clammy palm. "It *shouldn't* be the price."

"But it is."

I shook my head and slowly loosened my hold, his hair tickling under the pads of my fingers as I let go. "It won't be. I didn't even realize it was until you said it." Our gazes met. "But I...I want to *try* to continue."

He nodded, then knelt and collected all the beads that'd danced away from us. "Here," he said, pressing a bunch into my hand.

"Thank you."

"I couldn't do it anymore," he said, still kneeling at my side. "She and I parted ways. I only told my mama the other night, at the village festival. I imagine the rest of Waldau will know soon enough."

My heart beat hard against my ribs. I wanted to ask him why they'd parted ways, but the question didn't belong in that moment. I stared at my suddenly tingling hand, then shook it off. "Will you stay?"

And though I motioned to his cord and the work to be done beading it, we both knew what I really meant. Would he stay this time or would he trample over my heart and run away from me again?

Julian held my gaze as he seated himself back onto the stool beside me. "Oh, I'm staying."

So side by side, we continued threading.

The air crackled between us, neither knowing how to break through its silence. My hands grew sweaty as did my inner thighs, and the nape of my neck prickled with goose bumps.

I willed him to be the first to speak. And like he read my mind, he cleared his throat. "Are you looking forward to moving?"

"Yes. No. I'm afraid. Frau Weiß died a week after moving to a retirement home...the fear and the stress is what killed her."

Julian pushed two beads down to the knotted end of his cord and grabbed some more. "You're not putting your Oma into a retirement home."

"Herr Vogel also died a month after moving into his son's place." I dropped a bead and it rolled under Julian's chair. I left it there and took another. "I don't want to kill her."

He picked up the fallen bead for me and passed it over.

"You're wondering why I'm moving at all, aren't you?" I said.

"No, Lenny, I'm not. You've sacrificed enough to look after Oma. I'm just wondering how I can help you." He ran his fingers over the line of beads he'd threaded. "And why *you* are doing penance."

"It makes me feel less guilty for being selfish. For needing to move."

"You're the furthest from selfish I know. It's okay to need something for yourself—Oma would understand too."

She might understand, but that didn't mean I could risk the stress of it killing her. And that's why no one had told Oma our plans. Why no one would.

Julian and I continued threading as outside the shed, the afternoon turned to late afternoon, and late afternoon to evening.

When evening stretched toward the night, when my bird fluttered suddenly, daring me, I slid my foot over to the tip of his and touched it. He didn't respond; didn't nudge mine back or move his away. Maybe he hadn't felt it, except he had, and I knew it by the way his fingers stilled on the beads and his gaze shifted just a fraction as if he were looking at me out the corner of his eye.

Maybe he wasn't sure if *I* meant it. Maybe he was hedging his bets by keeping still. Or maybe he didn't want to give me the wrong idea. Yes, our friendship he wanted back, but just that. No footsies under the table. Nothing else.

My sandal *churred* over the ground as I rearranged myself, moving my foot back to safety under my stool.

I didn't want anything else either, did I? Shit. I wished I could have taken back that hurried retreat, because it seemed to suggest I did.

And I didn't.

I shouldn't.

Even with the light on, the night seemed to claim the room. After I tied the end of my cord and then Julian's, we stood, stretching our limbs.

"How do we do it?" I asked quietly, looking down at the smoky glass beads. "How do we get our friendship back?"

"Step by step. Spend more time together—"

"Doing what?"

"Whatever we want."

"Can we chat more?"

He let out a relieved breath. "Yeah, I'd like that."

We both looked at each other at the same time.

"What would we like to do next time?"

Julian smiled and it ached of relief. "We could go for a walk, eat with Oma...or maybe even watch a movie."

"A scary one?" I said before I could stop myself. I shouldn't have said it, but though I tried to tell myself it didn't matter, I liked his response.

He laughed, and there was a blush under the stubble on his cheeks. "Maybe."

Find A Lenny, Pick Him Up

"AH-HA!" CAME JULIAN's voice from around the twisting trunk of a Birch tree in the far back of our yard.

I dropped the giant wax mushroom I'd just pried off its metal stake. It rolled over tree roots and onto its red and white head in the grass.

"Find a Lenny," he said into my ear.

My skin started to prickle, but I was left no time to bathe in it. His arms came around my waist in a hug that whipped the air from my lungs.

Next thing I knew I was staring at Julian's shorts as his shoulder dug into my stomach. I was so close. I could poke out my tongue and touch the smooth skin that peeked out from under his T-shirt.

"Pick him up…" he continued, but the wind must have picked up his words and carried them off for how far away they sounded.

"Put me down!" I tried to sound mad, but it lost its impact when I laughed. It caught me by surprise—I couldn't help it. "I really mean it, Julian."

"Sure you do," he said. Then he moved toward the back gate.

Only once we were through did he let me down. "You've been working all week," he said. "Consider this an intervention."

When I protested, he shook his head. "Just a couple of hours off, okay?"

And I was too afraid to say no. Not afraid of him or what he might do—I was afraid of missing out. What was a couple of hours, if it cracked more of the ice between us?

I followed him to a quiet spot by the river and we lay back in the welcoming shade of a large chestnut. The smell of freshly cut grass surrounded us, and I breathed it in. Nice. A much welcome intervention. Julian linked his fingers and rested them under his head, and I wondered if it was the intense heat that made it so comfortable between us, or if we'd finally latched onto the thread of friendship.

Since the moment in the shed, Julian had come around every day. At first it was only for an hour, then two, and then it was half a day. Yesterday, we'd spent all the daylight hours together, doing chores for the move. It was somewhat forced at first, but in the end it was like riding a bike. We might have been rusty after years of not doing it, but a few rounds in, and it was coming back to us.

It helped that we followed two unspoken rules:

1. We never talked about the past.
2. We never talked about the future.

Julian gave a cat-like stretch, his corded muscles stretching.

And then he broke both the rules at once.

He rolled onto his side and plucked up a leaf that had fallen onto my chest. It was amber and rimmed with red. As he dragged it down my arm, it seemed to whisper: *things are going to change, no matter how much you might like to ignore it, the future is there, waiting around the corner... Where are you in it?*

Berlin, I answered.

And Julian?

I didn't know. Would this tentative friendship even survive the summer?

The leaf lingered on the back of my hand and Julian stared at me. "We should go camping again this year."

Bang! The past *and* the future in one sentence, and I wanted to pick myself up off the grass and walk away from it.

And I wanted to roll closer and will him to say more. More of both *then*s. The future then, and the past one too.

Remember, remember? Do you remember?

I rolled my head toward the sky. "I think we'd better head back for lunch. Oma will be waiting. Ben and Caro will be here soon as well."

He frowned and pulled the leaf off me. It dropped out of his hand like nothing more than a second thought. "We just got here."

"Yeah, well, I forgot about lunch."

Julian tried to grab my hand as I sprung up, but I smoothly twisted out of his reach.

"What was it I did?" he asked, scrambling to his feet before I could convince my legs I really did want to leave. But damn, they weren't having any of it. They only took me backwards a few steps until I hit the chestnut trunk.

"Nothing."

"Don't give me that."

I threw my hands up. "Are you so intent on bringing up the past? Do you need this talk so badly?" And I could have been asking myself for the *Yes!* that screamed in my head.

"Fine," I said, twisting half away from him and banging my hand against the peeling tree bark. "*Years*, Julian. It's been fucking years since...that day in the rain, on the hill...it ruined us. I never should have finished! Hell, I never should have started."

I lifted my gaze skyward, but there was no clarity to be found through the breezing branches. "Why couldn't I stop?" I choked on air as the rest of it fought to get free. "Why did you just *leave*? You never even answered a single e-mail...and now you're back, wishing for friendship?"

I shook my head. "You want the truth? The truth that you already know and seem to need to hear from my lips? Well here it is: I *was* hiding from you at the village festival. I was hiding because you broke...you broke *me*, and just seeing you makes me scared I'll break some more."

My chest was expanding rapidly with the great lungful of air I was sucking in as I forced myself not to fucking cry.

He tentatively came forward. I could see he wanted to reach out and lift my chin—make me look at him—but he left his hand twitching at his side.

"I don't know what to expect with this." I motioned to the space between him and I. "Us."

Is this friendship? Or more than that? What are we doing here? And if we are doing what I think we're doing, how will it end, when nothing else has changed?

"I'm sorry for hurting you," he said. "There are a lot of things I should have done differently, and so much I still need to do. I want a lot of things." Like I had, he motioned between us. "But if I can only choose one?" He stepped closer and lowered his voice. "It would be to have our friendship back."

He tried to catch my gaze, but every time he caught it, I broke free.

"I fucked up," he said. "It took me so long...I was afraid." His swallow was audible, and I glanced up. Julian had closed his eyes, his lashes just kissing his skin. "I was gutless."

He opened his eyes and I shifted my gaze. "But Lenny?" he said softly. "There were a lot of things I didn't fuck up, too.

Lots of things were great between us. I'm staying here, and I'm not going to give up trying until you've weighed all of those things and still tell me you want me gone."

I blinked and swatted the tear before it trailed down my cheek.

"I want to know why you left. Is it because it's icky?" And he knew what I meant. Not the G word, the C word. Cousins. "Am I the cuckoo in the nest for not thinking so?"

And I wanted him to say: *No, you're not put together wrong. Love knows no boundaries* or even *I don't care what the rest of the world thinks. Don't you care, either.*

Instead, he finally caught my gaze and trapped it with his damp one. "Some people think it's wrong. A lot, even."

"And you?"

He looked down at his feet or maybe it was mine or maybe it was the roots and bald grass between us.

His mouth parted, and shut, and parted again.

Maybe he wanted to answer: *It's taken me a long time to realize what other people think doesn't matter.*

But what he answered? What made me smile even though we were a long way off resolving the past? Simply this: "I want to watch movies with you, Lenny."

WE WALKED HOME to Oma and boiled potatoes and spinach. When we were done with lunch, Julian cleared the table. Before I could stand up, he rested a hand on my shoulder and spoke to Oma. "I want to know my fortune."

She reached for her crystal ball and raised a brow at him. "I thought you already knew it."

He smiled and although it was at Oma, his fingers pressed more firmly into my shoulder. "I'd like us all to be reminded."

Living With the Caro Monster

AFTER THE RIVER, after we'd broken our rules, after Oma had made me relive Julian's thirteenth birthday and fortune, Ben and Carolin returned home.

"I never backseat drive when *you*'re behind *my* wheel."

Ben crashed into the kitchen with my sis behind him. We all stared at him—his hair, to be specific, or the *lack* of it.

"What'd you do to your golden mop?" Julian asked, leaving my side and welcoming him with a hug.

"What I did," he said, glaring at me like it was all my fault, "was let your sister cut my hair."

"And I did." Carolin kissed Oma on the cheek, slipped out of her long-sleeved buttoned cardigan and peered into the crystal ball. "Whose future are you reading today?" She eyed me and gestured between her front teeth.

Damn spinach! I picked it away.

"You didn't cut my hair! You got *rid* of it!" He glanced at his reflection in the glass cabinets and shuddered. "You are *so* freaking lucky my papa rolled me over as a baby!"

There was a tense moment at the mention of his papa.

Then Julian rubbed a hand over Ben's smooth scalp. "Why'd you not stop her?"

Ben batted him away. "She said she was shaving the back bits. Then, in one quick flick of her minx-ass wrist"—he ran a hand over the middle of his head— "I couldn't just leave it like that."

Both my eyebrows lifted as I queried Carolin. To her credit, she was blushing furiously. "It looks *fine*."

"Why?" I asked her.

"Maybe I wanted to know what he'd look like if he went bald?"

Ben looked about a half-syllable away from throttling her. Julian laughed, tugging him back by the waist.

Oma raised her hands and the kitchen fell silent. "Carolin, Ben…do I need to lock you two in the attic?"

Julian and I shared a look and laughed nervously.

"Maybe that's a good idea," Julian said, then under his breath, just for me. "It worked for us, didn't it?"

The low timbre of his voice rumbled through me, beckoning me to follow it and remember that night: the anger, the hurt, the fear when Julian almost fell from the roof.

Carolin's haughty outrage quelled the memories.

"I'm twenty-six," she said, going to the cupboards and grabbing a bottle of sparkling water, "you can't put me in time-out anymore."

Oma cracked her cane on the kitchen tiles and swiftly stood. There was something distinctly Gandalf about her right now, and it had all three of us guys shrinking back.

Carolin, oblivious in her righteousness, twisted the lid off the bottle. Water fizzed up and dribbled down the neck.

"Carolin," Oma said, "don't you think, at the very least, you should apologize to Ben?"

Carolin's long hair tumbled over her shoulder as she glanced at him. "Ben and I never apologize to one another."

Her gaze almost looked wounded for a second, but then it disappeared behind a sly smile. "It's our thing, isn't it?"

Ben went to run his hand through his hair and stopped short on his smooth scalp. "Maybe we should change that."

She grabbed a glass. "What's the point? You'd be saying sorry every second sentence."

Ouch.

Julian looked at me out the corner of his eye, mouthing: "What the…?"

"I won't ask you again, Carolin," Oma said, moving to the drawer I locked at nights. "Is it too much to ask for a little peace in this house? Between the four of you, it's a wonder I haven't gone completely raving mad."

"More than you already are?" Carolin laughed, then she shrugged and turned to fill her glass, and my Oma sighed.

"If that's what you think. I can work with it."

I didn't even see how she got them, but suddenly she was behind Carolin with a pair of scissors in her hand.

There was nothing any of us guys could have done to reach her before it happened. Oma grabbed a large handful of red locks and chopped them off at her shoulders.

Carolin heard the snip, and froze.

By the time she turned around, Ben was hugging Oma and prying the scissors from her grip. He passed them to Julian, who stuffed them back in the drawer and turned the lock. The key was pressed into my hand.

Oma cracked her cane against the floor again. "Julian? Lenny?"

I was already on my feet, shuffling toward to her. Carolin's face was reaching the same color as her hair.

"Help me get Ben and Carolin up to the attic, would you?"

I nodded. No way was I going to be in her bad books as well.

But to the surprise of us all, Carolin came over to me, pried the key from my grip, grabbed the scissors from their place and took herself up to the attic.

Before it was Ben's turn to go up, he turned to me. "Please let us out in time to crash Nick's bachelor party?"

"That's not until next week."

He looked at me blankly. "Do you know Oma at all?"

I chuckled. And when he raised his brow again, I nodded. "I'll free you for crashing the party."

Oma prodded his shoulder to go up. "Nick didn't invite you?"

"It wouldn't be half as fun if he did. For any of us."

Ben creaked up the stairs. Just before he got to the top, Carolin turned around. Passing Ben, the scissors and glaring at each of us watching, she said, "Fair is fair."

Ben gripped the scissor handles, but my sister hadn't quite finished yet. "But just remember, you're going to have to look at me the rest of the night, all day tomorrow, the day after that. Next week—weeks—too. Whatever monster you create of me, you'll have to dance with her at Nick's wedding in front of the entire village."

Ben laughed. "I've lived with the Caro monster my whole life, nothing has ever stopped me dancing with you in the past. Nothing will in the future, either."

"You took a perverse pleasure in locking them up there," Julian said a half hour later as we sat on an old bench that overlooked the backyard, close to the house.

We sat there, not because it was warm, not because it was private, not because we had nothing else we could be doing—but because Ben and Carolin were strangely quiet and we hoped we'd hear them shouting from the garden.

No such luck.

Oma had taken a shot of schnapps and was out for an afternoon nap. Silence cradled us; it could have just been him, the barren backyard, and me.

"It looks strange without all the wax flowers in it," he said.

"Yeah," I said, lifting my knees onto the bench and hugging them loosely. His profile was softened in the orangey afternoon light. If it'd been two years earlier, I would have inched my feet over the bench between us until he picked them up and rested them in his lap.

I dropped my feet back to the ground, leaned forward onto my knees, trying to see through my sudden tension to the garden.

He sighed. "You want me to leave now, don't you?"

I could almost have laughed. He knew everything. "I just need processing time. To be sure I can do this again. With you." Without breaking what was left of my bird.

The wooden bench planks groaned as he pushed himself off. *Of course*, he said with his nod.

As he passed me, I snagged his hand and his fingers caught between mine. "Are you ever going to tell your mama?"

"Which part?"

I wanted to say *both parts*, but that would have been hypocritical. How could I expect him to tell his mama anything about us when I'd never been able to tell anyone myself?

I stared at his fingers and mine.

"The truth?" Julian said. "I still don't know how to tell her any of it. I tried once and..." He squeezed our fingers together. "She made me feel like it was so wrong. That *I* was so wrong if I thought like that."

"What changed?"

"I listened to her, and I was unhappy." His fingers drifted away, then he tightened his grip again, gaze locked with mine. "Take the time you need." His fingers slipped from mine. "I'll be here, waiting, whatever you decide."

Then he left.

And I needed to think. Really think about all those moments that had led to now. But I needed distance to do it. Enough space to give me perspective. I glanced at my shed where, in my cupboard next to the wax warrior, there was a set of keys to my new beginning in Berlin.

I knew just where I needed to be.

Later!

I DRAGGED TWO ten-liter tubs of paint and a backpack full of brushes and rollers out of the train. Right about now, I wished I'd driven and not left the car at the house.

Sure it was quicker on the train, but it came at a *heavy* cost to my back.

I muttered under my breath as I walked in the sweltering heat, the metal paint handles digging into my skin more painfully with each step. Sweat dribbled down my brow and I was drenched under my backpack.

Halfway home, a car slowed on the road beside me. I glanced over and there was Herr Koch winding the car windows down, a smirk on his face. He lifted his cap in "hello" and I managed a weak smile.

There were three free seats in his car, plenty of room for me and all my crap.

The smirk on his face told me he knew it too. "How's the place coming along?" he called out.

"Just. Fine," I said through clenched teeth. I'd arrived last night, and was happy to find an identical East German cabinet sitting in the kitchen. Ben and Caro had done an amazing job with the garden too, and last night I'd added the wax decorations I'd brought up. "You've seen the new and improved garden?"

"It's strange," he said, chuckling. "But whatever floats your boat. Guess I'll be seeing you around, Herr Krause. Later!"

And off he went, laughing, leaving me to splutter on his exhaust fumes.

When I finally got to the house, I dropped the paint and lay on the cool floor groaning. Not only was I hot and bothered, I was tired as hell. I'd camped in my sleeping bag in the newly widened living room and I hadn't found a position that worked for me. I wanted to blame it on the hard floors that still needed carpeting, but the truth was my mind was elsewhere.

Herr Koch's television had been on last night and, without curtains up, the light from the screen blinked patterns on my walls. The effect reminded me of some of the clubs I'd been in with Ben and Caro over the years. And the thought of clubs drifted to parties, and parties made me think of old traditions.

I rolled over and pushed to my feet. It was time to get painting.

I HIT MY biggest snag when it came to putting masking tape around the edges of the ceiling. I laughed and punched the wall.

Of course. I had no effing ladder.

Like Herr Koch knew exactly what I was missing, he'd set up a large ladder on his veranda, in a sunny spot where the sun reflected off the metal. It was a tease. I knew it. He was having his fun with me.

He waved at me from the veranda, sitting in his wicker chair with a teapot and cup on a small table in front of him. His glance at the ladder was subtle, but his grin was not. I swallowed a scowl, forced a smile back to him, and made my way to the neighbors on the other side of his place.

They weren't home. Neither were any at the next three places I tried.

The house on the corner with two large cherry trees out front proved more fruitful.

A middle-aged woman with greying red hair that reminded me of my Aunt Thomas answered the door. I immediately stepped back, my heart racing faster, and I had the urge to cringe as I waited for her to call me "Leonard."

I hid my shudder as best as I could. This woman was a little shorter than my aunt, and held more around the middle. She looked like the type that would hug you and stroke your hair if you needed it.

"Can I help you?" she asked, and her soft voice helped me to find mine.

"Uh, yeah," I said. "I'm moving in down the road, and I'm painting the insides, but I'm short a ladder. I wanted to ask around to see if I might be able to borrow one for a couple of days."

"A new neighbor, how lovely. I'm Kristina. And where are you moving in?"

I gave her my name and pointed in the direction of my house. "The other place Herr Koch owns."

"I know the one. Just a minute, I'll get the key for the garage. There's a ladder in there."

In five minutes, I was one ladder the richer. Kristina gave me a kind smile, and I knew she didn't mean it, but seeing it made me a little wistful. If Julian's mum had been more like this woman, things might have turned out differently.

"Thank you," I said to Kristina, and she waved it off.

"No problem, Lenny. Just a word about your neighbor though…"

I looked at her as she smiled sadly.

"What about him?"

"Well, as with any place we have our eclectic collection of locals. Like the guy that dresses like an elf and buys his two rolls at seven every morning from the bakery. And the girl across the road with tattoos sleeved down her arms. Your neighbor is one of the bunch. He's the cheeky one. He really knows how to wind some of us up the wrong way."

"I've noticed."

"But he's a good kind. Just lonely."

"Lonely?" I thought of him on his veranda with his tea. I'd never thought about who he lived with in that big old house.

"His kids have left. They travel all over the world, and since his wife passed away, he hasn't really known what to do with himself. So he stirs up a bit of trouble from time to time to keep occupied." She closed the garage door and glanced from me to the ladder. "Anyway, don't you mind him. Good luck with your new place. I hope to see you around."

I left with the ladder and a smile. When I passed Herr Koch, I waved right back at him, before moving inside my house and getting to work.

It took me all day and most of the evening to get the painting done, but the fumes were going to my head and I knew I would have to use the key Ben gave me to crash at his place for the night.

Before that though, I needed to measure the rooms for the carpet and eat something. I made a quick stop at the local supermarket and picked up some bread and cheese for a sandwich, and a six-pack of beer.

I ate my bread and cheese, measured the rooms, and then took the beers with me to Herr Koch's.

He answered the door, touching his cap as if he'd just pulled it on. "What?"

"It's a warm evening. Perfect for beer, don't you think?"

He frowned, looking from me to the beer like he didn't understand.

"I'd like to get to know my neighbors," I said, taking a step back to where the ladder still stood. I put the beer on the small table that held Herr Koch's tea earlier, took one bottle, and perched myself on one of the ladder's flat metal rungs.

"That's presumptuous," he said, taking a beer and sitting on his wicker chair.

I shrugged. "Maybe. Maybe not."

We both drank a few moments in silence. Then Herr Koch spoke. "When do you and your Oma move in?"

"End of August, hopefully."

He looked toward the rose bushes at the side of his neat garden. "Why Berlin?"

"I told you already. It's creative."

"There are other creative cities."

"Yeah, maybe, but..." I breathed in slowly. How to describe it? "It feels freer here. The city doesn't sleep and it's there at your beck and call. Even if I don't need everything it has to offer, it's nice to know it's there in case." I finished my beer, and grabbed a second one. "And I like it here," I said, motioning around us, "because it has the pluses of the village with all the other parts a short train trip away."

Herr Koch murmured and gave a small laugh. "Wish my kids thought that way." He took a large gulp of beer, then narrowed his eyes at me, as if calculating something. "But that's not the only reason you want to come to Berlin, is it?"

It wasn't. There was another small, teeny-tiny reason that was probably just stupid. And I wasn't going to share that with anyone.

"What"—I swallowed— "makes you think that?"

"I raised two kids of my own, and one of them does the same thing when he's telling the truth but not all of it."

"Does what?"

"Blinks fast like that."

I hadn't even realized I'd been blinking.

"Oh, uh, I—"

"You don't have to tell me," he said, and stood. "Thanks for the beer." Then he added with a growl to his voice, "But don't think buttering up to me is going to win you any favors."

~

WITH THE REST of my beers and some clothes in my backpack, I headed to Ben's for the night. There I ate cheese and salami from his fridge and drank the rest of my beers. Coupled with my tiredness, I was about ready to fall into a coma on Ben's bed.

Only, once I hit the pillow, I was wide awake again. Any time I tried to rest, I thought of *him*. What was Julian doing right this second? Was he sleeping already? Or going out with Ben and Carolin? Was he thinking of me as much as I was of him?

Perhaps he was sick with anticipation of what I'd decide about us? Or was he worried that I was out partying in Berlin and having the time of my life?

I leaned over the bed to where I'd dropped my jeans and fished out my phone from the pocket. I scrolled to his number and stared at it. I wanted to ring, just to hear his voice for a moment. Just to hear the way he said my name.

"Ah, fuck." I dropped back on the pillow. This was only the second day since seeing him. I breathed out slowly, placed my phone on the bedside table, and picked up the remote control for the television.

I hit the light switch above my bed at the same time I pressed the power button on the remote.

On screen two men were kissing. I laughed.

Snag

I DON'T KNOW how I got through the next days of painting and laying carpet, really. What with the lack of sleep, I probably seemed strange and spaced out, but meeting with the pastor at the church around the corner from my new house was about the last straw.

All I wanted was to find someone who could do a weekly house call, and who was moderately liberal. I mean, it was fine if they weren't the type to like it if Oma spiked their coffee—I'm sure we could work around that. But this guy couldn't even smile. He sat stiffly behind his desk with his fingers linked as if in constant conversation with God. And when I fished around for his thoughts on being gay—because I knew that level of liberalism was important to Oma—he just stared at me.

He was *still* staring at me.

I twisted on the hard wooden chair, my hands braced on the seat, the corners digging into my palms, and tried to concentrate on the calendar behind the pastor. It was of a bird with ruffled feathers, straining to fly against the wind. I let slip a nervous chuckle. Because my bird and I felt it.

Just slip off the chair and walk out of there!

I was just about to do that, when the pastor spoke. He leaned over the desk and gave a sympathetic smile. Or what I imagined he thought sympathetic was. "Your Oma opening up to Christ will change that."

"Fuck you," I said lurching up from my seat. "There's nothing to change. Jesus." I knew this was the worst place to swear and use His name in vain, but I was glad I did when I saw the way his mouth dropped. I stalked out of his office, not suppressing my shudder, and hurried outside.

A ray of sun streamed over me through a gap in the clouds and I stood in the spot as my body debated whether it wanted to carry on or fall asleep. It decided to drag my ass back to the house, where I sat in the middle of my carpeted living room and looked up other pastors in the area on my phone.

I rang. No others did house calls.

I rested back on the carpet and stared at the ceiling, at the wires coming out where I had to attach lights. I thumped a fist on the floor next to me. Stupid. I'd returned the ladder to Kristina already. I'd have to go back and get it again. But not today. I was too exhausted.

I felt for the phone I'd dropped on the floor next to me and picked it up. Like I did every day, multiple times a day, I scrolled to Julian's name and stared at it, wondering what he was doing at exactly that second. Then I forced myself not to dial, and scrolled back to Ben's number.

That one I hit.

He picked up on the third ring. "Hey Lenny, how's it going?" he called cheerfully down the line.

I could hear the rustle of wind and others in the background and guessed he was outside somewhere. "Okay. The house is getting there. The kitchen cabinet you found with Carolin is perfect. Where are you?" *Who are you with?*

"You're welcome." His voice seemed to get distant, as if he were talking to someone else for a moment. "I think we should set up in the shade. It's too hot here." Then he was back to speaking with me. "Just having a small picnic. Me, Caro, and um…" He hesitated, like he wasn't sure if he should continue or not, and I knew what that meant.

"Julian?"

"Uh, yeah. Just a sec…" More rustling came down the line. "Moved away from the guys, so we can actually talk."

"Where are you?"

"You know the spot by the river where we skim stones sometimes?"

Yeah, I did. It was the same spot where Julian had broken our two rules; the past and the future ones.

Ben continued, "I've kicked off my sandals and am dunking my feet in the water. Bless you, cool water."

I closed my eyes and imagined myself there too. "Sounds nice."

"Yeah. It is. Did you call for a reason? Or did you just miss me?" His tone got all fake-sappy at the end and I could see him waggling his brows as he said it.

"For a reason," I said. But, yeah, I did miss hanging with him. Going back to his place to crash had been strange without being able to shoot the shit with him. Ben was part of the Berlin I wanted. "I hit a snag with the pastor."

"Snag?"

"Yeah, I can't find one."

"That's a pretty big snag."

I groaned. "You don't say."

"You called for some of my all-knowing advice?"

I choked on a laugh. And then—"Actually, yeah."

Ben plotted on the other end of the line, murmuring incoherently. Then, "I got it!"

"You do?"

"Well…I mean, it's worth a shot."

"Keep going."

"Dylan. He's your answer."

"Dylan?"

A voice called out Ben's name in the background. I stiffened, because it wasn't just any voice. It was Julian's. He called again, and this time I was positive I could hear the smile attached to it.

Who's on the phone?

Julian was closer now, and he sounded almost breathless or...hopeful, maybe?

Ben must have lifted the phone away from his mouth, because I only faintly heard him. "Lenny," he said, and I held my breath. Waiting for what, I don't know. It was just—despite the distance, it was like I could feel him standing close to me. Shivers raced over my skin and my cock stirred to life when he said in a softer tone, the smile still there, "Say hi from me."

A part of me wanted to reach into the phone, grab him into a hug and say "hello" face to face. But another part was nervous, hesitant, and still not quite ready to risk doing this again.

Ben suddenly broke through the tension, his voice loud in my ear. "Did you hear that?"

I nodded, even though he couldn't see. "Ah, yes."

"Back to Dylan, then?"

"Back to Dylan."

"He's a friend of mine and Carolin's. Gay friend, actually, if, you know, you find you fancy him."

"Stop trying to set me up. I'm good."

"All right, all right. Just doing my job, making sure my best friend's set."

"He will be once he gets to Berlin," I said. "Now, this Dylan, is he a pastor?"

Ben gave a nervous laugh. "No. Actually, he's an actor. But he played Friar Laurence in a modernized version of *Romeo and Juliet* earlier this year."

"An actor? You want me to get Oma a fake pastor?"

"It might be a bit unconventional."

"A bit?"

"Lenny, shut up. Unless you have any better ideas?"

He had a point; I didn't. And it wasn't as if Oma was a strict believer in God or the church. More than anything, she just liked the company—and trying to tease as much as she could get away with. I shook my head as I heard myself agreeing to this plan. "Will he cost much?"

"He's an actor. He's scraping by. I think twelve euros an hour should do it."

Even twelve euros an hour was going to dig a hole in my shallow pocket. I pinched my nose.

"I'll um," Ben said then paused, "...I'd like to pay for it. Oma's family, you know. I mean, I don't have much, but I want to help."

"Thanks, Ben." My breath came out a little shaky, but I was smiling. I imagined him running his toes over the top of the water, blushing too. "So, how do I contact this guy? I want to interview him first."

"Got a pen?"

I rolled over and got up, moving to the kitchen where I had my to-do list on the cabinet, a pen on top. I flipped the list over and wrote Dylan's phone number on the back.

"He lives really close to Treptower Park," Ben said. "You could suggest meeting him at the little island in the park to talk."

I blinked and murmured something back to him. We said our goodbyes, and hung up. When the line died and the silence of the house took its place, I was left staring out the window, remembering that day in the paddleboat. Remembering that question he'd asked me: *In your future...where am I in it?*

Where indeed.

Lilies

I CLUTCHED DYLAN'S phone number and the to-do list and dreamed my way out of the house and into the front garden. I needed something to snap me out of imaging answers to Julian's question of the future and our roles in it.

Herr Koch strolling through the front gate did the trick.

It took me a moment to recognize him because his cap was off. He had dark grey hair that slightly receded in the front to make an M shape, but it was cut short to make it look good.

I shoved the paper in my pocket and folded my arms. "And to what do I owe this pleasure?"

He glanced toward the giant wax mushrooms around the tree trunks. "Herr Krause—"

"Call me Lenny," I said.

"And you can continue to call me Herr Koch."

"What can I do for you?"

"I was just informed by one of our neighbors that you saw Pastor Stein earlier." He had his hands on his hips, and I prepared myself for his disapproval.

"He's homophobic," I said, meeting his gaze and standing

as solidly as I could, as if that would give me a shield against whatever he'd say next.

"I heard you told him to F-off."

"And I'd do it again."

Herr Koch dropped his arms and surprised me by clapping. "That was the best gossip I've heard all year. At least since our local elf swung his sword at a drunken man attacking another man and really did save the day." He walked toward my wax lilies at the wall of the house and gently touched one of the leaves. "Pastor Stein is the only guy around here that I truly dislike."

Slowly, I moved over to him. He seemed to be taking the gay thing well. I motioned to the lilies. "I made these a couple of years ago. Oma doesn't see much anymore and she loves flowers... Why do you dislike the pastor here?"

He blinked away from the lilies to me. "We used to go to his church every Sunday. When one of my sons came out a few years ago, I didn't have anyone to talk to about it except for him. Let's just say, it was a very short conversation. I left and haven't been back since."

He shrugged and lifted his hand to his head, as if he'd forgotten he wasn't wearing a cap. He gave a short laugh and looked back at the lilies. "Family is more important than that shit."

I murmured in agreement, then felt a warm hand close down on my shoulder. Herr Koch pressed his fingers warmly. "You're an interesting tenant, that's for sure."

I shook my head, folded my arms and looked at him. "Are you unsure about me staying because you think I won't make the rent? Are you afraid I'm not reliable enough?"

"There's that, too."

I held my breath to protest, and let it out. "I always make sure the bills are paid. You'll see."

"This place is a lot of money for what you're making."

"What if I make you sure I'll have the money by sub-letting one of the upstairs rooms?"

He looked at me. "How would your Oma feel having a stranger in the house? Still homely then?"

I cursed and scowled at the white and brown façade of the house.

"But if you *do* want to sub-let to someone," Herr Koch said, "I have to okay them first."

"Okay them?" I repeated.

"Yes, you know, ask a few questions, see what they're like and if I like them."

"You're not going to make this easy, are you?"

"Where's the fun in that?"

I shook my head. "Kristina was right about you."

"Kristina? What has she been saying about me?"

"Just that you like to make mischief."

He let out a rumbling laugh, but didn't deny it. "You blinked again. She said more, I know it." Herr Koch pointed to the mushrooms. "How long does it take to make something like that?"

Kristina's words came back to me. *He's lonely.*

"Anywhere from a week to a month," I said.

"Don't they, er, melt in the sun?"

I shook my head. "These ones I made from carving wax. They melt at 104 degrees."

And though I was tired and a touch dizzy, I decided a little tour of the wax garden wouldn't hurt. He asked questions and I answered them. When I showed him the birdhouse I'd attached to the tree out in the backyard, I actually got a smile out of him.

He leaned against the trunk and took in the garden from a distance. "You're creative all right." It would have been a nice way to end our conversation, but he had one more question for me. A small, innocuous question. But that didn't matter. When he said it, it reminded me of *that* Christmas a long time ago. "What's the biggest thing you've wanted to make?"

Why Berlin

After another sleepless night at Ben's, I went back to the house with a bunch of Ikea light fittings and a hopeful attitude. On the plus side of things, I was close to getting the house ready for the final move. On the minus side, I was almost out of money.

I'd checked my online bank account, and it seemed that all the paint and carpet and gas to get here had put a none-too-shabby dent in my savings.

I had barely 600 euros left. And while I'd paid both the bond and one month's rent to Herr Koch already, I still had to pay the contractors for tearing down the wall.

And, of course, when I opened the letterbox, what did I find?

"Great timing."

I schlepped up the path staring at the contractor logo, wondering if I could wish it to hold something else—anything else—but the bill inside. I'd be happy for junk mail. Some useless two-for-one deal.

After letting myself inside the house, I carefully rested my bag against the wall that I'd yet to find the right wallpaper for. I had a few things to do: I needed to get the ladder from Kristina again before I could deal with the lights. I had to get through to Dylan. And I probably had to open this envelope.

Wriggling my thumb under the sealed flap, I ripped it an inch, but I couldn't go any farther than that. Instead, I slipped the envelope in the side pocket of my bag, and left to get the ladder.

I knocked at her door, and waited to see if I'd flashback to Aunt Thomas when I saw her. I didn't. But that was because she wasn't home.

I tried a few other doors, but it was ten o'clock on a Thursday and, well, yeah, I wasn't lucky. I kicked at a loose piece of gravel on the way back to my place. I could go out and buy one, but I didn't have the money for that and besides, I had a ladder back in Waldau.

On the last fifty meters to my gate, I fished my phone from my pocket and rang Dylan's number again. A groggy morning voice came down the line after the seventh ring. "Yeah?"

I introduced myself, and he perked up when I said I was Ben's friend and Carolin's brother. "I've heard a lot about you," he said.

I shook my head, imagining how Ben had talked me up as his single gay best friend. "Um, did Ben tell you we're looking for an actor?"

If I thought he sounded awake at the mention of Ben, now he was *really* awake. "An acting job? For real?"

"It's a small, weekly thing," I said. "But if you're interested in some work, maybe you'd like to meet and we can talk more about it."

"Yeah, sure, no problem. Just tell me when and where to meet you and I'll be there."

I saw Herr Koch sitting on his wicker chair with his cap and a teacup in his hand. Instead of continuing another ten steps to my place, I stopped.

I quickly finished up with Dylan. "I'm heading back to Waldau tomorrow, so how's sometime this evening?"

"That's just fine."

"Okay then." I gave him my address and we arranged for six o'clock.

Pocketing the phone, I opened Herr Koch's gate and walked up to his veranda. The ladder he'd had there a couple of days ago was folded against the wall of his house. The wooden boards under my feet groaned. Or maybe it was Herr Koch upon seeing me.

I pointed to his teapot. "Is there enough in there for two?"

"Do you always invite yourself to other people's morning tea?"

"Only people I like."

He blinked rapidly and looked toward the street, adjusting his cap. "What did I tell you about the buttering up business?"

"Is that a yes to the tea or not?"

He grumbled, got up, and disappeared into his house. He came back with a second teacup. Carefully, he lifted the teapot and poured me a cup. "It's black tea."

"Then I'll need a splash of milk and a little sugar," I said and sat down on the edge of the veranda. I caught him shaking his head at me.

"Your parents must find you a handful," he said, handing me the milky tea.

"I'm sure my Oma does."

There was a moment of expected quiet, and I sipped the sweet tea and watched a breeze comb through the grass and kiss the roses.

Herr Koch's wicker chair scraped over the veranda, and I looked over at him, shrugging. I wasn't sure why I felt the need to share this with him.

Maybe because he had lost his wife; his kids' mother.

Maybe I just wanted him to feel like he could share stuff with me too if he wanted.

Or maybe it's because he was a stranger, someone who didn't know me. Someone I couldn't accidently offend or hurt by talking about it. "My mama and papa died trying to get out of East Germany," I said slowly.

He rested his teacup on his lap and stared at it. "I'm sorry to hear that."

Another cool breeze brushed over the garden, this time tunneling its way under my shirt and bringing the scent of rain with it.

I looked at the sky. There was a stretch of blue still over us, but in the distance I saw clouds.

"It's why Berlin," I said. "You wanted to know why I want to live here, and it's one of the reasons. It's a teeny tiny one, and maybe stupid since I never knew my parents, but it's also why. They died trying to get out of my village, out of the East. There's this tiny voice in my head that says I shouldn't let them have died in vain, you know?"

I glanced over to him again. He was watching me. Listening. "But Waldau is also my home, where I grew up. I love it there too."

I gestured around us. "Berlin is feels like a compromise, it's both past and present—it's saying I love my Oma *and* I respect my parents. And yeah. It just feels right to be here."

A nervous burst of laughter left me, and I brushed the back of my neck and stretched. There came a clatter of china as Herr Koch set his teacup on the table. He looked like he wanted to stand up and move, maybe come closer, offer some kind of sympathy, but he hesitated and remained seated.

"I think you chose the right city," he said gruffly. "I love Berlin because it's the place my kids were born and raised and it's where I met my wife." He pointed to the roses. "Some of her ashes are under there, just as she wished. It's why I don't leave this place. It's why here."

I didn't know what to say. I could only nod. Then I moved over to his table and poured us both some more tea. We sipped for a while in comfortable silence. The clouds drew nearer; soon the sun was trapped behind them and a shadow fell over us.

I knew I had to put those lights up while there was still daylight to work by. It was going to be a dark evening.

"Do you know what time Kristina is usually home?" I asked.

"She works half-time; Thursdays is a working day. So not until four. Why?" The way he looked at the ladder, he knew why.

"I'm putting the lights in today."

"Go on," he said, gesturing toward his ladder.

I didn't hesitate to move toward it. "Isn't this against the rules of this game it is you're playing?"

He scowled, but behind it there was a cheeky grin. "Just don't expect anything else from me more than tea and conversation."

"Thanks," I said, quickly picking up the ladder before he changed his mind. The metal was cool on my skin as I hugged it to my side. "I'll bring it back before I leave in the morning."

"Heading back to the village?"

"Yeah, a guy I know is having his bachelor party tomorrow night."

"Close friend of yours?"

I laughed. He wasn't exactly a friend, wasn't exactly an enemy. "Nick? Nah. He's a frenemy."

'J'

———

After finishing the lights, I'd needed a few minutes to rest.

I lay down on the carpet and went over my plan to move Oma here. The house was getting there. Once the wallpaper had been done and our furniture was all in, it would pass as a replica.

Or I certainly hoped it would.

But would the move come in on budget? I cringed, rolled over to my bag, and pulled out the thin envelope. Quick and nasty, I tore off the top and pulled out the paper.

I scanned over the numbers, and lurched to my feet. Then I double checked I wasn't seeing things, and tossed the paper onto the carpet, right on the spot where the old wall used to be.

Eight hundred and fifty euros? That was more than double the estimate. I scrubbed my hands over my face. Ben had told me over the phone the wall had been thicker than they'd expected and that it'd weighed over a ton, but I hadn't realized what he was really saying until now. It was going to cost more.

Double.

I paced the rooms, looking out of the windows through the

rain. My wax flowers were the only bright, hopeful-looking things out there.

I stopped moving. That was the answer. I was going to have to sell some of the wax garden. Realistically, I didn't have time to start from scratch. Not if I wanted the money fast, which I did.

I rang Ben.

"You're missing me now, I know it."

I sighed down the phone. "You have no idea how much I could use a beer right now."

"If it helps, there'll be plenty of that tomorrow night at Nick's."

I moved to the window in the kitchen and sat on the wide sill. Rain pelted against the glass in a repetitive, soothing way. "It helps a little. Is Oma doing okay?"

"She's fine. She had one of her night terrors last night, but Caro got to her before she found a way into the knife drawer."

"How is Carolin?"

"She's um… you know, the same as always."

"You mean she's driving you crazy?"

"She definitely drives me crazy all right."

I laughed and swapped the phone to my other ear. "Oma hasn't had to stick you both in the attic again, has she?"

"No-no. We're behaving ourselves. Now what's up?"

"Are there any rainbows where you are?"

"Nope."

"Shame, I could use the pot of gold at the end."

"We could all use some of that."

Resting my head against the glass, I breathed heavily, fogging the glass. "I could sub-let one of the rooms upstairs. But I'm pretty sure Oma would notice a stranger coming inside the house all the time. The only people she's used to coming and going like no-one's business is me, you, and Carolin."

"And Julian."

I stilled. "Yeah. And him."

In the fogged glass, I drew a J. I could feel a tingle start from my fingers and move all the way to my bird. I liked the idea that formed in my head. It was dreamy and comforting. But…

I shook the idea away. "I need to make some money by next week. As soon as the rain clears here, I'm going to take some pictures on my phone and send them to you. Could you set up a bid over eBay for me?"

"Sure. What are you selling?"

"The mushrooms."

His response was to sigh. "I like the mushrooms. They're my favorites. Now I need a beer too."

"I miss you," I said suddenly, without the exaggerated sappiness we usually put in there when we said stuff like that. "I look forward to tomorrow."

"Me too."

We ended the call, and I continued to sit on the windowsill. It was getting dark quickly. I could go over and flick the switch and shed light in the room, but that required actually getting up. With my head still resting on the glass, I closed my eyes and drifted into a half-sleep filled with images of my friends and family and Herr Koch.

The sound of the gate creaking open had me jerking awake. I rubbed the sleepiness out of my eyes as I strained to make sense of the gate opening.

Oh, yes. Dylan the actor. Oma's new pastor.

I looked through the rain at the man coming up the path and my breath hitched. I couldn't see Dylan's face. I could only make out his dark hair. But that combined with the umbrella he carried…well, it was enough.

My bird fluttered.

Pastor Dylan

I watched the umbrella for a long, silent moment as Dylan shook the water off it, his back turned to me. I held the door in a tight grip, waiting for him to lean it against the house and come in.

Dylan finally put it aside, turned and held out a hand. I shook it, noting the gentle way he gripped back. Not all encompassing and firm like Julian would have held me. I blinked up at his face. He had the same dark hair, but rather than mussed, his was swept neatly across his forehead. His smile looked surprised.

"Come in," I said, gesturing to the empty hall.

"Thanks." He wiped his boots on the front mat and took them off after stepping over the threshold. "So you're Caro's brother. You don't much look like her. I was expecting red hair."

I led him to the kitchen and switched on the light. There was no furniture in here yet, but I figured we could lean on the bench. "Take after my father's side," I murmured. "You want a drink of water? It's all I have."

"Sure." I washed out the cup I'd brought with me and filled

it. Dylan continued, "Ben said you were an incredible artist. Did you make the garden out there?"

"Incredible artist? He really was chatting me up."

Dylan laughed, sweeping his bangs back. "He wasn't so subtle. Thought you and I might, you know, hit it off."

"Ah, Ben," I said, shaking my head. "It's sort of flattering he'd do that."

"I hear a 'but' coming."

I shrugged, and leaned back against the bench looking down at my feet.

"Let me guess: there's someone else, and he doesn't know about it. I hope it's not Ben, because crushing on straight guys—"

I let out a whooping laugh. "No-no. No. It's not Ben." And then, for the first time I admitted it to someone other than myself; the words came out of me heavy and syrupy, but they also left me feeling so much lighter. "But yes, there's someone else."

"Yeah, well. Look at you. I'm not surprised. Is it requited?"

"Guess you'd say I'd click 'It's Complicated'."

Dylan nodded and sent me a wink. "Okay. Gotcha. So... now it's my turn to impress you with what I can do, right?"

"Sounds like a plan."

Before I could give him a run down on what I wanted to hire him for, Dylan took over.

"I can do pretty much anything. I mean, when I get a role, I research and really try to get a feel for the character. I'm into method acting. For my role as a homeless kid in this indie film I acted in, I lived on the streets for a week, trying to immerse myself in what his life was really like.

"Some extra skills I have are playing the drums and bass. I'm bilingual and can also do a few dialects. Irish and Southern American is my forte, though I'm working on my Australian one."

"Well—" I started, but a nervous Dylan cut over me.

"I am willing to do anything except frontal nudity—unless it's really tastefully done. But even then, it wouldn't be my first preference."

"No!"

"No? Just like that? I guess I could—"

I laughed and clapped a hand on his shoulder, feeling him start under my touch. "This is not your usual acting gig, but I can promise you there'll be *no* nudity of any sort."

He settled against the bench, more relaxed now, though a light flush on his cheeks told me he was a little embarrassed.

"All right," I said, looking across the room to the window at our reflections. I told him what the plan was. What I wanted from him.

Dylan folded his arms and looked at me via the window. I could see him processing the challenge. "Every week for two hours?"

"That's right."

"Will you buy me the clerical collar and clergy shirt?"

I searched past our reflections, trying to see some of the garden. I glimpsed a spot of red. The mushrooms. I'd definitely need to sell them as soon as possible.

I turned to Dylan. "You'll have the clothes."

"And I'd probably need a bible too."

I couldn't help a grin at that. He returned it.

"Anything else?" I asked.

"When do I start?"

"In the next couple of weeks. I'll tell you exactly when later."

"So I'm hired?"

"You're hired."

He raised his arms and boogied his hips. "Pastor Dylan. I like it." He flashed me a broad grin and then looked around my empty house. "What are you doing tonight?"

"Just going to crash." Hopefully.

"If you want to do something else, there's this club that Ben and I like—they're having a band playing there tonight. If you want to come along, it'll be great to see you there."

I had to leave tomorrow, but the idea of a night out, living the Berlin beat was tempting.

Well, it was until he told me the name of the club.

I shook my head, probably a little too roughly, and wished him a good night.

I watched him and his umbrella shrinking down the path and then the street towards the train station. I shut the door and leaned back against it. I didn't want to go to *Die Kathedrale* and its haunting stained glass windows.

Neighborhood Elf

I woke up with a stiff neck from sleeping on the floor. I wanted to get an early start and hit the road before traffic got too crazy.

But while I knew I needed to hurry, I was nervous too. The sooner I was back in Waldau, the sooner I would have to face Julian and talk. Only, I still hadn't found the words I would tell him yet.

I rubbed my brow and moved outside into the pleasantly fresh air. The sky was blue and the garden held a yellowy aura from the early morning sun. I took my phone, trampled over the dewy grass and took snapshots of the wax mushrooms.

I held my breath and then sent the pictures to Ben.

A minute later, still crouched staring at the mushrooms, I had a WTF text back from him. *It's 6.40 in the morning!*

I sent back a smiley. I imagined him grumbling, but possibly smiling at the same time.

Reluctantly, I turned away from the mushrooms and went back inside. After I packed my sleeping bag and backpack and was heading for the door, I had another text. *Done. Up on eBay.*

I chuckled and locked up. From next door, the wicker chair

groaned, and one look over the fence, I saw Herr Koch with his tea and the paper. Damn! His ladder. I needed to return it.

Also, my stomach was grumbling something fierce. Breakfast was also an idea...

I stuffed my things into the car and grabbed my wallet. I'd make a quick trip to the bakery for some food.

A five-minute walk later, I was one of the two customers lining up. The delicious freshly baked smell of croissant had me breathing deeply and smacking my lips.

I ordered two of them.

Then two pumpkin seed rolls.

And then I added two muffins.

Maybe it was procrastination. Maybe it was the need to say goodbye properly, but I left the bakery, shoving change into my wallet and feeling good.

Bang!

I'd bashed into someone's shoulder. "Sorry."

I looked up. And there was the neighborhood elf.

The graceful, lean man swished to the side, his hooded cape fanning at the base. "No problem," he said, as he swiftly moved into the bakery, his sword jangling at his hips, high black boots clopping up the concrete steps. "No problem, at all."

I stared after him until I was looking at the door. I tightened my hold on the bakery goods, feeling the edges of the paper bag as it grated over my palm. I closed my eyes for a second as a rush of emotion came over me, and I was thrown back to that Christmas where Julian had dressed up as an elf. The Christmas he'd given me my first wax-sculpting set.

I hurried back, returned the ladder to Herr Koch, had breakfast with him, and hightailed it to Waldau.

It really was time to stop cowering and face him.

And I would face him, but first there was Nick's bachelor party.

This time it was just Ben and me fleeing over the paddocks and into the haunted wood with Nick at our heel, as was tradition.

We leaped over the fence and dashed past the first few trees to safety. A long screeching tone sliced through the night, bending around tree trunks behind us. Ben and I clutched each other. Sure we were big, strapping twenty-four-year-olds. That didn't stop the child in us rearing up as we shuffled closer together in the web of shadows that layered the haunted wood. *Oh my God, it's finally happening. The witch is claiming us after all this time....*

The screeches stopped.

"K—lo? Le—ny?" The voice was distant, coming in and out of focus.

It was Nick, surely. He'd set us up. It was—

A twig snapped.

We froze as the figure appeared.

"Julian," we breathed out together.

"You fuck!" Ben called to him, letting go of my arm. Wisps of moonlight stretched through the trees, making the smile on his face lose its cheekiness. Instead it looked milky and soft— maybe the haunted woods were magical after all. They seemed to stare right through my best friend. "I actually almost shit my pants."

But it seemed its powers were limited. "Charming."

"What was with the wounded dog howl-screech thingy?" I asked, swinging under a low branch, like *these woods are a piece of cake.* Like *I wasn't scared at the sound you made.* Like *see, it's just a playground to me.*

Julian's lip twitched. *You're a terrible liar. Give it up. You pissed in your pants a little, didn't you?*

I shook my head.

Pea-sized didn't count.

"I wanted to scare off Nick," Julian said. "He looked like he was going to climb the fence this time."

Ben slung his arm over Julian and inclined his not-quite-bald-anymore head to me. *Hurry up*, he seemed to say. *You know what happens next.* "You're right on time. Lead us back to your shed and please tell me you have beer in there."

"It's a house-truck now," I said, plucking my sweaty T-shirt from my chest. The air funneled around me, cool and refreshing.

"Upgrading, are we? Even better."

There was beer in the house truck, and whiskey too. Ben took one look at the dusty bottle in the hollow box under Julian's armchair, and decided he'd help Julian clean up a little.

"Whoop!" He jumped onto Julian's made bed, ruffling up the blankets. Then he bounced up and down on the mattress and wriggled back to the wall. "I think I've just solved your problem, Lenny!"

How could he be so carefree? So relaxed as he laid himself on Julian's bed, his sheets, his scent? There was no afterthought, no nervousness; he could sit there and drink his whiskey and be happy.

And I wanted to join him and couldn't, because my jumping on the bed spoke of so many other things. One glance at Julian and I'd become a provocation. And if I never looked at him, awkwardness would thicken the air, wrapping around my throat until I stuttered...

Julian seemed to get it. He pulled out a chair from the table. "Sit, Lenny," he said. Then to Ben: "What problem have you solved?"

Ben swigged whiskey from the bottle and hit the palm of his hand on the bed next to him. "We get some straps for this baby, and with the help of Oma's sleeping pills, we've found a way to move her to Berlin."

I sat, feeling Julian's knuckles at my left shoulder blade,

where he still clutched the back of the chair. Ben was waggling his brows, relishing his brilliance. It was a solid plan. "Okay," I said. "If Julian agrees—"

"I agree."

"Sorted," Ben said. "Then let's work out some details."

After discussing the move for over an hour, Ben's cellphone rang. He looked at his shorts, confused at first, and then he scrambled to answer it, pulling it from his pocket and leaping off Julian's bed. The whiskey bottle was dumped onto my lap.

"Caro? You okay?"

I rested the bottle on the table and listened in on the call. Ben sounded concerned, was Carolin okay?

It looked like Ben wanted to run his hand through his hair, but once he touched the very short blond bristles, he dropped his arm.

"Sure, yeah. I'll be right there." He found the shoes he'd discarded at the door and hooked one onto his foot, hopping to keep his balance. "No bother. Got it. Give me ten minutes."

He stuffed the phone back into his pocket. "Your sister is drunk off her ass," he said to me.

I leapt up and snagged my sandals.

"No, Lenny, you can't help."

"She's my sister."

"Yeah, exactly. She doesn't want you to see her like this. She's supposed to be the big responsible one."

"Then why you?"

"Because she's seen me drunk and worse. She holds the cards, so I'll have to keep tonight entirely to myself." He slipped into his other shoe. "She'll be fine, promise. I'll take her right home."

"Yeah, but—"

"I want her to trust me, Lenny. Please don't come."

Julian was at my side. "I'll make sure he doesn't. We'll leave

Caro her dignity." He cocked his head and looked at me. "Right?"

"Fine. But call me if it's really bad and you need help."

Ben thumped his hand to my back. "Sure thing."

And then he was out of the house truck and gone.

"She'll be fine," Julian said.

I gulped and then murmured aloud, "Yeah, but will I?"

Julian gave an uneasy laugh. Then he found his shoes and put them on. "Let's get out of here."

It was the first time in a week I'd seen him, and I didn't want seeing him to end already. "And do what?"

"The haunted wood."

"Haunted wood again?"

"There's a certain path in there I think we might remember."

My lips twitched into a smile and my hand tingled as I followed him out into the summer night.

I laughed the moment the dirt path disappeared into the barely touched woods. A nervous, uncertain laugh. "We don't have a torch."

Julian took my hand and squeezed. "I'll lead the way."

We stepped into the sea of silver trees. Slowly, we retraced very familiar steps. Steps I sometimes walked on my own, when I closed my eyes and went to sleep at night.

I drew my palm over the rough bark of every tree we passed.

"I want," Julian said, the pressure of his hand in mine increasing, "to tell you one of my memories of us as kids."

"Which one?"

"The one when I knew."

"Knew what?"

"That I loved you."

I stopped, hand trailing down the bark of a Birch.

Julian gently let go of my hand. He turned to me, his lips

moving shyly into smile. He wagged a gentle finger at me, the very tip scraping over my chin. "Before you say this is too much, let me say it's not the kissy-kissy sort of love." He cocked his head. Julian-so. "Not the you-brought-me-cake kind of love, either."

"Then what type?"

"The you-make-me-mad-but-I-can't-stay-mad-long type. Is that one okay?"

I slid down the Birch trunk and made myself comfy at its base. Resting my arms atop my knees, I looked up at him. "I'm listening."

Julian paced a few steps in front of me. It was his turn to jump for a low hanging branch and tag it. "Okay, here we go. It's the spring before I turned fifteen…"

THE PEBBLES JULIAN skimmed into the river got heavier and heavier the longer he waited. After each throw, he looked over his shoulder at the crest of the hill, shimmering silver in the moonlight. This time he'd be coming round the mountain when he came… Another stone… This time he'd be coming…

A cooler breeze rustled through the trees and a few drops of dew rained on him. He chucked the last stone, pulled up the lapels on his jacket, and stuffed his numbing hands in his jean pockets. The shit.

Why wasn't he coming?

He kicked at the grass until a tuft of dirt came up and his boots were muddy. Hadn't they been talking about this all week? They should have been in the graveyard already!

Heels sinking in the soft dirt with every step he took, he muttered under his breath and trekked to Oma's.

Why did Lenny forget such things? Was it because he didn't care about freaking Nick out at the Séance he and his friends were having? He'd better not have stashed the torches and recorder and planted Pastor Dieter's garden hose for nothing.

He slid over the hill and pounded down it to Lenny's backyard. And three steps from the base, less than a hundred yards from Oma's, his foot caught in a shallow burrow.

"Oh mother of fuck!" his roar carried in the air—must have, because suddenly there was a blur in Lenny's back garden. The sound of the gate squealing open. And—

"Julian?"

Whenever Lenny said his name, the mellow timbre of his voice made him forget. It was always just a second, and not more.

For a second, he couldn't focus on the pain ripping up his calf or the gust of wind that blew grit in his eyes. He couldn't think of anything. His mind was tingly, like it was asleep. It was like a drug racing through his body: Julian.

And then it washed away and the pain came back. With swearing, too. "This never would have happened if you'd met me!"

He pushed away Lenny's offer to help him and hobbled toward the back gate.

But his ankle had twisted nicely, and it hurt like a bitch, and Lenny wasn't listening to him. His best friend, almost but not quite as tall as him, hooked his arm around his waist and took the weight off his foot.

Julian let him have his weight. Let him struggle! *But Lenny was fitter than he looked.*

Julian wrapped his arm around Lenny and together they made it to the house. Oma watched them as they moved to the bench. "Sit," Lenny said.

Oma went to stand up and Lenny turned to her and said the same thing. He disappeared into the house and came back with ice. "Take off your shoe," he said, perching on the other end of the bench.

Julian propped his foot up on the offered lap, and the denim of Lenny's jeans scratched the back of his heel. Ice wrapped in a dishcloth came down on his foot and it grew cold and numb on the one side, while staying warm and sheltered on the other.

"Sorry I forgot," Lenny said, his voice breaking at the end. "I'd promised Oma we could watch fireflies tonight, and it took longer than I thought."

With a shrug, Julian looked out into the yard. "Fireflies? This time of night?"

Lenny pinched his big toe, grinning. "Want to see them?"

Oma shifted and stood up from her chair. "Lenny spent the day making my wish come true. He's a romantic, that one." She shuffled to some black wiring leading inside the back door.

Once Oma disappeared, he switched his gaze to the chestnut-haired boy at his feet, who had a smudge of dirt in a line under his eye and on the tip of his straight nose. "Romantic, eh?" Julian teased, wiggling his toes into Lenny's stomach and making him laugh, and squirm, and threaten to drop his foot.

Julian quickly stopped when his ankle reminded him it was still sore. His annoyance came back with the pain. "So much for getting revenge on Nick—"

Light sparkled in the corner of his eye and he blinked toward the sight in the backyard. Hundreds—thousands?—of warm orange lights blinked. In the grass, by the bushes, up the cherry trees, in a huge swarm in a hydrangea plant close to the back shed.

Their backyards were similar, with the same layout, almost. But here, in Lenny's garden, they could have been in a different world. The lights blinked gently...

They really could have been in a firefly nest.

He looked at Lenny. Firefly light reflected in his eyes, and the way he stared at the garden and squeezed Julian's big toe—Julian knew Lenny was feeling proud of himself. Was happy. "You did this for Oma?"

"She wanted fireflies," Lenny said. Then he chuckled. "I 'borrowed' all of the Leike's fairy lights. This was the closest I could get."

"It's beautiful."

"THAT WAS THE moment all the mad was washed out of me, and I felt it," Julian finished, now crouching in front of me at the foot of the Birch. He reached out and touched my stomach. A light stroke to my bird. "Right there."

I wound my palm around his finger and lifted his hand to

my mouth. I placed a kiss at the tip of his finger, grazing my teeth over his skin just enough for him to shiver.

I wanted to ask him to take me home, to come into my bed and just stay the night with me, him, his warmth, his scent wrapped around me until morning. I wanted to remember what it felt like to have him that close again.

But Ben was home. He occupied the other half of my bed. There was no room, and only questions if I stayed with Julian.

I tugged him forward into an awkward hug. But I didn't want awkward, so I pushed myself away from the Birch trunk and sank down until I was lying on the cool dirt, pulling Julian with me. On top of me; our bodies molded into a full-length hug, arms coming around each other as I twisted to let him hold me back. My leg slipped between his and he pressed his legs together, locking it in place.

He was aroused; I was aroused; and we pressed ourselves closer to feel each other, but nothing more. This was a hug. Both of us knew what it meant. It was me embracing us again.

Me telling him how much his memory meant to me.

Me telling him that this moment—the moment his finger had touched my stomach—this moment was the one when I knew I loved him.

Not the you-brought-me-cake type of love. That had always been there.

Not the kissy-kissy type either. That had been there a long time too.

But the you-make-me-mad-but-I-can't-stay-mad-any-longer type. That one was new.

Scared of a Different Color

THE HAUNTED FOREST turned from silver to the color of ink.

And despite the dark, and the branches that creaked, and the rustling, whispering leaves, and a small breeze that spooked an owl into hooting—despite all that, I wasn't scared to be there.

Well, I *was*, but it was scared of a different color.

It was a scared that curled my toes and made me hard. A scared that had my heart thumping to an invisible beat and my tongue on the tips of the lyrics. A scared that made my breath come out uneven and had my bird leaping from the nest, diving down to my feet and swooping back up again.

It was a scared that made me nip at Julian's ear and whisper, "I like learning things about you that no one else knows."

He twisted us, putting his back against the cool earth, his hands rubbing over my shoulder blades, my sides. He pulled at the damp, soil covered T-shirt.

I rested my arms on the ground by his head, my fingers could just comb through his thick hair as I looked down at him. "Tell me more."

Slowly, he slipped one of his hands under my T-shirt and

pressed firmly at the base of my back. The pressure was firm and his hand was warm, and in the touch—the way he paused —there was a question: *Are you ready for the past now?*

I nodded and my body shifted against his, relieving—and building—the tension between us. It almost hurt how much I strained against my shorts. The groan he gave suggested it was the same for him.

"And the kissy-kissy sort of love? When was the first time you knew you wanted to kiss me?"

"That day in the theatre when we were mocking Ben and that girl? God, Lenny, I wasn't really mocking them. I wanted to be doing all those things with you. Wanted to kiss you. And then you pulled away, and my sweaty, shaky hands found their way into the popcorn and I had to start pelting you with it for fear of what my hands might do otherwise."

He slipped his other hand under my shirt and skated it up to my neck, where he clasped and I shivered. He pushed me down until I molded into him, my head tucked into the crook of his neck. "You have no idea what these hands want to do to you, Lenny."

I kissed his neck, darting my tongue out to taste him. Sweet and salty and earthy. It was a small kiss, but he arched under me, nudging my cock at the same time.

Vice-like, his hands clamped me to him. "You want more?"
Yes.

"Okay, but first, can I ask something?"

"Ask me."

He shivered, as if my words tunneled under the collar of his shirt and crept towards his straining cock, teasing him at the tip.

"Will you go camping with me this summer?" It was my turn for his words to slide and slither over me, gripping my cock and pulling.

"How about after Nick's wedding?" He pressed into me

some more. "Just you and me?" I added, and he jerked his hips, moaning.

In my head his next words were: *That'd be bloody perfect.* They were meant to be hot and juicy as they slid over me, taking me so deep I wouldn't be able to hold back from exploding.

Instead, what he said stuck like ice to the sensitive skin and pulled so hard it brought tears to my eyes. "Be nice to share that tradition one last time before you leave."

"Leave," I repeated, rolling off him. My back hit the ground. A pained laugh escaped me. We might have been ready to talk about the past, to accept it, even, but what of the future?

The future is there, waiting around the corner… Where are you in it?

Berlin.

And Julian?

Would this tentative…would this love survive the summer?

I sat up, gripping my knees and catching my breath. When Julian reached out to touch my cheek and ask me if I was okay, I pushed to my feet. "I should get home. Just in case Ben needs help with Carolin."

He was on his feet in a second. "Let me walk you there."

I let him, and we drifted into safe subjects. Then Julian opened the gate, and after I passed through, he kept staring at the attic.

The urge to ask *Lenny for your thoughts* came over me and I repressed it with a grimace. But I didn't have to wonder long. He caught me watching him and shrugged. "I was thinking of the fight we had that night."

He didn't have to add anything more. We both knew he was referring to the fight after his mama had caught us watching porn. "What about it?"

Julian said his next words carefully, bordering on hesitantly.

"You were upset, but it wasn't just that I told my mama you brought the porn, was it?"

"Did you think it was?"

"No."

"You never said anything."

"I thought about it," Julian said. "I almost did. But I guess a part of me wasn't sure you knew if you were gay. And another part didn't want to know if you did."

"Why not?"

"Because I was scared. I didn't want my hopes dashed. They were what I was living on back then."

Verses With a Side of Massage

"WANT TO watch a movie?" Ben asked almost the second Julian walked into our kitchen the next day dressed in shorts and a monster T-shirt like the one I'd bought him years ago.

Julian quickly found me playing cards with Oma and raised a brow. "Do I want to watch a movie?" He hummed, but I could see he was hoping I would want to. I smirked.

"I think you do," I said. And then in front of all my family, I smiled up at him across the room. "Especially because it's something scary."

Even across the room I saw how his green eyes darkened to the same inky color as the haunted wood the night before. But even as one part of him seemed to smile deeply, there was a twitch to his brow that said he didn't understand why we'd left things so abruptly last night.

I'd tell him later, if we got any chance at being alone.

"You can count me out, kids," Oma said—not that she'd have watched anything anyway. "Pastor Dieter is coming around for more of my coffee and a game of poker. I want to squeeze more information out of him about his replacement. I really have to insist this next pastor be a trained masseur."

Carolin dropped the butter knife she'd been using to spread jam on her bread. It clattered against the table, staining the tablecloth. She tried to rub it clean. "A masseur?" Her *what-the-fuck?* glance at Ben, Julian and then me, had me suddenly roaring with laughter. The table jiggled and our card game was lost.

"Why yes," Oma said, leveling me to mere laughing whimpers with her glare. "I'd like my verses with a side of massage. I think I could concentrate better on them that way."

Julian snorted. "Tell me how that conversation goes." He took my sister's bread and pinched a bite, winking at her. "So what's the movie?"

Ben waved an old disc at him.

Julian shuddered, and I could read his ambivalence from here. "Looks freaky."

It was. And bloody too.

My sister and Ben shared the only throw blanket we had and hid behind it.

When I clutched Julian's arm into a death grip at the next scary part, Julian left the room, returning with a fresh tablecloth from the linen cupboard. "Was the only thing I could find," he said, draping it over us.

Covered from view, the gentle weight of Julian's hand skimmed over my thigh and rested there. Just like that, the movie wasn't so scary anymore. He raised a brow. *Is this okay?*

My answer was to slip my hand under his shorts to the rim of his boxer-briefs and pull at the tiny hairs there. He hissed in a breath and, when Ben glanced at him, said, "This film is freaky as shit." He swung his gaze casually to me. "I love it. You?"

He emphasized his question by dragging his hand farther up my thigh, over my shorts, to the crease of my leg and crotch.

"Best film ever," I agreed, and boy what an effort it cost me not to gasp. Sweat started to bead at my hairline.

"But," Julian added, "there are a few parts that confuse me."

"What parts?" I said, slipping a finger under his briefs toward his inner thigh. "Maybe I could explain them to you."

"Bet you could. You know what this movie night needs? Snacks." And he slunk out of my grasp. "Lenny, help me."

I followed him to the kitchen. I could hear Oma and Pastor Dieter laughing from the bench in the backyard, and knew we were alone.

I reached to the top cupboard for some cups, but Julian whisked me around, pinning my arm to the cupboard as he kissed me hard and sucked my tongue. He pressed his warm length closer and closer to mine, stealing away my breath. "What the hell was that in there?"

"Thought you loved it?"

He ground against my length. "Does that answer that?"

I nodded and rubbed back, eliciting a groan from him. "I didn't want to leave like that. Yesterday, I mean."

Julian's breath tickled over the side of my neck. "What happened? More importantly, what happened *since* then?"

"You left. I went to my work shed and finished Oma's beaded door. When I stowed it away, there it was, the first little wax warrior I'd made, sitting cushioned in silk, in a much-loved leather case." I pushed us apart so I could see his face. "I looked at it and I just knew."

He cocked his head. "Knew what?"

The wick was burned, but the wax had barely melted. I always wondered why that candle never stayed lit at Christmas. And it was you, wasn't it? Had to be. *You snubbed out the flame every time. Then, that moment in the attic, when the box of Christmas decorations fell and spilled over the floor—you took it.*

Almost ten years you've had it.

To Julian I said, "That if I asked you, you'd say, yes."

"Asked what?"

"I don't think that would matter." But I had a question in mind: *Would you come with me to Berlin?*

He cupped the back of my neck and brought our foreheads together. Our noses bumped. I could feel his kiss before he gave it, and then—

My phone rang.

It startled us apart. I quickly picked up.

Ben's voice skipped down the line. "Can you also bring Caro and I some coke and cookies?"

"Seriously?" I rolled my eyes at Julian and mouthed Ben's name. "You couldn't get off your lazy ass for a second to come to the kitchen?" Which was good, actually, because who knew what they'd have walked in to? Why did one thing have to right itself only to show there was so much more at stake?

If they knew, what would they think? That Julian and I were wrong? Icky?

Would they try to convince us to stay apart?

"Our lazy asses are very happy right where they are," Ben said, "breathing life into your cushions."

"I don't know if I should feed that mouth."

"You know you love it."

Julian reached into the fridge, pulled out the coke and started filling two glasses for us.

"Looks like Julian has read your mind," I said, pulling down two extra glasses. "Coke is on its way."

Julian backed out of the kitchen, grinning at me, and suddenly I wished I didn't have to leave for Berlin tomorrow. I wanted to steal some time just the two of us.

I grabbed the tin of cookies.

Guess it'd just have to wait until I got back. Nick's wedding.

(Berlin)

OKAY. OKAY. OKAY.

THE ISLAND AT TREPTOWER PARK HADN'T CHANGED.

There were more people picnicking, more paddling boats on the water, and more clouds dancing across the sky. But the trees were exactly the same, the air tasted the same as it lightly breezed over Ben and I, and the grass tickled at the rim of my shorts just like it had back *then*.

If I listened hard enough, I thought I could almost hear my sister's singing sailing over the smooth river water.

I felt for the paper I had folded and tucked into my pocket, and brushed my index finger over the edges. I'd been in Berlin four days, finishing up my and Oma's new home, and every day I carried the paper.

Note, actually. Six words had been scrawled on lined refill, using one of my thick sketching pencils.

Ben shifted next to me, as if no position on the bank was comfortable. The ground was a little bumpy and dry after the summer, but comforted by good memories, it was easy to over-look. Though every now and then, the image floating in my mind had a melancholic aftertaste.

Ben stroking Carolin's hair...Julian resting against the tree trunk…and whenever I looked back toward the bridge, there was Ben and Carolin, huddled under his T-shirt in the rain.

"I think I'm gonna grab us some beer," Ben said and hopped up, using my shoulder as a brace.

Then he was gone and I was left alone at the water's edge. I glanced at Ben's figure shrinking toward the beer garden and fished into my pocket, taking out the note.

When I'd gone to pack Oma's beaded door, there'd been an envelope on my work-shed table. It sat perched against an old roll of partially faded wallpaper that matched the pattern in our house entrance.

I unfolded the note, reading the words again, loving the sprawling handwriting. How many more times would I read this note? I knew the words by heart, but somehow it was more real seeing it in his handwriting. My bird took a little dive each time I read it.

I want to be your David.

"What's that in your hand?" Ben motioned to the note with an incline of his head as he passed over a bottle of Pilsner.

I took the bottle and rested it between my knees as I slipped the note back into my pocket.

"It's…it's…" My lips stretched into a smile. God, I wanted to tell him. Wanted my best friend to know. To *not* care.

And to care—the happy kind of care.

But Julian… It wasn't just for me to tell. "It's nothing."

"Doesn't look it."

"It's a secret," I said. "For now only." *I hope.*

I expected him to try and tease it out of me. Ben loved a good secret. But he didn't. He nodded somberly, and stared at his beer, picking at the label with his thumb.

"I guess we all have secrets. I get it, man." He partially shifted his head toward me and looked up out the corners of his eyes. There was something strained in the way he breathed, and I shifted to face him. Before I could ask him what was up, he said, "I have a secret of my own."

I raised both brows and kept things friendly by nudging him in the side. "Yeah?"

"Yeah." He took a large drink of his beer. "Do you remember when we met at *Die Kathedrale* the last time?"

"You were upset about the girl you thought was about to dump you. Olivia, right?"

He glanced to the river. "Nah, her name wasn't Olivia. Do you remember what I said to you? Exactly?"

I thought back to the moment, twisting my beer bottle as I did as if it would help bring back the details. "You said you thought she was the one and that you thought you'd fucked it up."

His Adam's apple bobbed in his throat. He took another large gulp of beer and continued to pick at its label. "I said she *is* the one."

I didn't mean to huff, didn't mean to be rude or annoyed, but the sound came out. Or maybe the truth was I did mean to be annoyed, I just hadn't intended on showing it.

Ben glared at me. "What the fuck?"

In the deep pools of his eyes, I saw my shadow looking back at me. And he was shaking his head at me.

I bowed away from his gaze. Fuck. What a dick I was. "Shit, Ben. Sorry." I stared down at my bottle. "I guess I didn't believe you'd met the one, because if you had, I thought you'd have introduced her to me, you know? But that's crap. It's not like I ever tell you about my—" I swallowed "—about my relationships."

Ben nodded, and the small smile he gave me said it was okay. He picked the ground for a stone and hurled it into the river. "I never introduced her to you, Lenny, because I didn't have to." His breath shuddered out of him as he looked at me. "It's Carolin."

At first I thought he was having me on, that it was a joke, but when his lips didn't twitch upward, when he didn't hoot out in laughter...when he stared right back at me, I knew this was real.

"Carolin? But you...you fight. All the time. You..."

"It's her, Lenny. It always was, and it always will be." He found another stone and threw that. "Say something."

"I..."

"*Please,* say it's okay." His voice cracked.

I knocked my beer over as I swallowed him in a hug. "Okay. Okay. Okay," I said. I squeezed harder. "I'm just...speechless."

His laughter burst out of him and shook the both of us. He thumped me on the back and slowly we pulled apart. Ben's eyes glistened and his lip wobbled. He pulled up his T-shirt and used it to dab his eyes. "Shit, she said I'd cry. Why does she always have to be right?"

I laughed. It was like Ben had passed his bird over to me to take care of for a few precious moments.

But now he was waiting for it back and all in one piece. I gave it back to him as best as I could. "I think Oma knew all along," I said. "She said Carolin would have more than a romance. It makes sense that you are her love story."

"How so?"

"You're the only guy that could ever be worthy enough for it."

He blushed.

"So does she feel the same way?" I asked. "When did it... you know, *happen*? And what do you mean she was going to dump you?"

I shifted my leg away from the puddle of beer I'd spilled.

Ben finished the rest of his bottle. "She was going to dump

me because I was too chicken shit to tell you about us. I kept putting it off. She said she'd tell you, but I—I needed to be the one, you know?"

I snorted. "She has you wrapped around her little finger. No way she would have dumped you. Nicely played, Carolin."

That got me a deep punch to the shoulder. Then he grinned. "It's true."

I rubbed my hands and looked at him over my fingers. "Now, how did it happen?"

"I guess it's always been happening, but things came to a head earlier this year. You want to hear this?"

"Yeah. But leave out the sordid details."

He smirked. "I'll just think those parts."

BEN STILL HADN'T *properly found his voice.*

Caro swung off the horse and batted his offered hand away. Her cheeks were flushed from riding. She blinked, and Ben thought he saw her blush. But she quickly turned toward Kasper, the horse, and drew the reins over his head. She handed them to Ben, and he hated that she wore gloves, because their hands bumped and he wanted to be touching her.

"Let's find a quieter spot to tie him up," she said.

Nodding, he clutched Kasper's reins tighter, glancing away from Lenny and Caro and the haunted forest behind them.

He didn't reckon he'd ever felt like this. Caro had made him feel some wicked things before—God that was for sure—but this topped them all. *Somehow, she was squeezing his heart and blowing gently on it at the same time.*

He wanted to choke and laugh and fucking giggle *all at once.*

The moment he'd seen her cantering across the paddock, in her jockey costume, hair a fiery red in the night, streaming behind her…

He twisted, his gladiator sword clanking against his shin armor. Thanking the stars it was night and Kasper would hide him, he quickly rearranged himself. He led Herr Braun's chestnut horse a few steps down the fence, feet unsteady over the grass.

"I'm screwed," he said to Kasper under his breath.

He looked back. Carolin tucked her jockey whip into her boot and shook her head. Then she smirked at Lenny. How that smirk had taunted him in the past. How much he'd hated and loved it at once.

"Have fun in there," Caro said to her brother. "If we're not here to see you come out, we'll meet back at the Leike's after-party."

"Don't get too scared," Ben added and winked—but his words seemed forced, and the wink robotic. He wiped one sweaty palm over the strips of material that showed through his costume. His other hand slipped down the reins.

Caro jogged to his side, her gaze slowly working down him. "Gladiator, eh?"

If she wasn't holding his heart so tight and breathing so warmly on it, he might have managed to waggle his brows, thump his armor and tell her he knew she loved it. As it was, his usual jokes were being juiced out of him.

"Hot jockey, eh?" he said back to her as the shouts of the villagers behind them dulled and they approached a bend in the paddock, curving around the haunted forest. There was a second paddock here that would work for putting Kasper in until morning.

Ben opened the latch of the gate and walked the horse in. He made quick work of unbridling him and stashed the gear in the corner of the paddock, under the hedge that lined the far side. He chucked his gladiator helmet with it; the sweat was making his hair stick to his head.

He loosened his hair with his fingers and faced Caro, who'd been quiet, watching him the whole time. Suddenly, he was unsure where the bloody hell to put his hands. He decided on the hips.

Caro leaned back against the gate, taking out the whip from her boot. She fiddled with it. Then her voice came over to him softly. "Hot jockey?"

He laughed, nervously, glancing at the whip. "Come on, Caro. I know I always say the wrong thing, but that's a little extreme, isn't it?"

She lightly tapped the end of the whip against her leather glove. Without looking up from it, she said, "You don't always say the wrong thing."

He moved in front of her, and she tilted her helmet down so he couldn't see her eyes. "Did I...did I say the right thing just now?" he asked, gently pulling off her helmet and hanging it on the fence.

Hair curtained the sides of her face, and he just...he needed to pull it back. He reached out and his fingers threaded through her hair as he pushed it back.

Her breath hitched and she looked up at him. "Ben?"

"I hope these words are also right, because you're the most beautiful woman I have ever seen, Caro." He cupped her head, leaned down and kissed her. Soft lips grazed his with a small gasp that he felt drift in him all the way to his toes. "I've dreamed of doing that a long time."

He closed the rest of the distance between them, meshing their bodies together, his hard against her curvy, soft, energetic, demanding.

Their kiss deepened and Caro wrapped her arms around his neck, the whip dangling down his back as they tasted each other. She pressed herself against him and he groaned, lurching to pull back.

"You don't—?"

"Oh, I do."

"Then—"

He came in and kissed her again. Lightly, he drew away. He touched the side of her cheek, and then pinched the tip of her pointed nose. "Because I need to know, Caro. What about you?"

"Me?" she said, folding her arms, the whip jutting upwards between them, close to his face.

"I want you to be my last first time."

She blinked rapidly, coyly looking down, her lips spreading into such a shy, beautiful smile; he just had to kiss her again. "Me too, Ben."

And that was it.

They were tangled in each other's arms again, kissing, exploring, hands roaming to touch each other's skin. He lowered himself to the grassy ground, Caro coming with him, slowly pulling off his armor. It was too cold outside for him to undress her, and that was fine. This was fine —perfect.

She straddled him, looking down, wonder showing in her big green eyes *and the way her dark eyelashes kissed together when she blinked. She rocked against him and Jesus—it was too much. He came up onto his elbows and she bent and kissed him, a wet, teasing touch to his lips.*

"I'm going to make you come in your pants," she said in his ear. Then laughed as he groaned. She grated against him again.

He grabbed one of her wrists and lightly bit each finger before breathing on her palm and kissing it. "Do you mind dropping the whip, Caro?"

She laughed again. This time with more confidence. Then she shook her head. "No, I sort of like it. Be good, Ben. Be very good to me."

"Always."

LIGHT BLAZED ACROSS Herr Koch's garden from his front rooms, warm orange outlining the grass and the rose bushes. It reached out to me, beckoning, welcoming.

Still hazy with the revelation of my sister and my best friend being in love with each other—and the beers Ben and I had shared to celebrate the news—I wasn't ready to go to sleep. I wanted to do something with my nervous energy.

Chatting to Herr Koch sounded like a fine plan.

I rang the doorbell. His footsteps thudded down the hall and then air sucked around me as he opened the door. "It's you," he said, and motioned me to come in.

"Yep. I'm back for a couple of nights."

I followed him down hardwood floors to the kitchen. His was at the back of his house, a mirror image of mine, with white walls and family portraits hanging from them.

He motioned for me to sit at a sturdy, long wooden table that looked like it should seat ten. "Cup of tea?"

"How about a beer?"

He shook his head and brought out two bottles from his fridge. "You can hardly sit still. What's up with you?"

And I couldn't hold it in anymore, I wanted—needed—to share, share, share! I told him about Ben and Carolin and as I did, as I delved back into old memories, I wondered how I'd never seen it before.

Suddenly, my beer was finished, and I wasn't talking about Ben and my sister anymore. I'd mentioned Julian already a handful of times, and my free hand was resting on my pocket with his note.

"Anyway," I said, pulling away from saying too much. "Ben's family. I'm so happy for him."

"Another reason for Berlin," Herr Koch said. It wasn't a question; he knew from the way I'd told him everything that it was a fact.

"Yeah."

"And what about sub-letting? Have you thought any more about that?" He chuckled. "What am I talking about? Now that I know your real plan, I know you couldn't possibly get away with someone else living there with you and your Oma."

My hand was in my pocket now, the note beneath my fingers. "Actually. Maybe I could."

He took my empty bottle and moved into the kitchen to get me a fresh drink.

"Huh," he said, the fridge squeaking. "Well, you're creative. That's for sure." Then the fridge shut, followed by the sound of the bottle opener snapping the lid off the new beer. He came to my side and handed me the cold bottle.

Then that cheeky grin was back on his face as he made sure I knew where we stood on the whole matter. "You just remember, Lenny, I have to okay them first."

Part Three

LOVE NEST

And Then The Wind Changed

WE ARRIVED BACK in Waldau on Saturday afternoon and hurriedly dressed for Nick's wedding. Suit, tie, dress coat, the whole hog. Ben even folded a piece of cloth into my breast pocket.

"When it's our turn," he said, "you're buying yourself a new suit."

I choked on the raisin bread I'd been stuffing into my mouth, spraying crumbs over my front.

Ben hit me once on the back, harder than he needed to. Then said with a grin. "Get used to it."

I brushed my front, and Oma came up to me and pinched my cheeks. "Better."

"Crap," Caro yelped, pinning pearls to her hairdo. She grabbed her purse and held it under her chin as she did the last touch to her hair and walked out the door. "We're going to be late."

We were just in time.

Ushered inside the church, Ben, Caro, Oma and I sidled into a free space on some back pews to the right.

It took me no more than ten seconds to spot Julian. He sat

with his mother in one of the middle rows on the left. From here, he was just an arm in black, dark hair that shimmered under the lights, and a collared neck. Flowers, lining the aisle, brushed against his arm as he turned suddenly, scanning the crowds.

Just when the music began, when we all stood and the bride walked down to Nick-the-groom, Julian found me. The bride cut through our connection, and we found it again immediately. We continued to stare at each other even when the rest of the crowd followed the trailing gown to the front. Then, as we all reclaimed our seats, he winked.

It was fitting, and perfect. He was giving me back something he'd taken from me in this very church.

I acknowledged it by shyly smiling back at him, but it was prematurely wiped off my face when Aunt Thomas twisted and, following Julian's gaze, glared at me.

Oma touched my sleeve, smiled, and patted my arm.

I didn't see Julian again until the reception in the village hall.

THERE WAS SOMETHING brewing in the air. It was like the music tightened around us, pulling Julian and me closer and closer. We couldn't resist taking that extra glance at each other across the dancing crowds, or grazing our fingers as we passed drinks, or laughing out loud and using it as an excuse to clutch the other's shoulder and let our breaths bump into each other's ears.

I didn't dare drink any wine, I felt heady enough without it.

Tonight, the air was thick with the promise that something special would happen.

And then the wind changed.

Perhaps it was the slightly burnt smell coming from the

kitchens that was off, or the cool breeze that rushed through the room as the doors opened and banged shut. Perhaps it was the change from the musician's flute to the viola, but suddenly, the hairs on the back of my neck bristled.

I cradled my drink and glanced across the table at Oma chatting to Herr Leike about the village play. She looked up at me and winked. "You should get up and dance, boy."

"You want to dance, Oma?" I asked, extending my hand toward her.

She batted it away. "Dance with someone your own age."

I rolled my eyes, ate another square of apple strudel, and wiped my mouth with a purple serviette that matched the violet sashes around the cream bouquets of lilies that had been making Carolin's eyes water most of the evening.

Over the rambles of the crowd and the viola, I thought I heard someone call out "Len."

Following the sound to the table on my right, I started when I saw a familiar male face. Nick's cousin Theo waved back at me and stood, as if to—

No, no, no, please don't come over. I really didn't want to talk. No matter how charming he could be...

Theo continued to skirt his way around his table, and a syrupy sludgy feeling filled my stomach. I hadn't spoken to him since, well, in *years.*

In fact, I'd hoped I'd never see him again.

Crap. He was definitely moving in my direction.

I slid off my chair and sidled past Nick and his best man, Thomas, towards the dance floor. Searching for Ben and Carolin, I hoped I'd be able to ask Carolin to dance and avoid Herr Theo. The song ended, and I stumbled into Carolin's old friend Anita and her four-year-old.

"Sorry," I murmured, and hurried toward the side of the room where large burgundy velvet curtains were drawn over the windows.

I was tempted to hide behind them and wait the evening out if it meant avoiding awkward conversation with Theo, but Ben snagged my arm just before I reached the velvet safety.

"Where are you off to?" he asked, and turned us both toward the dancing crowd. He rested an arm on my shoulder and pointed toward Carolin, who looked like she was helping Tina out with her wedding dress so it wouldn't get trampled on when she danced.

"It's strange being able to dance with her like this," Ben said, and I heard the smile in his voice, "in front of you all."

"You'd have danced anyway," I said, shifting slightly and hoping Theo didn't spot me.

"Yeah, I know, but it's more freeing now. And it's a bonus not to have to hide when we kiss."

"You can feel free to keep hiding—" That earned me a swat to the back of my head.

"So you've told Oma?"

Ben snorted. "Not exactly. We were planning to tell her after the wedding, but she caught us making out against Pastor Dieter's house on the way to the reception. She waited until we finally noticed we had company, and then slapped her cane against my ass. 'Like a *mosquito*,' she said, and I swear-to-God, her grin was equal parts holy and hell. Then she left us gaping like fish and murmured 'That's one down.'"

"One down?"

Another swat came to my head, then Ben rested his hand there. "Guess you're next, Lenny boy."

Me, next. I searched for Julian on the dance floor.

He spun his mother and she laughed. He caught me looking at him over Aunt Thomas's shoulder and a smile lit his face. *Later*, it seemed to say. *Later, and it'll be you and me dancing, Lenny, just like it always should have been.*

Then Theo came into my wonderful view breathing apologies to Frau Rohr after treading on her toe. I yanked Ben with me and moved behind a large square pillar.

"Are you hiding from someone? Not Julian again, I hope. Thought you guys had made up?"

I let out a nervous laugh. Oh, we'd made up all right. Kissed and made up. "Nah," I said, and patted the off-white pillar. "This is just a better place to chat."

Ben frowned, but it melted off him as he noticed Carolin coming toward him. Theo, thank God, was still stuck talking to Frau Rohr, and Julian had danced closer to us. Each time our gazes clashed, he grinned and it was making my bird flap like crazy.

Then suddenly he was close enough I could hear his deep voice as he murmured things to his mama.

Carolin slunk into Ben's embrace and stood with us, watching our neighbors and friends as they danced and ate and sang and drank.

Carolin gave a melancholic sigh. "Who would ever have imagined Nick a married man?"

"Lenny?" It was Theo's voice coming over the heads of a group of bridesmaids.

I cowered farther behind the pillar and shook my head at Carolin's questioning brow. "Talk to me, and don't stop. I don't want to talk to the guy."

My sister laughed. "What could we tell him, Ben?"

"What about telling him that you weren't actually drunk the night of Nick's bachelor party...that really, you were calling me for a booty—"

"You're helpful, guys. Real helpful."

"Maybe talking to Theo won't be quite as bad, then?"

I weighed up the options. "How about," I said, smirking at Carolin, "you tell me why you shaved off Ben's hair. The truth."

She stroked a hand over Ben's head. "I'm sure you don't really want to know."

Ben straightened and snagged Carolin into a bruising kiss. "Dammit," he said, "there's more to it than wanting to know what I'd look like bald, isn't there?"

She bit her lip. "Um, it doesn't really matter."

"I'll be the judge of that," Ben said.

"But you're biased."

"Then Lenny will be the judge, won't you?"

I leaned back against the pillar. "Sure thing."

"Fine, I'll tell you why, but God help you, Ben, do not interrupt me again." She might have sounded intimidating if she could have held her smile in cheek. "Let's see, it was about two weeks ago…"

A YOUNG TWENTY-SOMETHING blonde with angel earrings stood next to the exact same kitchen cabinets as the ones at home. Carolin sidled up to her, skirt catching on a lampshade and almost tipping it over.

The market was so full of used furniture there was barely space to walk. The lamp wouldn't have been the first thing she'd knocked over. Luckily, Ben was behind her, catching things as she went. She threw him a grin, and focused on Angel Earrings.

"What do you want for the cabinet?" she asked, touching the criss-crossed glass doors. The one back in Waldau wouldn't survive the trip—if they could even get it off the wall. No, this was perfect.

"Hundred euros," Angel Earrings said, making Carolin balk. Was she kidding? This was old East German crap; they were a dime a dozen…

Of course, she didn't say that because this was the first time in a week of hunting she'd spotted one.

"I'll give you twenty euros for it," Ben said, inspecting the piece critically. He took out his keys and pressed into the wood. "The wood is rotting."

"Rotting?" She frowned.

Ben gave her a sweet smile. A little too sweet if you ask her. "See how easily my keys press into it? This cabinet doesn't have a long shelf life, dear."

Carolin's eyes widened. Dear? He just freaking called her dear?

She scowled at Ben as he continued to barter for the cabinet. Continued to call her dear, and flick his hair out of his eyes like they only did on modeling ads.

Ben might have got Angel Earrings down to twenty-seven euros, but her temper flared in equal amounts.

Outside, after they'd stuffed the thing into Ben's car, he raised his hand for a high-five. "Score, right?"

"You were trying to score, all right," she muttered, bypassing his hand and jumping into the driver's seat.

He didn't seem to notice, still gloating from his bartering skills. Flirting skills more like it. She ran her hands over the steering wheel and rested her head back against the headrest.

She was being ridiculous. She knew it. That wasn't Ben. It wasn't.

It was just…she was a couple of years older than him—what if he decided she wasn't the one? What if he decided he was too young to settle? Sure he'd had many girls before her…but what if, in the end, she was just one on the list?

"What's next on our Oma list?" he asked, blue eyes smiling at her like they always had—even when they'd been at each other's throats. Which they often still were.

She swallowed a sigh and looked away from him, out onto the street. He was beautiful, and kind, and so full of love… She didn't want to only have a piece of it. She wanted the whole thing.

She wanted to be the only one he said "dear" to.

"What's up?" Ben asked, sliding his fingers to the nape of her neck and massaging. His touches never ceased to send wonderful shivers through her.

"Do you remember when Dave dumped me and I came around to your place a complete mess?"

His hand stilled. "Yeah. I remember."

"I thought he'd broken my heart."

Ben's jaw clenched.

She looked down at her hands gripping the steering wheel. "I was wrong. He didn't break anything. He'd have had to really have it for that."

"Where is this coming from, love?"

She choked on his soft "love." Taking his hand from her neck, she kissed his knuckles. "Do you remember when you took me to Oma's?" She chuckled, but the memory was a sensitive one, and what he'd done for her meant everything. "You were so freaked out, you didn't know what to do with me, and every time you said something sweet, I just cried harder."

Ben let out a soft breath. "Yeah. I didn't know what to do. I hate seeing you sad."

She laced their fingers together. "It was the same night Lenny came out to me and Oma and I found out you already knew." He went to say something, and she shook her head, stopping him. "You remember what I said to you that night?"

"Caro, how could I forget? It was the first time you said you loved me. And then you tore me to shreds when you joked about not meaning like that." *He leaned over and kissed under her ear. "Like this."*

"I lied, Ben," she said slowly. I loved you for real in that moment. Like this. I just couldn't say it.

She wanted him to get it right away. Wanted him to tell her he loved her. But instead he curled a finger under her chin, made her look at him, and then kissed her. A tender kiss that said so much and wasn't quite enough.

A car horn blasted beside them, the driver pointing to the parking spot. She sighed and drove to Lenny's soon-to-be new home.

"Please say that list is almost done," Ben said when they finally trudged back to his place after a long, long morning.

Carolin laughed. "Just you getting a haircut. Then we can drive back to Oma's."

He snatched her into an embrace on the stairs leading to the kitchen. Pressing her against the wall, he kissed her. She moaned and arched into him. "We have time for this?" he asked, hand sliding under her skirt.

She laughed. God, yes!

Oh, but no, not really. Dammit. "Sorry. Haircut and then we have to hit the road before we hit the worst of the traffic."

"How about we skip the haircut and—"

She laughed and kissed him back against the opposite wall. "I'll make it a quick trim and then we'll see."

"I love it when you raise your brows like that. Sexy as fuck."

"Kitchen, Ben. Now."

She cut his hair. Trim here…a bit there…

"Are we…" *she drifted off and cut some more.*

"Are we, what?" *Ben asked, craning his neck to look back at her.*

She straightened his head, and continued to snip-snip. "Are we going to tell Lenny soon?"

Ben went quiet. What did that mean? Did it mean he didn't want to? That he wasn't sure where they were going together? That it wasn't going to last?

Stop it; this is Ben. This is right.

"Soon," *he said.* "Just got to find the right moment, you know?"

She swallowed, so glad he couldn't see her.

"Just need to shave the back," *she forced out of her tight throat, and picked up the electric shaver.*

"Then I'll be irresistible to women?" *he said, chuckling.*

"Irresistible to me, you mean."

He choked on his laugh and swore. At the same time, he jerked and the shaver met the back of his hair, nicking a large chunk. "This is one of my 'say the wrong things' moments, isn't it?" *he asked.*

She stared at the bald spot. Crap. How could she fix it?

Picking up the scissors again, she tried to make the nick less obvious—but it wasn't working.

She switched the shaver on again. The silver lining, *she thought before she winced and shaved up the middle of Ben's head,* is that at least now there might not be so many cute girls fawning over him…

"So what's the ruling? Am I forgiven? Or do Ben and I need another night in the attic?"

"Somehow," I said, over a loud roar of the cheering crowd that happened every time the newly-weds kissed, "I don't reckon that's quite the punishment we thought it was."

Carolin giggled and Ben's wide smile said it all. My best friend leaned over and kissed my sister. "Oh, yeah, we made up all right." To Carolin, he said, "Calling her 'dear' meant nothing. Sorry you got upset."

She reached out, touched his hair and grimaced. "Yeah, me too."

"Really, Caro? You're so asking for it." He picked her up and hurled her over his shoulder. "You can stay like this until you finally figure out how to say sorry. Even if it was partly my fault and an accident." He grinned at me. "She's quite the handful, this one."

I laughed. "That's for sure. Hey, can you check if Theo's gone?"

Ben peered around the corner with Carolin pummeling his ass. "Seems that two bridesmaids are keeping him occupied. He looks miserable."

"And you really don't," I said.

"What can I say? I love her in better and worse."

Carolin's gasp had Ben tensing. He didn't stop her when she pushed herself off him. But he waited, hands clutched tightly against his sides, making the material taut beneath them.

"Say it again," she said.

He held her gaze steady. "I love you, Caro. I knew it since I was fifteen, when you couldn't find my bird for the top of the Christmas tree and you cried. But you never gave up looking; you just did it through your tears. And then you found it—somehow it'd come out of its box and was laying between the wall and the shelf in the attic—and you took it and you couldn't bear to look at me, and you carried it downstairs and placed it on the top.

"Yes, there have been other girls in my past, but I've always measured them up to you, and all of them failed. It was only ever about you."

Carolin kissed him and didn't stop.

I inched around the pillar, eager to give them some privacy.

Julian danced closer to me, and when he found my gaze at his next turn, I slipped him a wink. Poor Julian obviously wasn't expecting it from me, because he lost his footing and quickly had to catch his mama and hold her close. "Sorry," he said to her.

"You even stumble with grace. You're just too good a dancer to waste on me," she said. "How about you find yourself a nice girl and spin her around?"

"Nah, thanks. I'm good."

She frowned. "Are you still upset over Liddie? She was a very nice girl, but there'll be others. I still don't understand how she could have broken it off with you."

"She didn't, Mama. I told you, *I* broke our engagement."

"Well that I'll never understand." She shook her head and cupped the side of his face, smiling proudly at him as only a mama could. "You're too good to be sitting all night without a single dance like *some* people."

Julian looked honestly confused. I shook my head to tell him not to bother asking, that I knew exactly what she meant, and it just wasn't worth it, but he didn't see me. "Some people? Who?"

Ben stiffened next to me the moment she said it, "Like your cousin, for instance."

Julian stopped dancing and stepped back, his hands loose on her arms and sliding off her. "Sorry?" he asked again, as if he must have misheard.

"Well, you know. Because of his preferences. It'll leave him a lonely young man tonight."

I looked away from them; no matter how inappropriate

Aunt Thomas was, the truth remained: it wasn't likely I'd be dancing with my partner in Waldau tonight or any other night. These events always would be somewhat lonely.

And it was okay. I was okay with that.

Apparently others weren't though.

Carolin hissed and I snapped my gaze to her and Ben, who were glaring at Aunt Thomas with a frightening passion. I nudged Ben in the side. "Don't worry about it," I said under my breath.

My head swung back and my bird soared to my chest when Julian said, "Maybe *I'll* dance with him."

All the air had left me and for a moment I forgot how to get it back. I sought for his gaze, pleaded with him to look at me and *say it again, please*, but his eyes were steady on his mama.

"You're too nice, Julian," she said. Then, with the worst timing possible, the music stopped, and she finished, loudly in a suddenly quieter room, "But it would make it look like you're sinking to Leonard's level."

My throat dried up—not at her words, because I'd heard them from her before, but from the sudden surge of support that spilled around me. Oma cracked her cane against the floor, parted the dancing crowd, and came charging.

Carolin sprung toward Aunt Thomas with murder in her eyes. Ben locked his arms around her and pulled her back, suddenly whispering in her ear. With a growl at our aunt, she nodded. "Yes, do it. Make it good."

"Oh, you betcha I will." Ben let her go. Then there was pressure on my hand, and suddenly Ben was yanking me to his chest. He started to dance, tugging me along to keep up.

"What—?"

"Shut up and dance, man," he whispered in my ear. I did, but when he tried to twirl me, I clocked him over the back of his head. He smirked. "Okay, okay."

"But thanks," I said, and moved with him. I kept twisting

my head to look at Julian. Oma had just reached them both. But in the end, it wasn't Oma who gave it to Aunt Thomas.

It was Julian.

He closed his eyes and stepped backwards. The step was small and pained, and he said a lot with it. His mama must have understood too, because she hurriedly moved forward to close the distance, but it was too late.

"Oh, Mama," he said, voice breaking. "There aren't any girls that I want to dance with."

Ben moved us right into Aunt Thomas's view, and she blinked from us to her son. "Are you saying—?"

"Yes. I am."

"But that was just a phase, wasn't it?"

Julian looked down at his leather shoes, and rocked back on his heel. He dug his hands into his pockets and jiggled nervously.

I needed to be beside him, supporting him.

I stopped dancing, but as I let go of Ben, Julian looked at me and shook his head. *Not right now*, he said.

He focused on his mama and smiled sadly, then retreated a few steps. "It was never just a phase. I tried for you. But that was why I broke my engagement to Liddie."

Aunt Thomas opened her mouth, and Julian stopped her. "No, don't say anything. Think about it and we'll…we'll talk later."

"Julian," she said, but he'd already turned. Most people had resumed dancing and parted for him to escape. When Aunt Thomas tried to follow, she found herself trapped behind swishing skirts and pressed tuxes.

Ben finished dancing the song with me. "Did you know about Julian?"

"Yes," I said.

He thought about it before nodding slowly. "I get why he didn't tell me."

"You do?"

"Yeah, he's interested in me."

I laughed and led him back to Carolin. "No, no. Don't count on it."

"You sure? Because all this is hard to resist."

I rolled my eyes. "Oh Ben, what would I do without you?"

He sighed. "I just don't know."

Carolin snorted and slipped her arm around Ben's waist.

"I think I'll leave you to it. I'm going to go check on Julian."

"Should we all come?"

"Too many people." I shrugged, grinding my heel against a shriveled balloon. "I mean, it's just…I've been there. So maybe it's best if it's just me."

Carolin nodded, and Oma suddenly appeared cracking her cane against my butt and making Ben smirk.

"Hurry up and get going already," she said, and as I twisted to go, she touched my arm, and then flattened my collar. "Make sure he knows just how much we love him."

"Julian?"

He stood with his back against the church wall, the light from the nearest lamp falling softly over him.

"Julian," I said again, this time more than a whisper.

He lifted his bowed head, and I moved to him.

"I hoped you'd follow," he said. His eyes were dark, but I felt his tears on the pads of my fingers as I brushed my hand over the side of his face.

"I'm so sorry, Julian."

His breathing shuddered on my neck as he rested his forehead against my shoulder. From the hall came the sound of music and cheering, and then the clock chimed in the tower above us.

Eleven o'clock.

A couple left the wedding, laughing and slurring, and Julian stirred. I kissed his head and whispered in his ear, "Shall we get out of here?"

I led him through the village and back to his place, but once there Julian shook his head. "I can't stay here tonight," he said.

I squeezed his hand. "Come and stay at our place."

He brought both our hands to his brow. Slowly, he slid us over his nose to rest at his mouth. He kissed my knuckles, his lips warm, soft. His green forest eyes pleaded with mine to lead him somewhere we could both be lost for a night. I got it. I understood.

I pressed my lips against his. "Can we take your house truck?"

XOXOLLLLL

I TOOK HIM to the exact spot he'd stayed in the last time we'd both been here: the little nook at the bottom of the hill.

It'd been a long, nervous walk into the woods with our flashlights. We knew the path like the back of our hands, so it wasn't getting there that had our birds lodged in our throats.

We set up our tent and I stashed our stuff inside, then ducked out of the tent opening.

Julian stood, staring down at an old tree stump, hands deep in his pockets.

"Julian?"

He scrubbed his face with his hands. "Last time we were here, Lenny…it was the second time I'd been so unbelievably jealous."

I wrapped my arms around him and rested my forehead against the back of his head, breathing in the soft, clean scent of his hair. "I'd hoped so."

"You did?"

"You've no idea how much." I nipped at his hair and pulled it gently between my lips. It tasted like his smell. "What was the first time you were so unbelievably jealous?"

He turned his head to the side, and a small smile tugged at his lips. "It's why I remember Jessica Kolb's full name. How could I forget? She was there touching you, when I could only ever do that in my head."

I clutched him tighter, thinking back to all those times, those hundreds of times where I'd been touching him in my head too.

"I got your note," I said in his ear and smiled at his answering shiver.

"And?"

I loosened my arms and moved until I was standing on the stump in front of him. He looked up at me, and I tugged him up. The space was limited and I slid my leg between his to make us fit. "I don't want you to be my David."

"You don't—"

I placed my fingers over his parted lips and his breath drifted through them. He held my gaze, uncertain and curious, then raised one brow.

I replaced my fingers with a slow kiss. He sighed into it, sinking against me, arms warm around me, hands threading through my hair. I groaned and nipped his lips, pressing myself as close as I could to his firm, aroused body. One gentle thrust of my hips had us doubling our grips and deepening our kiss.

The air whispered sweetly and moonlight trickled through the trees lining everything in silver. I gently pulled back, skating my hands down his shirt. "I don't want you to be my David; I want you to be my Julian."

"Oh, Lenny," he said softly. "I've not shown it well, but I've always been yours."

He kissed me then, and this kiss was new; it was confident and daring and felt like an exclamation mark to his admission. My bird hopped up and down inside, excited, ready to leap from the nest again and soar through me.

"Always yours," he said again and that was all it took. I needed him close, close, closer.

One by one I undid his buttons, then slipped my hands onto his stomach, sliding them over his chest. My hard cock strained in my pants and I thrust against his hardness, reveling in the strangled sound Julian let out. I kissed his throat and up his jaw and a soft puff of air skated over my cheek.

I pushed the shirt over his shoulders and it fell to the base of the stump in a crumpled heap.

Julian gently rid me of my shirt and then he gazed at me with such a longingness and heat that I almost spilled in my pants. I took one of his hands and pinched them to my nipple, massaging it. Julian sucked in a breath, then gripped the back of my neck and kissed me hard, tongue meeting, tasting, sucking mine.

He kissed his way down the sensitive side of my neck, and I fumbled between us, hooking my fingers into his waistband. His shiver echoed through me, and I opened his pants. Then hesitated.

He rested his forehead against mine and we both looked at my fingers, so close to touching him, the fabric of his under-wear shifting.

Is this okay?

Julian kicked off his shoes, peeled off his socks, removed a condom from his pocket, placing it at the base of the stump, and then moved my hands back to his pants and helped me push them to his ankles.

I'd seen him naked countless times before, but never so exposed. He placed his palm over his upward curving cock and tugged himself, eyes never leaving me. I swallowed hard, kissed him softly, then stepped off the stump and circled him.

"You're beautiful, Julian," I said to his back. With the tips of my fingers, I trailed a line down his toned back to the crest of his ass. His Australia-shaped birthmark was darker against his flesh, and I outlined the puckered skin. How many times had I dreamed of him like this?

I gave in to one of my fantasies. One of the many things I wanted to do with Julian. Sliding my hands to brace his hips, I bent down and kissed it. He inhaled sharply, and his muscles tensed as if to hurriedly turn around, but I tightened my grip and kept him steady.

I kissed the mark again, slowly making my way toward his hip. Then I came full circle. He looked down at me, eyes glassy in the moonlight.

"My turn now?" he asked, stepping down from the stump.

"Well—"

"That was a rhetorical question. Hop up on the pedestal, Lenny."

He pulled me up onto the stump and kissed me and my cock strained so hard to be freed.

I tried to shove my pants off, but Julian batted my hands away and did it for me. Then his hands clasped my backside and ran down my thighs, urging me to wrap my legs around him. His stomach was hot and hard against my crotch as he carried me to another stump a few feet up the incline.

He set me down, dropped to his knees in the leaves and dirt that collected at the base of the hill, and ran his hands down my thighs, slowly parting them. His lips skimmed down my smooth skin that ached for his touch, bursting in goose bumps whenever he went.

Then his hand curled around my cock and squeezed lightly. I thrust into the touch, then choked on a moan when his tongue slid once around the tip of my cock. "Julian," I whimpered.

He slowly sucked me into his wet, warm mouth, humming my name back to me, and I arched into him, needy for more of his words making love to me. "Say more."

Is this how you imagined it would be? His next hum said, wrapping around me as good as his mouth.

—No. This is better.

His hums, his hands on my nipples, and his mouth around my cock pushed me to the edge. I clutched the tree stump, digging the rough back into my skin as my head rolled back and I thrust into his mouth.

He moaned around me and I glanced down at him as he jerked himself, hand moving in time to his mouth on me.

We were loud in the night. And I wanted us louder. I wanted to hear Julian gasping my name while I let my words caress him, bringing him closer and closer—

I gently pushed against Julian's shoulder, moving him back until I popped free from his mouth, and a breeze rushed to take his place.

"Lenny?" he asked.

"Lie back, Julian." He lay on the flat ground, and I sank to my knees. My leaking cock dragged over the hairs on his leg as I kissed up his thigh. Then I stretched myself over him and kissed his neck.

A leaf lying close to us caught my eye. I picked it up and teased its pointed tip against his nipple, drawing an X and O. He squirmed and jerked under me, his cock dueling with mine. With my free hand, I took us both and squeezed. Julian murmured my name again, and with our lengths touching, slippery from both our beading tips, I slowly stroked.

With each stroke, I marked a cross on his nipple that soon turned into an L.

His hand came up to his chest, trapping the leaf and my fingers. I quickened my strokes, and Julian gave a silent cry, his lips parting.

"I want your hands on me this time," I said. "And I don't want you to let go. Ever."

He gasped and then his hands were on me, hard and firm

and tugging me close to him. He pushed my hand off of our cocks, clasped my shoulders, and pushed me flush against him.

His lips crushed mine. "Not touching you back was the stupidest thing I've ever done."

Angling his chin, Julian sucked on my earlobe, gasping as my responding thrusts grew more aggressive. He did it again, scraping his teeth this time and running a hand over the swell of my ass. He slipped to my crease and lightly trailed a finger over me. But it wasn't nearly enough. I ground us hard together and slapped my hand over his at my ass, pressing him closer. Right to where I wanted him.

His breath caught, and the way he gently prodded at my entrance, I knew he was asking: *Are you sure?*

"How's ten years of sure for you?"

He responded with a half laugh, half moan, then he took his hand from my backside and slid a finger into my mouth. I sucked and lined his finger, watching lust darken his eyes.

I moaned softly as he arched against me, his hand back at my ass, finger nudging my entrance. "Yes. More."

He pushed deeper inside me, and it was hot and made me even harder, and it wasn't anywhere near enough.

I kissed him and reached for the condom close to the first stump. Julian lifted onto his elbows. "Don't you need to be stretched more for your first time?"

I gripped the condom and the corner of the foil dug into my palm. "It's…" Suddenly I didn't want to say it.

"It's what?"

"It's not my first time."

Julian didn't say anything, he fell back on the soil and leaves, and ground his palms over his eyes. The laugh he gave didn't sound humored.

I sat back on his thighs and closed my eyes. "It was—"

"Dammit. I don't want to hear it." He tried to roll away, but I pinned his shoulders down and looked him in the eye.

"Don't tell me you never fucked your fiancée."

He drew in breath to throw something back at me, but then he slowly exhaled and his tensed shoulders sagged toward the ground. "You're right." He blinked. "It's my fault for taking so long." His jaw clenched. "I hope, at least, whoever he was, he was good to you."

I kissed his brow. "I can read you, you know, Julian. Relax, it wasn't Theo."

He choked as he exhaled. "Thank fuck for that."

Because I knew, deep down, he really did want to know, I told him what happened in Berlin that trip. How I thought it was a new beginning for me.

His arms wrapped around me in a hug. "Did you get your new beginning?"

"No." I shifted out of his embrace enough to draw lazy patterns over his jaw. "I thought I was closer when I started the move to Berlin. It was—*is*—meant to be my new beginning. But I think, first, I have to resolve the past before I can move on." I stilled my finger on him. "Why did you come to my bedroom that New Years?"

"You know why," Julian said.

"Did you know I was awake?"

"I did."

"Why did you leave?"

"It's always been the same reason. My mama…she doesn't have anyone else. When she told me it was wrong, that what I was going through was just a phase that I'd get over if I tried hard enough—if I loved her enough. I knew I had to try." His arms came off me and he scrubbed his hair. "It was earlier this year when I knew I couldn't do it anymore. It wasn't all bad with Liddie, you know. She just wasn't…she could never be *you*." He glanced to the foliage. "Do you think…"

"Think what?" I asked.

261

He closed his eyes. "I want a new beginning with you, Lenny. Can we have that?"

I leaned in and kissed each eyelid, then his lips.

"You said," Julian whispered, tracing a hand over my back, "if you asked, I'd say yes."

"I did."

"Ask me to move to Berlin with you."

My bird swooped suddenly inside, stealing all my words to sing: *Julian, you have no idea how I've longed to ask you that.* I pressed my length against his and kissed his breath away, taking it for my own. Where was that leaf? I wanted to mark every inch of his body with L for Lenny. Because wherever he went, I wanted to be with him.

"Ask me if we're going to tell our friends and family about us."

My throat tightened as well as my stomach, and I sat up. "Are you sure?"

"Yes."

"I'm nervous."

"We'll do it together."

"Okay."

I lay back against him, our cocks meeting again. I rocked against him and he bit his lip, titling his chin up in his passion. The moonlight emphasized his lust, and his lust was for me, and it was the most erotic thing I'd ever imagined.

"Anything else I should ask?"

"Yes," he moaned. "Ask me if we'll make love now."

"Will we make love now?" I said in his ear.

He groaned, tightened his grip on me and rolled us. "Yes. But I *am* preparing you properly."

He shimmied down my body, kissing his way there. Gently, he lifted my knees up, exposing me to him. His nose grazed over my cock and he flicked his tongue over my entrance. My hands hit and clutched at the soil as I controlled myself from bucking.

He did it again, a long, sensual swirl of his tongue that just pushed in—

I cried out with the flare of arousal. *Don't stop. It's too much. Stop. No, don't stop!*

His hot, moaning breath vibrated over the skin, danced deep in my balls and inched up my cock.

With the next thrust of his tongue came a finger too. That's when I lost it, whimpering at him to put on a condom, to come inside me. But first, I pulled him against me. "That was... was...unexpected."

"Just one of the things I've fantasied about doing with you," he said, finding the condom.

"Fantasied?" I asked breathily as he tore open our pre-lubed protection.

"You've no idea how much I want to do to you. You're in my thoughts every time I've jerked off since *forever*. That night we watched porn? It was you, Lenny. Knowing what you were doing next to me...God, I wanted to grab you to the sofa and... *everything*."

My heart beat triple-to-one with desire at that revelation. I took the condom, placed it on his hard tip and worked it on him, loving the way his eyelids fluttered as I caressed him.

"Will you do one of my fantasies now?" I asked.

He gazed down at me with half-lidded eyes. "Anything."

"I want to see you."

Julian bit his lip, and then kissed me, hands digging into me. Lifting my legs, he angled himself at my entrance and eased the head of his cock inside me. I rolled my head back and *felt* the stars that sprinkled the sky above me.

"You okay?"

I tilted my hips up. "Deeper, Julian. I want you all in." *In this, and in my life.*

He sank into me with a careful thrust and a gasp. I clenched around him as he breathed through his teeth. "You feel so good, Lenny."

He rocked slowly in and out, fingernails lightly scratching my hips and backside with every thrust. My hips bowed up and he plunged deep, drawing a sharp, needy moan from me. His eyes flooded with passion and need and elation, and he thrust deeper, harder, faster, taking me in his hand in the same loving rhythm.

Sweat pebbled at my brow as I rode the mounting pleasure, but I couldn't hold on much longer and I said as much. Julian's strokes quickened, cock hitting my prostate over and over and over. My pleasure soared and then shockwaves blasted through me as Julian gasped and stilled, cock pulsing in me. "*Lenny.*"

And at my name, I came with him, ten years' worth of orgasm pouring between us.

Herr Koch Meets Herr Thomas

AFTER, WHEN Julian had helped me off the ground and brushed me free of leaves and dirt, he wrapped an arm around my waist and kissed the top of my head, his chest warm against my back.

"You're so beautiful," he murmured in my ear and I responded with a stupidly large grin in the dark.

When a chill breeze made me shiver, Julian pulled me into the tent. He searched our stuff and hummed. "Did we pack a sleeping bag for me?"

I'd hurried to grab the camping gear and only my sleeping bag made the journey apparently. I grabbed my bag and unrolled it over a foam mattress. "Guess you'll have to share mine."

A devilish spark filled the inch of space between us and Julian made quick work of snuggling into the sleeping bag with me, his heat and mine meshing together, legs tangled, my head resting on his chest.

We left the door unzipped to look up at the stars; and it was just like the first time Julian and I had camped together in our backyard, only without Ben asleep at our feet. I felt comfortable in his arms and on the edge of bursting out into a hearty laugh.

"Still want to go to the stars?" Julian asked, and it made me smile that he too was remembering that night.

"If I do, are you still offering to piggyback me?"

Julian laughed and at that sound something fluttered and twisted in my belly. It was my bird, tweeting, laughing, singing.

It was my bird, finally healed.

In the morning, we went straight from the camping grounds to Berlin. We were halfway there anyway; it just made sense. That, and I really wanted to show Julian the house in Berlin.

I wanted him to see the new beginning I was carving for myself, and I wanted him to beg to be in it.

He did beg.

He didn't fall on his knees or do anything dramatic, but he did beg.

I saw it.

In his eyes as he took in the garden and the front of the house, the way his gaze lingered on the upper rooms as if he were trying to figure out which one might be mine. Which one might be *ours*. His face lit up with hope and he bit his bottom lip. His hand found mine and, still taking in our home, he threaded his fingers in mine and squeezed.

I heard it.

In his voice hitching as he asked, "Can we go inside?"

I felt it.

In the tight hold of his hand. In the way he wouldn't let go so I could unlock the door.

I tasted it.

In his kiss. The soft way his lips brushed over mine as he took my hand with the key...

His begging was loud and clear, and now I wanted it to stop. I wanted him to look at our house and *know* it was our beginning. Know that we were going to share not only these rooms, but also our lives. I wanted to see that confidence. I was done with wishes. I wanted reality. I wanted *this* reality.

I looked to our hands and the keys, and moved us both to the lock. Together we unlocked and opened. I placed the keys in his hand. "This set is yours."

He pocketed them and kissed me again. "Oh, they are so mine."

I laughed, and then my gaze caught on Herr Koch's roses leaning in a breeze, and I cursed.

Julian frowned and looked over his shoulder. "What?"

"He has to okay you."

"Who?"

"My landlord."

Julian pressed his hands on my shoulders. "No problem. I'm sure we can butter him up."

"No, that won't work," came a hearty male voice. Julian and I jumped apart and watched Herr Koch push his way through the gate. His cap was black today, casting heavier shadows over his face and making it hard to read his expression.

"Herr Koch, this is Julian Thomas."

Herr Koch lifted his cap an inch in greeting and swung his gaze right back to me. "So you've found someone to share the rent, I see."

I shook my head. "This is my boyfriend, and yes, we'd like to live together."

My landlord narrowed his eyes on Julian. "I don't like to be buttered up, Herr Thomas. That doesn't work for me."

"What would work for you, Herr Koch? I'd like to get your okay."

Herr Koch nodded and paced the path in front of the veranda. He was scanning the garden, and there was a glint in his eye. He was amused—he was going to make this difficult.

"I like people earning their 'okay'," he finally said. "Are you helping Lenny move his Oma?"

Julian nodded. "I'm going to do whatever I can."

"Good. That's a good start."

Herr Koch looked at me and I could see the grin twitch in his cheek. "Help him move her here, and then be on the lookout. I'll give you a nod for 'okay' and shake my head if…well, you know what that means."

My hands balled at my sides and a hot flush of anger ripped through me. I didn't want him to play the cheeky old neighbor, didn't want him to wind us up, not about this. "Don't be such a bored old man. Just say okay!"

What I said must have hit him hard, the way he stumbled back a step. He quickly readjusted his cap.

Although I meant the words in the moment I'd said them, now I wanted to swallow them. But it was too late. They were out there. I looked at his face, and knew I'd hit a sore spot, and I cursed myself some more. "I'm sorry. I shouldn't have said that—"

"A nod or a shake of my head," he said quickly, and turned his back on us. "You'll find out which it'll be soon enough."

Are You Ready?

THE DAY BEFORE the scheduled move to Berlin, Julian and I called a family meeting—including Julian's mama. It was set for four o'clock. We waited in my bedroom, nervously kicking my old soccer ball between us as we sat on the bed, straining to hear their footsteps as they gathered.

"Are you excited about Berlin?" Julian asked, hooking his bare foot under the ball and slowly lifting it to the bed. His foot grazed my knee and I grabbed it, making him laugh.

"I can hardly think about being excited at the moment," I said, looking toward the door. "Not until we…"

"Yeah."

"You think they're all there now?"

"It's ten past. I think so."

I swung my legs off the bed, battling the urge to throw up in my wastepaper basket.

Julian laughed, brushed the back of his hand against his eyes, and laughed again. He shoved himself off the bed. The mattress bounced and the ball dropped off it. "Fuck, I'm nervous."

I wiped my hand on my shorts and held it out to him. He

threaded his fingers with mine. "We can do this," I said, words hovering between certainty and uncertainty. "Worst comes to worst, we still have each other, right?"

He drew me into him and we danced a few quiet steps. My breathing calmed. "Right. We'll still be us, with or without them, Lenny. I promise." He brushed the pad of his thumb over my lips and kissed me. "Ready?"

I shook my head, but walked with him to the door. "Let's do this."

Downstairs, everyone had gathered in the kitchen. Julian and I walked in and sat on two chairs at one side of the table that seemed to be reserved for us.

"We asked you all here," I said, looking from my sister and Ben closest to us, to Oma and my aunt opposite, "because we…have something we'd like to say. We…" My throat seized up with panic and I glanced at Julian. We might make this work together if they rejected us, but Caro, Ben, Oma…it'd break my heart to lose them.

Julian looked at me as if the rest of the room didn't matter. "You okay?"

I touched his knee under the table, where he clasped it. His tremor passed through me, mixing with my nerves and making my bird throw up inside. I wanted to lean against him and have him lean on me too.

Oma rubbed her crystal ball with her thumbs and looked up at me. *Are you ready?* she seemed to be asking.

I squeezed Julian's hand and nodded. "I'm okay."

"What is it, Julian?" his mama asked, dabbing at her eyes with the cuff of her sleeve. "Why'd you ask me over here?"

"Let them speak in their own time," Oma said, letting go of her crystal to rearrange her scarf. A wobbly smile—something I hadn't seen often before—stretched across her face. For a second it made her look a younger, shyer version of Oma.

Carolin sent me an encouraging, curious smile. The way

she straightened the wrinkles in the tablecloth told me she was getting impatient, maybe even nervous. Did she already suspect?

Ben wore a lazy grin and twirled my sister's shoulder-length hair around his pinkie. His addiction to touching her was sweet, and it made me hope harder that he'd be okay with Julian and me. His friendship was the reason I'd not completely broken when Julian left for the Army, when he left for college, when he got a fiancée... I caught his gaze and silently begged him to understand. To be okay with it.

"Oma," I said. I swallowed and tried again, pointing to her crystal ball. "You once read into our future love life. I asked you if you saw the person I was going to be with." My words came out shaky and I stopped to take a breath, feeling the air tighten in my pause, as if my family was starting to guess where this was going.

"You want me to take over?" Julian whispered.

"Not yet," I said to him, and then continued, "You said to me that I'd tell you when I've found him."

I raised my chin and glanced at each of them in turn, lingering on Oma who still wore that wobbly smile. "Well I found him a long time ago. Then he found me. And now we've found each other."

I turned to Julian, his eyes the color of the grass by the river where he'd said it perfectly: *I want to watch movies with you, Lenny.* "I want to watch movies with you, too."

He let go of my hand under the table and brought his to my cheek, wiping away a tear that leaked out of me. "Scary ones," he said and smirked.

But when his warm words went away, a cool silence filled the void, making me shiver. I stared down at the tablecloth and moved my toes over to Julian's. He nudged me back. *It's okay, we'll get through this*, it seemed to say.

But he didn't *look* okay at all. He was staring at his mama, face blanched with anxiety, and his grip on me tightened. I slid our chairs closer together and circled an arm around him so that he could lean on me.

Aunt Thomas was shaking her head. "This is a joke."

Julian's back heaved and I felt his silent sob. I held him tighter, bringing his head to rest on my shoulder.

"Hey-hey," I said into his hair, desperately wedging my toe between his as if it would help. As if it made the words *we'll get through this* true.

"Oma?" I whispered. "*Please.*"

She released the tablecloth that she'd been using to wipe away her tears and found her cane and then her voice. She pointed the cane at Aunt Thomas. "Let me give you a piece of advice. These two boys are happy together and they have been in love for a long time. There is no changing that. No changing them. The only thing that can change here is your attitude. Find a way to accept this, Nadine, or you'll have lost both the men in your life."

"I...It's true?" Aunt Thomas didn't even seem to have heard Oma.

Julian lifted his head. "It's true, Mama."

She sniffed. "And here I thought I raised such a good son."

My chair screamed as I lurched from it. There was nothing but red and the pounding hurt inside. I had been holding Julian as he'd started to break, and it was *her* fault.

I lunged toward her, hands coming up to push her out of our house. Out of our lives. *Out, just get the fuck out.* How dare she! How could she? Julian was perfect. Just perfect and—

Someone grabbed me from behind, tightening his hold over my chest and pulling me back against his. "Cool it," came Ben's voice gently in my ear. "Let her go."

Carolin was in front of me, pulling at Aunt Thomas's arm, forcing her out. "I may look a lot like you," she said, "but I will never, *ever* be so cold."

I stumbled back with Ben, only now hearing how ragged my breath was, only now tasting the tears on my lips.

Ben loosened his hold once my sister came back in. "She's gone."

"Julian?" I said, reeling out of Ben's grip. I moved over, straddled his lap and hugged him. I didn't give a shit about how close we were and how it might look. I rested our foreheads together. "I'm so sorry."

His shoulders shook, but he nodded, our noses bumping. "It was what I expected...I just hoped I'd be wrong."

We stayed like that for a long time, and when we finally parted again, we were back in Oma's kitchen.

It could have been any other day.

Ben peeled potatoes, humming off-key as he winked at Carolin. My sister scrubbed the dishes, stopping only to flick bubbles at him; snorting with laughter when some landed on Ben's lips and he kissed it back to her. And Oma sat in her chair gazing out the window, the afternoon light softening her features, its warmth making her eyes drift shut.

I shifted on Julian's lap, kissing him one more time before getting off him.

"Get a room, guys," Ben shot at us, flinging over a dishtowel.

"You too, dick-a-roo," I threw back at him.

He came over, giggling, and snatched back the dishtowel. "Dick-a-roo?"

Julian snagged the towel back and whipped him on his butt. "Hey, my guy learned name-calling with the best."

"True that," Ben said, then he hooked an arm around both our necks. "I just want to say one thing, guys."

"What's that?"

He winked at me. And said to us: "It's okay. Okay. Okay."

Red Umbrella

OMA'S MUSIC BOUNCED around the kitchen and I switched it off. She, Ben, and Carolin had gone to the village play, while I used the time to make sure we were ready for the move. Tonight.

God, I needed Herr Koch to give us a nod. I'd sent him an apology letter along with a wax lily and I hoped he forgave me for lashing out at him; I just couldn't handle any more obstacles between me and Julian, and I wanted to be with him. Every damn night. But also, Oma needed me and unless Herr Koch's nodded, I'd not earn enough for him to extend my contract.

I emptied my shed and placed everything in boxes in the rental truck that Ben had hidden at the dead-end street around the corner. My wax Julian warrior I kept tucked into my personal suitcase upstairs. Just in case...I couldn't lose that.

A hand pinched my nose, coming from behind me. I twisted. "Hey, Julian."

His gaze met mine and it looked worn and tired, but there was something happy and hopeful clinging to his smile.

I lifted my hands around his neck and massaged him,

slowly moving down to his shoulders. I leaned in and kissed him, and just the brush of his lips over mine had me needing him closer.

He broke free of the rapidly intensifying kiss, and took my hand. "I want to go for a walk with you."

We left the house, Julian snagging the old red umbrella on the way.

The air was fresh and dry, and there wasn't a cloud in the sky as we climbed up the grassy, yellow-weedy path to the hill overlooking Waldau. The taste of fall hit the back of our throats and lent quickness to our steps.

Near the top, but not quite, in the spot where I always came to think—in the spot where Julian and I had been almost exactly five years ago—we stopped. A bird chirped. The grass whispered with a breeze, tickling against our ankles.

Julian passed the umbrella to his other hand and dug the tip into the ground, staring from his feet to the village below. I stepped behind him, slipping my hands around his waist, and rested my chin on his shoulder.

His free hand met mine around his middle and rested there. As he breathed in and out, our skin rubbed lightly—a caressing presence.

"Berlin is the right move for us," he said, his words rumbling low through me. I liked his "us" so much, I pressed my lips to his neck—*thank you.*

He lifted the umbrella and pointed it toward my house, and then in a wide circle around Waldau. "This is—was—a big part of who we are." He arched the umbrella toward the river. "Where we swam in summer." He moved it to a grassy field behind the abandoned school. "Where I tried to teach you how to ride a bike."

"And failed." I laughed. "You dragged me and my bike back to Oma and said I had to change my jeans because the ones I was wearing weren't any good at bike riding."

Julian chuckled, the pressure of his hand tightening for a moment. He pointed the umbrella to the graveyard. "Where I used to practice the trumpet, and you and Ben said I was really close to waking up the dead... Then there is where I cut my hand and had to go to hospital; when I came back and was in too much pain to leave my bed, and you snuck to the side of my place, leaned against the fence and shouted out funny shit Oma had done through the window until my mama scared you off."

His swallow was loud and I detected the barest trace of a sniff. The umbrella was now pointing toward a little stream that forked off the river.

"That's where we built and raced boats we'd made from walnut shells and leaves," I said.

He nodded, his hair brushing the side of my face. "And here?"

I laughed. "Where Ben dropped the watermelon we'd meant to take to the village picnic, and instead of just leaving it there, we hunched down and dug our fingers in it, eating whatever we could off the path. I think I ate some grit that day."

"It was worth it." He swung the umbrella toward the village square. "And when we were older...this was where we both got so drunk the first time that we threw up in the gutters...where we practiced driving without our anal instructors—"

"And where I got my first ticket for driving illegally." I moved my hand, pressed against his thin T-shirt, and clamped it on top of his. "You were hilarious trying to weasel my way out of it, though. Sweet." I kissed his ear and he leaned his weight back against me.

"There's a lot of us down there," he said, swinging the umbrella up over our heads and opening it. "Which is why this is the perfect place."

I nuzzled into the nook of his neck. "For what?"

His body stiffened in mine, a shallow breath left him as he opened his mouth and then he hesitated, closing his mouth again. From here I could just make out the corner of his lips turned up in a smile. I wanted to know what brought it there.

I kissed under his ear. "Lenny for your thoughts?"

Julian relaxed against me, rested his head back on my shoulder and stared up at the umbrella. The sun filtered through it, casting a warm, serene glow over his face. His smile widened and he threaded his hand, between mine, through my fingers resting on top of his.

When he spoke, his voice was soft and low, and I felt the words rumble right through him to feed my bird. "Ask if I love you."

I spun him around and the umbrella dropped to our side and rolled a few feet from us. There was no preamble; I cupped his cheeks, light with stubble that perfectly prickled my palms, and kissed him.

"I love you too," I murmured and we fell back against the grass. I lay on him, my heart resting next to his, his hands threaded with mine, my gaze blinking down to his, his toes peeking through his sandals trying to touch mine, my knees sliding between his, his tiny hairs whispering over my skin.

Thank you for your thoughts, my body wrote against his. I kissed him. "Here's your Lenny."

Love You

THE MIDDLE-OF-THE-NIGHT MOVE to Berlin went without a hitch. Almost.

Ben and Carolin and two of their friends had packed up all our furniture, stacked it into a rental truck and driven it up to Berlin with a two-hour head start. Using pictures Carolin had, they set up the furniture at the other end. Ben had bribed all of his old roommates to come and help them, and twenty minutes before Julian and I arrived with a sleeping Oma in his house truck, they were ready.

The only hitch came when Oma's sleeping pills wore off while we were carrying her up the garden path of our new Berlin home.

Her arms twitched where I held her. I shared a panicked look with Ben, at her feet, and Julian, bracing her back. Would she notice any differences in the garden with her poor eyesight? Or would she only see the large pink and purple lilies perched close to the wall of the house, under the window, just like usual?

Oma laid her groggy eyes on mine. "Did I have another night terror?"

Sure, why not go with that? "Just a little one. We're putting you right back to bed."

"Put down my feet, Ben. Julian, let go. I can walk." They gently put her to the path. Ben gulped audibly and darted his gaze to Carolin holding the door open. I supported her up the path. Her nightgown billowed in a breeze and her curls bounced up and down. Her socks were dirty by the time we made it to the threshold.

I think all of us held our breath when Oma walked inside. Carolin had turned a small lamp on dim, giving just enough light to be able to pick our way around without having the full brunt of the main lights.

I turned to shut the door behind us. I didn't know what gave me the feeling Herr Koch had been watching the whole event, but when I looked up, I saw him staring back at me from over the fence.

I raised my hands into the air. *And?*

He spoke, and his message carried over the garden to the front door, just loud enough for me to hear it. "It's always been a nod, Lenny. Right from the beginning. I just liked playing the bored, old man card."

I looked down. I was sorry I'd said that. I liked Herr Koch, cheekiness and all.

"We're good," he called out as if he could read me.

I swallowed the lump in my throat and nodded toward him. *See you tomorrow, then,* I waved to him, then stepped back and shut the door.

Oma shuffled a few steps over the carpet, then she braced a hand on the wall to keep herself steady. She stared at the wallpaper; the one Julian had found for us.

She rubbed her hand over the floral print.

I glanced at Julian slipping out of his shoes. He frowned when he looked up at Oma, then sent me a reassuring smile. *It'll be okay.*

"Right," Oma snapped. "I need my beauty sleep, and by the looks of you all"—she squinted at us one by one—"you need some too."

She crossed her arms and opened her mouth to say something, then shut it again. Then she moved toward her bedroom. "But I want to see *all* of you for breakfast after the new pastor has come by to introduce himself."

Oh, shit, the pastor! Dylan. Had I told him he'd be starting tomorrow already? Ben found my gaze and winked. *It's sorted!*

"Pastor Dieter promised he was an expert masseur, too. So finally I'll get my verses with a side of massage."

Ben's eyes widened. "What the—?"

Carolin shut him up with a kiss.

"I'll pick up rolls from the bakery," I said, and kissed Oma's cheek goodnight.

She kissed mine back and said softly. "I love you, my dear. I love you all."

"You think she's buying it?" I asked Ben once her bedroom door shut.

Ben leaned against the wall, knocking the clock there. He straightened it. "She will until our fake pastor shows up and doesn't know a thing about massage." He shook his head. "How the fuck will we persuade Dylan?"

"It's an acting job," Carolin said, linking an arm in his and moving them toward the front door. "We pay him to do it. Now, if we're coming over for breakfast we'd better hurry back to your place for some shut eye." She pulled him into her. "No sleeping in tomorrow. We've got to be here extra early to make it look like we're living here."

Ben scowled at me. "You so owe me."

I so did.

I moved to them and locked them both into a hug; Julian joined us, and we huddled like old times, our giggles and chuckles bouncing off each other. We'd done it. There were still things to sort out back in Waldau, but we'd made it here.

To Berlin.

To my new home.

To my new beginning. With Julian.

I squeezed the back of his neck and he squeezed mine. "To us," I said. And I meant: To Ben and Carolin. To me and Julian. To best friends. To siblings. To Oma. To *love*.

"To us."

～

OMA LAY ON her side, curled up, and hugged the fresh blankets to her chest. Through the wall, she heard her kids cheering.

She smiled.

- THE END -

Acknowledgments

Thank you first to my wonderful husband, your support is what enables me to write and I love you for it.

Big thanks to Natasha Snow for the amazing cover-art of the second edition.

Cheers to Teresa Crawford for doing rounds of content editing with me. To editor Lynda Lamb, for going through and fine-tuning the text—and keeping me encouraged. Thanks to Vicki Secretarial Enterprises for proofreading the first edition.

Thank you to *Devil In The Details Editing* for copy editing the second edition.

Another cheers to all my betas readers, Vicki Ventriglia, Seiran Allen-Field, and to those others who read through and helped me shape the first edition and second edition of this story.

Finally, thanks to all my friends—you know who and how awesome you are!

Anyta Sunday

HEART-STOPPING SLOW BURN

A bit about me: I'm a big, BIG fan of slow-burn romances. I love to read and write stories with characters who slowly fall in love.

Some of my favorite tropes to read and write are: Enemies to Lovers, Friends to Lovers, Clueless Guys, Bisexual, Pansexual, Demisexual, Oblivious MCs, Everyone (Else) Can See It, Slow Burn, Love Has No Boundaries.

I write a variety of stories, Contemporary MM Romances with a good dollop of angst, Contemporary lighthearted MM Romances, and even a splash of fantasy.
My books have been translated into German, Italian, French, Spanish, and Thai.

Contact: http://www.anytasunday.com/about-anyta/
Sign up for Anyta's newsletter and receive a free e-book:
http://www.anytasunday.com/newsletter-free-e-book/